THE LEGACY OF OGMA

THE LEGACY OF OGMA

BOOK ONE IN THE WEAPONS TRILOGY

E. A. RAPPAPORT

iUniverse, Inc.
New York Lincoln Shanghai

The Legacy of Ogma
Book One in The Weapons Trilogy

iUniverse books may be ordered through booksellers or by contacting:

iUniverse
2021 Pine Lake Road, Suite 100
Lincoln, NE 68512
www.iuniverse.com
1-800-Authors (1-800-288-4677)

Because of the dynamic nature of the Internet, any Web addresses or links contained in this book may have changed since publication and may no longer be valid.

ISBN: 978-0-595-46404-3 (pbk)
ISBN: 978-0-595-70191-9 (cloth)
ISBN: 978-0-595-90698-7 (ebk)

Printed in the United States of America

Copyright # TXu-1-248-367

Library of Congress Control Number: 2006902609

Cover painting by Christopher Moeller. www.cmoeller.com.

Special thanks to Dana Moreshead and Kathleen Marinaccio. www.fishbraingd.com

Visit www.owlking.com for the latest news about The Weapons Trilogy

For My Daughter, Hannah

Contents

CHAPTER I

HALIA'S DISCOVERY

Halia neither heard nor saw any sign of her pursuers after an hour of crawling across the forest floor. She was relieved that they had either given up or lost her trail, but she wasn't about to turn back, Arboreals or evil spirits be damned. The small village of Hillside had nothing to offer her other than a somewhat decent meal, which she had already taken. Besides, she was used to being on her own, having fended for herself since becoming an orphan more than two decades ago. Convinced that she was alone, Halia rose from the ground and continued knee-deep down a shallow river, hoping she wouldn't get lost.

As the last fingers of sunlight released their grip from the tops of the trees, Halia removed a small bundle from her cloak and peeled back several layers of cloth. Inside were a small piece of cured venison and a slice of bread, the only food she had eaten in the past three days.

"This was my grand theft from Hillside," she thought. "If I had known the village captain was completely intolerant of all crime, I would never have taken this meal, despite my hunger."

While occasionally glancing backward, she devoured the food, finishing it in a half dozen bites. Halia bent over to take a sip of the cool water and immediately noticed something nearby that wasn't a natural part of the forest. Keeping her sharp eyes affixed to the mysterious spot, she headed cautiously downstream.

Before long, Halia saw the ruins of an old castle, almost completely obscured by vegetation. She waded ashore, pushing her way through an overgrowth of reeds, where she found a carefully hidden jumble of logs randomly tied together with a few strands of rawhide. Halia stepped onto the makeshift raft, stamped her foot a few times, and determined it to be in good enough condition for use on the river. Though there was no one else within miles of her, she declared, "Transportation, 'tis my lucky day, though I would have given my last meal for a horse instead."

"Nevertheless," she thought, "there is bound to be civilization somewhere downstream, and this heap of wood will bring me there faster than I could ever walk."

With darkness rapidly approaching, Halia knew her travels had ended for the day and was glad to have found shelter. Although she didn't believe the ghost stories told by the villagers in Hillside, she had heard of sabertooths stalking the woods at night. Unwilling to fall prey to a ferocious beast while she slept, Halia quickly inspected the surrounding area. "One can never be too safe," she told herself, "especially with only a flimsy knife for protection."

Nothing much remained of the ancient castle. A few moss-covered stones here and there marked what used to be the entrance. The northern wall, mostly intact, rose twelve feet from the ground, but the other three walls had long since collapsed, their remnants scattered about the forest floor. Half-buried mounds of rubble separated the rooms, which otherwise blended together in a sea of weeds and vines. The ruins fascinated Halia as she slinked back and forth examining the structure in detail. The more she searched, the more she hoped she would find something of value.

In the fading light, a curious stack of brushwood caught her interest. She dragged away a few of the larger branches, uncovering a stone staircase hidden beneath the debris. Excited by her discovery, she hauled the remaining branches away from the stairs and dislodged a couple of torches, just what she needed to light her way in the dark depths beneath the castle. "Once again, luck is with me," she said to herself. Without further delay, Halia pulled a tinderbox out of a small pouch on her belt, lit one of the torches, and descended the stairs.

Long and narrow, the steep staircase ended abruptly in a puddle of water beside an open doorway. What should have been a door instead was a mess of splintered wood and bent steel, having been hacked to pieces by someone in the recent past, judging by the lack of rot. Just beyond the pile of rubble, a gaping hole opened in the ground—a sprung trap, as wide as the stairway and more than ten feet deep. Halia thrust the torch forward, illuminating a large room. "The treasury," she exclaimed, fingering one of the larger pieces of wood, "and in finding it, I am not alone." Her heart beat faster, knowing there must be something of value in the room that would satisfy her desire for riches.

Cautiously stepping over the broken door, Halia knelt at the edge of the hole and peered down. Large spikes littered the bottom of the pit along with the remains of the false floor that had given way when two unsuspecting individuals stepped onto it. Their bones lay impaled on the bed of deadly spikes. "You were not fleet of foot to have fallen into such an obvious trap," Halia told the pair of skeletons before gently leaping to the other side of the pit. Her feet barely made a sound when they touched the floor of the chamber.

At first glance, the room appeared empty, looted many years ago by treasure hunters. Cobwebs crept up the sides of the chamber, and a layer of dust lined the floor, thinner toward the center and heavier at the base of the walls. The only indications that this room had ever been a treasury were the two partially destroyed wooden chests. Halia circled the enormous containers, imagining the vast amount of gold they once held. The locks, which had protected the substantial treasure ages ago, still performed their duty, forever prohibiting anyone from separating the lid from the trunk. Their function was now moot, however, since all four sides of the chests had been demolished, much the same as the door to the chamber.

Not a single brass coin remained of the original treasure. "The men who found this room before me were quite thorough, if unskilled. Fortunately, they left a few torches for me." Halia made a pass around the room, lighting the torches in the holders mounted on each wall. With her hands free to perform a more detailed investigation, she continued slowly around the perimeter, running her fingertips along each crack, chip, and crevice. When she reached the far corner of the room, she stood staring at a tiny gap between the floor and the wall that didn't exist elsewhere. "Nor were you observant," she murmured with a quick glance at the pit of skeletons.

Halia set both hands firmly on the wall and gave it a slight push. Nothing happened. She moved her hands lower, took a step backward, and pushed harder. The wall began to tremble faintly as dust fell from small fissures appearing in the stone. Halia stepped away and traced the new set of cracks with her finger. Just as she had expected, they formed the outline of a door about seven feet high and three feet across. Placing her hands in the center, she threw all of her weight against the wall.

With a low grumble, as if it were upset at its discovery, the secret door swung inward, revealing a passage leading deep into the darkness. Halia grabbed the nearest torch and waved it around, illuminating a long corridor. The flickering light faded into the distance without yielding any clue as to its final destination. A dull reflection on the ceiling, however, alerted her to a possible trap.

Halia tossed the torch onto the ground under the reflection with no effect. "I need something heavier, and I know just who can help," she thought, peering back toward the entrance of the room. She promptly returned to the pit by the door, climbed over the side, and, holding on to the rim with her hands, dropped to the bottom. With a momentary shudder of disgust, she hoisted one of the skeletons off the spikes and said, "You may be of use to me."

She threw the bones out of the pit, but the skull came loose and hit the ground with a dull thud. It rolled along the floor between the spikes before coming to rest with its empty eye sockets fixed on Halia. "You need those bones no longer," she explained as she began looking for a way out of the pit.

Hoping to climb up the side, Halia searched for a handhold of any size but found none. She tried to jump out but came up just short of the rim, needing a little more height on her tall frame. "I shall not remain in this grave with riches so near," she promised herself, glancing at the bed of spikes. "I do hope you can support my weight." Halia gently stepped onto a couple of the duller spikes, leaped upward with all her might, and barely caught hold of the edge of the pit. With a sigh of relief, she pulled herself out of the hole, lugged the remains of the body back to the secret passage, and threw it into the corridor. No sooner had the skeleton hit the floor than a heavy iron plate fell from the ceiling, crushing both the bones and the torch with a sickening crunch.

Halia snatched a pair of torches from the holders and stepped into the corridor. Her eyes darted from the floor to the walls to the ceiling. Methodically, she inched her way along the dark passage, throwing a torch to the ground, warily placing one foot in front of the other, and finally retrieving the torch. She went on and on, throwing, walking, and retrieving until her caution paid off at about two hundred paces when the torch landed with a peculiar thump. She scanned the ceiling and determined it to be solid rock, so she stomped on the ground near the torch and almost fell when the false floor collapsed into a pit filled with iron spikes. Only her superb reflexes allowed Halia to hop back just in time to avoid falling to her death.

The new pit spanned the entire width of the passageway and was easily twice as deep as the first. Halia had no choice but to jump across or turn back. She briefly considered retrieving the other skeleton in case there was a trap on the other side, but her curiosity got the best of her, and she decided against it at the last moment. Backing up a few feet, Halia ran as fast as she could and sprang over the hole, landing in a circular chamber eight feet in diameter. Her feet hit the slick marble floor and flew out from under her. Halia slid sheer across the room and smacked into the far wall. "This is no ordinary treasure chamber," she thought, "and it had best hold a worthy reward."

The walls, polished and devoid of dust, were identical to the floor except for a set of engraved symbols. Halia ignored the writing, partly because she couldn't understand the strange language, but mostly because her eyes had focused on a small chest resting on a beautifully carved dais in the center of the room. It was no larger than a plump tomcat, the perfect size for holding a golden crown or a bejeweled necklace. "You are well protected," Halia complimented the chest as she knelt beside it, "but you shall yield your treasure to me."

A Terun padlock, nearly unbreakable and frequently booby-trapped, secured the lid of the chest. Halia dropped her torch beneath the lock and leaned in for a closer look. This one was definitely booby-trapped, but she didn't care. A snarl crossed her face as she remembered her ex-friend Nervos, the Terun thief who had taught her how to pick this type of lock. She had learned much from Nervos but had never enjoyed the subterranean lifestyle of the Teruns. Their friendship lasted several months, ending when the Terun framed her for a series of thefts in the surrounding settlements. No wonder he was willing to give a fledgling thief such specialized knowledge. Halia had realized then that the only person she could ever trust was herself.

On her knees, Halia edged around to the side of the chest, removed a small metal file from her belt, and began to prod the lock. Within seconds, a poisoned needle flew out of the keyhole and hit the wall behind her with a slight ding. Next, Halia pulled a metal lock pick from her belt and inserted both the file and pick into the keyhole. With a few expert twists of her hands, the lock snapped open, and her face brightened. "Treasure!" she exclaimed in delight. "I shall go hungry no more."

Halia yanked off the lock and threw back the lid of the chest. She imagined herself wearing a jewel-encrusted crown, dressed in the finest silk clothes ever made, and carried on top of a gold-trimmed chair by four porters. She saw all of the townsfolk crowding around her, fawning over her, and asking her for favors. She pictured herself receiving invitations to the grandest balls in the land, mingling with nobles and royalty. Then she peered into the chest. Her head slumped down, and her jaw dropped in a look of severe disappointment. "Once again, my dreams are shattered," she whispered softly to herself.

Regaining her composure, Halia reached into the chest and lifted out a solid crystal sphere about the size of a newborn kitten.

Chapter II

Arwold's Vow

Coming from a long line of renowned warriors, Arwold had grown up with a blade in his hands. On this misty evening, he bore his family sword, a magnificent two-handed claymore with a well-honed blade nearly five feet in length. A small crystal sphere capped the end of the leather-wrapped hilt. For a brief moment, a tiny spot of blue light glowed off-center in the sphere. Arwold, however, didn't notice the glowing light. He was too busy blocking an awkward punch from a crypt ghoul, an animated, flesh-eating corpse brought to life by a necromancer. With his considerable battle skills, it didn't take long for Arwold to assess the strengths and weaknesses of his opponent. He was confident that this fight would soon be over.

The ghoul came at him, fiercely clawing with its rotting, moldy fingernails. Arwold parried the blow and followed through by hewing the arm clean off his decaying foe. The severed limb flew at him, hit his steel breastplate, and made a reddish-brown smudge on his otherwise spotless armor. Arwold grumbled in disgust as he threw all of his weight forward and swung sideways at the corpse. The claymore bit deeply into the rotting flesh and came out the other side, cleaving the ghoul in half.

Arwold looked at the stain on his armor and frowned, having no rags to wipe off the blood. He reached down to tear a piece of cloth from the upper half of his former opponent and noticed both sections of the body moving toward him, evidently expecting to continue the battle. Arwold grimaced as he sliced repeatedly into the remains of the creature until it finally lay motionless on the ground. "'Tis not right to bring such a creature into existence," Arwold thought, "but now I have given it the peace that it so deserves."

Surrounding Arwold, four other warriors, somewhat less proficient than he, nervously battled a dozen more crypt ghouls in a small graveyard outside the town of Krof. The mercenaries, trained in armed combat, would have done well against human foes, but fighting the living dead made them uneasy at best. It wasn't only their superstitions about being in a graveyard at night or the sight of the putrid flesh barely clinging to the bones of their gruesome opponents, but also the rank smell, the overpowering stench of death that permeated the battlefield. To make things worse, an unusually heavy fog was rolling in from the Sinewan River. Although a gentle mist was a normal sight near the river at dawn, it would occasionally drift over the land on warm summer evenings such as this. Of course, the men knew the night mist was no coincidence and believed there were foul deeds afoot.

The four warriors fought valiantly at first, but as the night grew darker and the fog grew thicker, they began to succumb to their fears.

"Arwold, let us return in the morning," a haggard fighter begged. "No man should touch the earth in a graveyard once the sun has set. It shall bring us nothing but bad luck."

The others, apart from Arwold, nodded their agreement.

"Nay, we must not let these unholy beasts reach the streets of our fair town. Stand your ground," declared Arwold as he positioned himself to take on two more of the creatures, "and know that good shall prevail on this night."

His men looked about anxiously as they backed away from the river, trying to avoid becoming lost in the dense patches of fog, which seemed to follow their every move. The ghouls pressed forward after them, oblivious to their surroundings. As he was retreating, the haggard fighter managed to chop a hand off his opponent. With renewed confidence, he advanced on the creature, thinking he might actually defeat it. The disembodied hand, however, shuffled toward him on its fingers and grabbed his ankle. He looked down and screamed in horror. Never had he seen such an appalling sight. The warrior tried shaking his leg, but the hand refused to release its cold grip. He reached down with the tip of his sword and tried frantically to pry it loose. Meanwhile, the ghoul that he should have been paying attention to lunged at him. He lost his balance and fell backward under the weight of the creature. Two more ghouls immediately dove onto him and began ripping into his exposed flesh, devouring each piece as they tore it from his body. The sight of this infernal feast was too much for the other three warriors, who threw their weapons to the ground and ran from the battle. Surprisingly, the ghouls didn't pursue them. Instead, they changed their focus to Arwold, their only remaining foe.

Arwold was furious. "First," he thought, "the vile necromancer had the nerve to defile Krof with his presence, and now my own warriors are deserting me." Arwold stood tall, fixed a strand of hair that was out of place, and yelled, "Stand, men! We shall defeat these foul beings! You must not fear evil!"

Those last few words had come straight from his father, the great Ardune, "Fracodian-Killer." They gave Arwold a flashback to his youth when Ardune had spoken that exact same phrase almost twenty years ago.

As a child, Arwold had shown an interest in weapons since before he could walk. By the time he turned five, he had begun his formal training. Many people in town believed the boy was too young, but Ardune knew his son was ready. Arwold took to the sword well and was soon able to best some of the more experienced warriors, vindicating his father's judgment. At a time when other children were just beginning to read and write, Arwold was learning combat techniques and practicing his form daily. Finally, after Arwold had turned eight, Ardune felt it was time for his son's first outing.

A small group of Fracodian raiders had recently ransacked a caravan outside of Krof. Most of the merchants escaped with their lives, but the bandits had stolen all of their goods and horses. Ardune expected that the attackers must have been a small group of nomads since his militia had wiped out the entire Fracodian population native to the forests around Krof. Defeating these Fracodians would have been a trivial task for the captain of the guard, but Ardune thought it would be a good learning experience for his son and decided to handle the matter himself.

When Ardune first told him of the mission, Arwold was thrilled. He had always dreamed of the day when he would fight alongside his father. He bounded into the armory and equipped himself with his finest armor and sword. He would prove how capable he had become by killing more Fracodians than his father did. When the two of them were riding out of town on their warhorses, Arwold was proud. He sat up straight on his mount, smiled broadly, and waved to the admiring townsfolk. He imagined their shouts of "Ardune!" were actually "Arwold!" Nothing could stop him. When they approached the Fracodian encampment, however, Arwold had a feeling he had never been aware of before. It began with the almost imperceptible turning of his stomach. Then, the hairs on his arms and legs stood on end and his heart began to beat faster. When he dismounted, his legs felt like two flakes of gold leaf, and he almost collapsed, recovering just before Ardune noticed. He straightened up, eked out a weak grin, and hoped his father didn't realize that he was so scared.

In a small clearing, three pug-faced Fracodians sat around a campfire, making a disgusting scene as they dined on a few rabbits. One tore a leg off, stuffed it into his mouth, and ate the whole thing— bones and all. Another preferred the ribs, crunching away on the tiny delicacies. The final Fracodian just ripped meat from the carcass and swallowed it without chewing.

As the father and son team approached, the Fracodians dropped their meal, grabbed their spiked clubs, and let out grunts of delight at the thought of mauling some humans. They approached the pair recklessly, believing a lone man and a child were no match for themselves.

Ardune pushed his son out in front and whispered, "Capture one of them alive, Arwold. We must learn if they are scouts in advance of a larger band of raiders."

Arwold watched the hairy fiends closing in. He saw their muscles bulging, their menacing eyes sizing him up, and their mouths drooling. The young boy froze. He wanted to move. He wanted to raise his sword in defense, but his limbs wouldn't obey him. Try as he might, Arwold could do nothing more than stand and stare as they drew closer.

"What do you wait for, Arwold?" yelled his father. "Attack those filthy animals!"

Arwold wanted to teach the three evil creatures a lesson for assaulting the merchants and stealing their goods. He wanted to prove to himself that he was a young man instead of a child. Most importantly, he wanted to impress his father, but it was no use because fear had completely paralyzed his body.

The Fracodians were a few paces away and advancing quickly. It would be seconds before they were upon Arwold with their deadly weapons, and Ardune hadn't budged from the spot behind his son. The warrior still expected Arwold to overcome his fear. The first Fracodian raised its club and began to smirk, thinking how easy it would be to kill these two wayward humans.

"Human scum!" the Fracodian bellowed, its foul breath slapping Arwold in the face. The young boy wrinkled his nose in disgust, but didn't otherwise make a single movement.

Then his father spoke the infamous words: "You must not fear evil, Arwold, for it has no power over the good at heart." Ardune placed a hand on the hilt of his sword.

The Fracodian swung its weapon straight at Arwold's head. In the last instant before the club hit his son, Ardune flicked his own weapon, the family claymore, into its way. The two weapons bounced off each other with a clang. Continuing his swing in a circular motion, Ardune brought his sword up and around through the neck of the Fracodian.

"I am disappointed in you, Arwold," his father admonished as he speedily dispatched the second Fracodian. "You will be disciplined for your lack of action." Ardune knocked out the remaining Fracodian, pounding it firmly in the head with the crystal sphere at the base of the claymore. He heaved the limp body onto his horse and said, "Tie up the horses they stole, then gather what you can of their loot and return everything to the merchants. Do not take long, for you shall have extra chores tonight—cleaning and polishing all our weapons and armor." Ardune trotted back to town without a single glance at his son.

When his father was out of sight, Arwold finally moved. First, he screamed, both in frustration and in anger. He cursed at himself and at the dead Fracodians. Finally, he took out his own sword and violently hacked at the bodies on the ground.

"Never again shall I fear anything!" he swore.

Those memories made Arwold even more resolute in his stance against the crypt ghouls. With extra energy and a few well-placed blows, he minced the ghoul nearest to him. Arwold turned to the creatures mauling the fallen warrior and roared, "Filthy beasts! You shall never again feast on human flesh." He kicked them away from the body of his comrade and carved them into small pieces. Arwold no longer had any conscious thoughts about the battle; his body was a machine hacking away at the crypt ghouls. Mud, dried blood, and rotting flesh covered his previously shiny sword and armor, but Arwold was completely unaware of his appearance. He had but one overriding goal in his mind: find and destroy the necromancer responsible for bringing these unholy creatures to life.

In the murky distance, the dim figure of the necromancer waved his arms in a mystical formation. He called out a few magical words, threw an object toward Arwold, and vanished into the darkness. The object, a large human femur covered in a sticky black liquid, seemed to hover in the air for a moment before it landed beside Arwold's feet and began transforming into a skeleton. It attracted bones from the dead bodies lying on the battlefield as if it were a powerful magnet and they were made of steel. Some came with sinew still attached, and others popped clean out of their former bodies. Bones from the feet, leg, hips, hands, arms, ribs, and a skull all merged into a single hideous entity nearly seven feet tall.

By this time, Arwold had destroyed the last of the crypt ghouls and turned his gaze to the spot where the necromancer had stood only moments before. "Hide if you must, wizard," shouted Arwold as he held up his claymore. "Upon this sword shall I bring you justice!"

As soon as it had fully formed, the skeleton grabbed the nearest weapon from the ground and wildly attacked Arwold. The warrior easily blocked the blade and followed with a swift counterattack, breaking a few of the skeleton's ribs. "Those cowards," he thought. "If they did not leave me to fight alone, I would have rid the world of that evil necromancer today. Now I have lost him again. I swear next time he shall not fare so well."

Arwold's clean-shaven face showed no sign of emotion as he raised his sword for another attack. "At least I will get some good practice finishing off this infernal creature."

CHAPTER III

THE EIGHT SCHOOLS OF MAGIC

Minaras leaned out of his second-story window and inhaled the fresh morning air. The salty smell invigorated him, although the overnight rains had diluted it somewhat. Below him, the Sinewan River surged higher than normal as it rushed to deposit its excess storm water into the Great Ocean, just visible on the horizon. Between his house and the ocean, the old wizard could see dozens of fishing cottages rising from the Anxiar Delta on stilts, and behind them, the sails of Seaton's fleet growing smaller as they headed for the prime fishing grounds of the southern waters.

"The Giant Fluke must be in season," Minaras thought. "Has it been a full year already? It seems like yesterday that Thulin and Oswynn began their studies, and yet they have barely completed a single subject."

Absently turning around, Minaras swept a stack of papers off his desk and replaced them with a heavy tome. He dropped into his comfortably padded chair and thumbed through the chapters, each describing one of the eight schools of magic:

Alchemy—the study of liquids and potions
Necromancy—the study of death and the dead
Conjuration—the study of imbuing everyday objects with special

powers
Elemental—the manipulation of the four elements: Air, Earth,
Fire, and Water
Illusion—the study of disguise and deception
Sorcery—the summoning and control of spirits
Thaumaturgy—the study of blessings and miracles
Transmutation—the transformation of one or more objects into
another

Leaving the book open to the chapter on necromancy, Minaras
rose from his desk to prepare for the day's lecture. He walked past a
wall lined with spyglasses, sextants, and compasses on his way to the
back of the room, where he grabbed two large beakers, two stirring
rods, and two granite mortars. Minaras placed one of each item onto
a pair of tables in front of his desk. Then he rummaged through the
pockets of his robe until he found a flask of white pebbles and divided
them evenly between the mortars.

Minaras returned to the back of the room and removed a human
skeleton from a large trunk. The bones looked real but were replicas
made for him by a local transmuter. The work was skilled, yet not
quite the quality that his former partner was capable of creating. The
skeleton brought back memories of the days he used to travel
throughout the land, battling fierce creatures and finding lost treasures. A spark came to his bright blue eyes as Minaras ran a hand
across his head, wondering where the time and his hair had gone. He
neither felt nor looked half his seventy years. The old wizard had
shared fabulous adventures with this old partner, Sigmus. Between his
elemental magic and Sigmus' transmutation, they made a formidable
duo. One of Minaras's favorite combinations was to throw a stone
into the air and cast his "Flying Boulder" spell, causing it to increase
in size as it flew. Sigmus would then transform the boulder into the
shape of a spear. Neither beast nor building could stand in the way of
the massive projectile.

Minaras sighed when he realized that it was nearly time for his lecture. As if on cue, Thulin arrived, carrying extra parchments and

quills for his notes. In his late teens, Thulin was almost as tall as Minaras, but had a lighter frame and a scholarly look. He quietly took his seat at the table and laid out his papers, careful to avoid touching the glassware.

Oswynn, five years younger and a head shorter, strolled into the study a few minutes later, still munching on his breakfast biscuit. As soon as he stepped into the room, he took one look at the beakers on the table and blurted out, "I have had enough of alchemy. It is the weakest of all the schools!"

Minaras hung the skeleton on the wall behind his desk before calmly responding, "Alchemy may be the easiest to learn, Oswynn, but it is in no way weaker than any of the other schools of magic. I have heard tales of an alchemist so powerful he could bring down an entire mountain. Magic is but a tool for wizards to use. The energy from within us determines how weak or strong a spell will be. Learn how to harness your energy and you will be able to work wonders using even the simplest of spells."

Oswynn gave a skeptical look to his master. "Even the lowest peasant knows that alchemy is the weakest of the schools and elemental the strongest. Minaras is either mistaken or trying to trick me into enjoying the unworthy subject. An alchemist would never be able to destroy a mountain," thought Oswynn, shaking his head as he fell into his seat beside Thulin.

"Why do you not teach us elemental magic and forgo the other schools?" asked Oswynn. "Are you not the greatest elementalist in the land? Why bother with anything else?"

"It is true that I, like most wizards, have chosen to concentrate on just one school of magic, but there are a few who are adept at two or three. I have even heard legends of a powerful mage who had mastered all eight schools many centuries ago. Ultimately, it is your choice, and I would not be a good teacher if I did not give you a broad range of knowledge on which to base your decision."

Despite his explanation, Minaras couldn't wait to begin teaching the fundamentals of elemental magic.

"As it so happens," he said, "you will be studying necromancy today."

Oswynn's face brightened with the good news, but Minaras didn't notice. He had already buried his head in the old tome and began the lecture with a dry reading. "Necromancy is magic dealing with death and the dead. Although it is its own school of magic, necromancy is closely related to both sorcery and alchemy." He continued quoting from the book in a bored monotone, not once lifting his eyes to his students.

Thulin listened attentively to his master and took frequent notes, glancing back and forth between the papers on his desk. He always understood the theory, but there was something missing in practice. He was like an aspiring artist who knew the names of every color in his palette but was unable to combine them into a coherent picture.

Oswynn was the exact opposite. If he were an art student, then he wouldn't be able to tell you the difference between crimson and scarlet, orange and ochre, or yellow and dandelion, but he could use those colors to form a painting of the sunset that rivaled the beauty of the real thing.

Once again, Oswynn didn't appear to be listening to his master. During the lecture, he focused exclusively on the items in front of him and kept playing with the water. He shook the container, then stirred the liquid with the glass rod and watched the water spin into a small vortex before finally settling down. Thulin glanced over at him with a frown. "Put the beaker down, Oswynn," he cautioned under his breath, "and listen to our master."

Oswynn flicked some water at Thulin with a smile and immediately pretended to listen to the lecture. Thulin wiped his arm while continuing to take notes. He shook his head, wondering why Minaras put up with such a disrespectful peasant, one who never seemed to take his work seriously. When his master paused ever so briefly, Thulin lifted his eyes from the page and caught a glimpse of Oswynn's rough, calloused hands. "Return to the farm where you belong," he thought, "you would be better off weeding than wizarding."

Minaras continued reading about necromantic theory for a full hour before it was time for his students to try some magic on their own. Oswynn was half-asleep but perked up when he heard the sound of the book closing.

"You will find some bone fragments in your mortar," said Minaras. "You must first crush them into a fine powder and then—"

"Using what?" interrupted Oswynn.

Minaras quickly realized his oversight, pulled two pebbles from a pocket in his robe, and chanted, "*Aweaxan stan lang. Aweaxan stan lang.*" At the completion of the spell, both stones elongated into cylindrical shapes. Minaras held them in his outstretched hand, nodding at Oswynn. The younger apprentice got up and retrieved a pestle for both himself and Thulin.

"That was a transmutation spell," he whispered.

Minaras continued his instructions. "When you have finished crushing the bone fragments, take one ounce of the resulting powder and stir it into the water with the following incantation, '*brim hweorfan blaec awendan*'. This will turn your water into Dark Whey, a common component used in many necromantic spells."

Oswynn pulverized the small pieces of bone in his mortar. Then he grabbed a handful of the white powder, threw it into the beaker, and shook the mixture while chanting the magic words. Instantly, the water turned black. "This is no fun," he thought. "Why can we not raise the dead or make that fake skeleton walk around the room? Why else would it be hanging on the wall if not to be animated? Necromancy is just as boring as alchemy."

Thulin wasn't as successful as Oswynn with the spell. After crushing the pieces of bone into a beautiful powder of uniform texture, he measured exactly one ounce, carefully poured it into his water, and meticulously stirred it with the glass rod to the same rhythm as his chanting. A beaker of cloudy water was his only reward. He kept stirring and repeating the enchantment with no effect.

"Why does this not work? I followed the instructions precisely," whined Thulin.

"Give up, Thulin. Your parents may be the greatest conjurers in the land, but magic is not for you," teased Oswynn, provocatively shaking his beaker full of the inky black liquid.

Overly angered at Oswynn's gesture, Thulin quickly responded, "At least I am no farmer. I shall succeed in converting this water into Dark Whey."

Thulin rummaged through his notes. "I must have forgotten something. Maybe my measurement of the powder was off by a fraction." To compensate, he added a pinch more and continued stirring. Nothing happened.

While his students were hard at work with their experiment, Minaras gazed through the open window at the noon sky. The river had ebbed, and Minaras could just make out the distinctive smell of low tide, a combination of mud, seaweed, and mussels drying in the sun. Eventually, his mind returned to the lecture, and he shuffled around the table behind Thulin and Oswynn. "How do you fare with the spell?" he asked, glancing back and forth between the two of them while peeking at the door through the corner of his eye.

Thulin looked up from the table and began, "My water remains cloudy—" but Minaras cut him off before he could finish his complaint.

"Keep trying, Thulin. This is fundamentally important to understanding necromancy. Now, I must attend to an errand. The village of Two Rivers is unable to contain its floodwaters, and I must train their local elementalist before the excess water destroys their crops. You two will research the mystical properties of bone powder and complete a full paper on your findings by the time I return this evening."

A moment later, he was gone, leaving his two students alone to complete their work. Thulin rifled through his notes with one hand and constantly stirred, chanted, and added bone powder with the other. He continued his attempts to create Dark Whey for the better part of an hour, but was unable to turn the water gray, let alone black.

"You have too much powder in your water. Spill it out and try again," offered Oswynn, genuinely trying to be helpful.

Thulin glared at him. "I know what I am doing. Should you not begin your research as our master ordered? Or can you not find your way to the library?"

"As you wish," said Oswynn, jumping up from the table and accidentally spilling his beaker. The black liquid oozed onto Thulin's notes and dripped onto his lap. Oswynn grinned as he skipped out of the room, forcing Thulin to clean up the mess before he could return to his failed spell.

Later that evening, Minaras had yet to return, but the two apprentices were used to his absence. It was much more common for him to extend his outings by a day or two than to shorten them by an hour. After giving up on the Dark Whey temporarily, Thulin brought his dinner upstairs to the library, where he found thousands of books packed into shelves, stacked randomly about the floor, and hidden under a circular table. There were only two spots in the entire room noticeably devoid of clutter: the first was the entrance to the room and the other was a small section of the back wall containing nothing but a painting of a doomed ship navigating a stormy ocean. Thulin shook his head at the mess. "If Minaras were to organize his materials instead of haphazardly throwing them about, he would have a truly impressive collection. The dust covering the less used tomes makes it even more difficult for me to conduct any type of ordered research." Even so, Thulin always managed to impress his master with the results of his assignments, and he vowed to do no less this time.

Both apprentices sat with a plate of food, a mug of cider, and a book in front of them. Thulin poured through his selection, *A Treatise on the Relationship between Alchemy and Necromancy*, occasionally taking a bite of meat or bread. Oswynn, however, was almost finished with his meal and had yet to open the large tome next to his plate, a lengthy catalog of alchemical components. He swallowed his last bite, looked up at Thulin, and remarked, "I grow tired of all this dreary studying." He pushed the book to the center of the table. "You may enjoy the endless lectures and reading, but I want to learn powerful magic, transmutation or elemental."

Without taking his eyes off his page, Thulin answered, "Do not worry Oswynn, our master shall teach us all we wish in due time." Still absorbed in his reading, Thulin pushed the book back to Oswynn without missing a single word. "Start reading now or you shall not finish your work in time," he ordered.

Oswynn thumbed through a few pages, not paying much attention to the contents. "This is of no use to me. It is but a dull list of ingredients, and I wish to learn spell-casting." He turned and stared at the painting in the back of the library. The ship called out to him, begging him to save it from its treacherous journey. "I do think I could teach myself if I had the proper materials. Perhaps there are books of more interest in the back room," he said with a mischievous gleam in his eyes.

"Oswynn, you know Minaras has expressly forbidden us to enter his personal archive," warned Thulin.

Oswynn looked at Thulin and let out a snicker. He continued flipping through the pages of the catalog with barely a glance at the words.

CHAPTER IV

THE WIZARD AND THE WARRIOR

It was a very busy night at The Weary Traveler, the only tavern in the border village of Farset. Calan, the innkeeper, Corselle, his wife, and Mena, his daughter, were having a difficult time keeping up with the demands of all their customers. Mena constantly rushed back and forth from the tables to the kitchen, while Calan and Corselle cooked everything in sight, hoping the food wouldn't run out. The family dog wisely retreated to the outdoors early in the evening.

"I shall be glad when these traders have left for Two Rivers," Mena said on one of her frequent trips into the back room.

"'Tis quite demanding on us when the traders are in town," her father agreed, while simultaneously stirring the contents of two large pots, "but they offer good merchandise this year. I should have expected they would arrive early with all the mild weather we have seen."

"If you had expected this, then you should have prepared better," scolded Corselle, waving her carving knife in his direction. "All our small game is gone, and we are almost out of venison."

"Will we have enough to last the night?" asked Mena.

"I do hope so. Our guests have had a long journey from Foxmoor," said Calan. Then, with a glance at his wife, he added,

"Tomorrow, I shall set out more traps, and Mena shall make an extra trip into town."

"Must I?" Mena whined. "With our extra business, I was hoping to look for some new fabric."

"The traders will be here for a few days," said her mother. "You shall have time enough to shop once our cupboards are full."

With a nod at a pile of untouched food tucked away near the fireplace, Mena asked, "Could we not use some of his meal tonight?"

"No," Corselle said firmly, "he will be here soon. Do you think he would not notice if anything were missing?"

Mena shrugged her shoulders, picked up two plates of venison, and dropped them off at a table in the corner of the dining area. Four hungry men dug into the food, remarking on how well it had been prepared. The voice of a young boy interrupted them.

"This be Xarun's table," he said, peeking around the room. "This comes from a plant found only in the wastelands."

He dropped a bracelet of braided twine on the table and added, "Four coppers."

"The badlands are a dangerous place, even for a caravan of armed men," warned the merchant. "You should not leave the safety of your village."

"Nothing dares to bother us here or in the wastelands. Xarun has seen to that."

The merchant nearest him dropped a shiny brass coin into this hand and asked, "Who is this Xarun and why do you say this is his table?"

"Xarun sits in the corner seat every night. If he sees you here, he will crush you with his bare fingers. I heard he single-handedly fought off an entire band of marauders, and he once pulled a tree from the ground to battle a vicious sabertooth that roamed too close to town. The cat only escaped with its life because Xarun had to carry an entire family to the healer."

"This Xarun sounds like a reasonable man," said the merchant.

"He tore down their house when they ran out of food during the feast in his honor," continued the boy. "And do not ask about his master who went missing when I was a baby."

"Then let us hope we finish our meal before he arrives."

"And there is enough for him to eat," added a second merchant.

"Here! Here!" the four men shouted and continued eating.

The boy glanced back at the door and scurried away as a huge figure appeared. Xarun stood in the doorway, a veritable bear of a man, both in size and personality. He stood just over six feet tall, weighed nearly as much as two men, and had very few patches of skin that were not covered with thick black hair. His massive chest and arms had been a testament to his physical power ever since he was a young apprentice to the local woodcutter.

Xarun let out a quick yawn, rubbed his eyes, and boomed, "Who be at my table?"

Mena rushed up to him and explained, "Good Xarun, I am sorry, but the traders arrived today, and we were not ready for them. Do forgive us."

He gave an angry "humph" and ambled toward his usual table in the corner of the room. The four men sitting there were halfway through their dinner, but it was his table and he was hungry. Xarun growled, "Your dinner be over," lifted the entire table into the air, and spilled everything onto the floor. The plates, mugs, forks, and knives clattered as they hit the ground by his feet. The traders rose silently from their chairs and left the room. One look at the warrior was enough to convince them that the stories they had just heard were true.

Xarun replaced the table and sat down as Mena rushed into the kitchen. Without a moment's delay, she returned with Calan and Corselle carrying the food they had set aside for him. Together, they laid out a meal that could easily have fed a family of eight: two different cuts of roasted venison, three lamb chops, two loaves of dark bread, several bowls of vegetables (destined to be untouched), a huge pot of savory stew, and a plate of fresh fruit. In their haste, however, they had forgotten to bring him anything to drink.

Reaching over to the nearest table, he seized a silver mug from another merchant, who pretended not to notice. Xarun emptied it onto the floor and banged it on the table to catch the attention of Mena, who was apologizing to the displaced traders. "I be adry!" he yelled. The young woman excused herself from the men and immediately ran to fetch Xarun some of his favorite ale.

In the meantime, the big warrior began eating his dinner. He munched on the end of one of the breads, but realized he was so thirsty he couldn't take another bite. "Where be my ale?" he cried out, launching some crumbs from his mouth.

The refreshing drink Xarun was hoping for didn't answer his call. Instead, a pouch of coins landed on the table in front of him with a loud clink. A man, buried beneath a dark brown robe, approached the table. In his left hand, the wizard held an intricately carved wooden staff about five feet long. Images of wispy creatures covered the shaft, each inlaid with two tiny citrine eyes. The wizard pulled back his hood to reveal a pair of tan eyes set into a timeworn face. Although his rough, wrinkled skin made him appear quite old, Ahriman was only in his mid-thirties.

"I have need of a talented warrior," he began in a gruff voice. "Everyone in this village says there is none greater than you."

"They speak true," Xarun replied, grabbing his fresh mug of ale from Mena, who had just returned. He gulped down half of the drink and wiped his mouth on his arm.

"I need no coins. Begone, wizard!" he commanded with a wave of his free hand. He had suffered through enough distractions for the night, and now it was time to eat.

The much larger man failed to intimidate Ahriman. He rested his staff gently against the table and defiantly sat across from Xarun, drawing a fierce stare from the feasting warrior. "Would you not like to earn some extra gold?" Ahriman nodded at the bag of gold on the table. "This would be but a small portion of your reward. You could have all the riches you desire."

Xarun tore into a lamb chop. Without dropping the piece of meat, he pulled aside the next person to pass by his table. "Lay your coins here, peasant," he commanded, pointing at the table with the bone in his hand.

Quivering, the man reached into his shirt, pulled out a few brass coins, and dropped them onto the platter as the warrior had ordered. "G ... g ... good Xarun, I ... I do obey. 'Tis all I have." Xarun waved the man away, polished off another lamb chop, and gave the wizard a greasy sneer.

Ahriman was neither impressed nor disgusted by Xarun's behavior. He stared back at the big man, coldly and silently.

Xarun's mood dropped a notch when he realized the wizard wasn't going to leave him alone to enjoy his meal. He finished eating and pushed the plate of empty bones to the side. "What do you want, wizard?" he demanded. "I have much to do."

"I assure you, what I offer will be more exciting than sleeping the entire day and bullying the locals at night."

"He looks like a Ferfolk," thought Xarun with a scowl. The Ferfolk were a tall, sturdy race with tough, leathery skin as thick as a good suit of hide armor. Their strong, powerful limbs and natural resistance to the effects of magic made them exceptional warriors. "There be no Ferfolk wizards," he decided with a shake of his head.

Having finally gotten Xarun's attention, Ahriman asked. "What do you know of the Arboreals?"

"Arboreals keep to their forest," Xarun replied without hesitation. In all the years he had lived in Farset, the Arboreals had never attacked the village, either directly or indirectly. One or two would show up each year to trade with the humans, but that was the full extent of their interaction.

"Humans and Arboreals have been at peace with each other for centuries, but tell me what you mean by 'their forest,' Xarun? Do you not realize they have been expanding their forest into human lands for ages?" Ahriman's lips curled up into a slight grin as if he enjoyed taunting the big warrior.

"Expanding into human lands?" echoed a shocked Xarun, his demeanor changing from one of amusement to one of concern. "How can this be?"

Ahriman had hit a nerve in Xarun and he knew it. The wizard leaned forward and asked, "When you were a child, where was the boundary to the Arboreal Forest?" Ahriman paused, allowing Xarun to squirm. "And where is the boundary today?" he continued.

Xarun leaned back in his chair and folded his arms across his chest. With a furrowed brow, he kept his eyes on Ahriman and thought back to his childhood. The boundary had seemed much farther away when he was younger, but he always believed that was because of the natural tendency for everything to appear larger to a child. Certainly, the village itself seemed to be a limitless spot for exploration and adventure when he was growing up, while now he knew it to be a relatively small habitation. Could the same also be true for the border, or was the Arboreal Forest drawing nearer to Farset?

"Many years ago, there was another human kingdom between here and the Arboreals," explained the wizard. "That kingdom has long since disappeared. A sea of vegetation now covers what once was a grand castle and acres of farmland. The Arboreals have no intention of—"

"I shall start not a war!" Xarun interrupted.

Ahriman shook his head. "Allow me to finish, for you will soon understand that I do not desire to wage a war against the Arboreals. I merely wish to recover a unique item they took from us humans. The object in question is held inside a small fortress close to Farset."

"Inside an Arboreal fortress!" said Xarun with a roar of laughter. "Where be your army?"

Convinced that he had succeeded in persuading the large warrior to join his cause, Ahriman picked up a bright red apple from the plate of fruit and sat back in his chair. "I assure you, we will not need an army … if you are as capable as I have been told." He took a bite from the apple. "The two of us should be just enough to slip into the fortress and retrieve the small trinket. You might even get to try your axe against a few of the Arboreals. They are not unskilled with a sword."

Xarun smiled as he lifted the pouch of gold and threw it back to Ahriman. Then, snapping his fingers at Mena, he yelled, "More ale! My friend be adry!"

CHAPTER V

CIVILIZATION

Halia lay wet and shivering on the raft. It had been a chilly night, made worse by a passing shower. She rolled over, catching a face full of the warm, early morning sun. Staring upward, the treetops seemed as densely packed as ever. "I hope this river does not head south," she thought. "If I become lost in the Arboreal Forest, I shall never see civilization again. That would be just my luck after finding this treasure." Halia removed the crystal sphere from her pouch and held it up to the sky, gazing at the clouds through the transparent glass. "This must be worth something to have been hidden so well."

The raft began to move faster, caught in a strong current. Halia replaced the sphere in her pouch, afraid it would bounce out of her grip and into the water. She got onto her knees and looked ahead. The once meandering river appeared to be wider than she recalled, and she hadn't seen any whitewater, until now. "I may need some type of paddle—or perhaps a better raft," she thought as water splashed up between the slats. Using her hands, Halia tried to guide the raft toward the shore. She was almost there when she noticed a wild boar drinking from the water downstream. Her stomach growled, causing her to wonder how difficult it would be to capture and kill the animal for food. "'Tis but a brainless beast," she whispered and frantically splashed her way to the riverbank. "At least I shall not die hungry."

Halia pulled the raft out of the water and dragged it into a patch of tall reeds, where she had a momentary vision of the raft's former owner lying on his deathbed of spikes. With a quick shiver, she said, "I promise to return for you," and quietly crept toward the boar.

Drawing closer and closer to the beast, she pulled the small knife from her belt and looked at its slender blade with a frown. "Wild boars are dangerous when angered. This tiny weapon had best be enough to pierce the thick hide on its neck." Halia crouched low to stalk her prey, creeping slowly along the ground. "Perhaps this shall turn out to be an easy meal." Suddenly, a slight breeze drifted past, not more than the puff of a baby's breath. The boar, detecting a strange scent, darted into the woods just before Halia was within reach.

Halia dashed after the animal, which ducked under a clump of vines and through a small bush as if it were sprinting across open land. She kept a close eye on the beast and did well to follow it as long as she could, but the boar finally escaped when a thicket of wild roses snagged her cloak and held it fast. It took several minutes to pry her clothing loose from the mass of thorns. The result of her hunt was nothing more than a plethora of small cuts along with a torn cloak. She trudged back to the raft, dejected and hungrier than ever. From then on, she ate only the few wild berries she was able to find growing along the banks of the river. "This is your fault," she scolded the water.

For more than a week, Halia drifted downstream, growing more hungry and tired with each day. Soon, she no longer cared where the river led, as long as it was dry. She dreamed of returning to Hillside or even the barren desert to the west. Her spirit was broken and her clothes were a mess. A thick layer of river muck permanently covered her pants, her boots were coming apart, and her cloak was shredded. Halia had also given up eating berries. It was too tiring to bring the raft ashore and secure it only to collect a handful of the small, sour fruits. She merely lay on the raft, floating with the current, day and night.

Just when all hope seemed lost, the trees of the forest began to thin out and patches of farmland dotted the landscape. Halia had reached the outskirts of Seaton. She sat up and looked at the distant city. "Civilization at last!" she said to herself in a cracked voice. "Now I shall dry off, eat a decent meal, and get a good night's sleep."

For the last time, Halia steered to the edge of the river and dragged herself onto the shore. Happy to be off the water, she kicked the raft and watched it disappear downstream. A moment later, she began walking the remaining distance into town. At first, she had to crawl, her weak legs buckling under her light frame when she tried to stand. As feeling slowly returned to her limbs, she straightened up and continued toward the city. Halia slogged through muddy streams, across a smelly sheep pasture, and even past a field of compost heaps, but it didn't matter to her. She would soon be in her natural environment. It was there that she could take what she needed and blend into the background. "Why did I ever leave Zairn?" she wondered. "Instead of heading inland, I should have hidden in the outskirts and returned after a month."

Halia passed dozens of outlying farms and peasant homes on her long walk. She could have stopped and begged for some food but instead made a beeline into Seaton, stopping once when she spied a nice gray cloak hanging out to dry and decided to exchange it with her set of rags.

By nightfall, Halia had reached the city proper. The sun had set, and the merchants had closed their shops. The taverns by the harbor, however, were drawing large crowds of sailors and traders intermingled with the occasional landowner or lesser noble. Halia naturally gravitated toward the docks district, thinking it the most likely place to find some desperately needed money.

Finding a shadowy spot in which to hide, Halia sat and waited for a suitable target. First, she saw two groups of sailors pass by, but it was likely that only one or two of the men in each group would be carrying any coins. It would be too risky for her to approach them and try to guess who had the money. Next, a merchant who had just closed his shop was heading to a tavern. He would have been a good target except that behind him was a pair of city guards. Using good judgment, especially given her dire need for food, Halia continued waiting. It wasn't long before a group of three well-dressed traders heading in her direction rewarded her patience. Halia wrapped herself in the gray cloak and walked tentatively toward the traders, trying to stifle her growling stomach.

The hood of her cloak, large enough for a Ferfolk, drooped over her face and made it quite difficult to see. "I must take care tonight," she thought, "I am tired and hungry, which will lead to mistakes." She took the small knife from her belt and held it tightly under her sleeve. When she was within two paces of the group, she pretended to accidentally trip and bump into one of the men. At the exact moment of impact, her hand darted out from her cloak to the man's belt, made a quick slice with the knife, and withdrew before he noticed anything.

"Pray pardon, good sir," Halia apologized hoarsely as she recovered from her mock fall and stepped to the side. She continued walking without glancing back, hoping that she hadn't been seen. When she was a few paces away from the group, Halia let out a smile. Hidden in her hand was a pouch full of shiny coins.

"Stand, thief!" A faint shout echoed in the distance as a hooded figure dashed down the dimly lit street holding a small object clutched tightly to its chest. The figure turned the corner and, not looking where it was running, bumped straight into Arwold, who was on his way home from an early dinner.

Arwold grabbed the thief and pulled back the hood to reveal a thin boy of no more than nine years. "Where do you run, lad?" the warrior asked, already knowing that the child had stolen something.

"I ... I be on my way home," the boy answered.

"You do seem to be in a hurry to get there. Perhaps you have taken something that did not belong to you?"

"N ... n ... no, sir," he said, trying to squirm out of Arwold's strong grip.

The tall warrior frowned. "Dare you speak lies to me? I know what you have done! Do you think I did not hear the call for help?"

The emaciated boy gave Arwold a look of desperation and pleaded, "Prithee good sir, hurt me not. I want only food ... for my family. We have had nothing to eat since—"

"Nay, do not speak to me of reasons!" Arwold tightened his grip on the child. "I shall deliver you to the constable at once! Beg for his mercy if you wish."

"You must not! My family will starve without this bread." The boy struggled to no avail. "Let me go, and I promise never to steal again. I be telling the truth now. You must believe me!"

Arwold wouldn't listen to the boy's pleadings. Stealing was stealing, and it was against the law in Krof. He lifted the boy into the air and carried him to the nearest guards. If he didn't teach the child a lesson now, who knows what atrocities he would commit in the future? By the time Arwold handed him over, the boy was crying, thinking of the cruel punishment that awaited him. The warrior then continued on his way home with a slightly springier stride, content that he had made his town a little safer tonight.

Back in Seaton, Halia removed a few coins from her newly acquired pouch as she walked toward the Misty Shores tavern. "Now for some fresh meat, a good drink, and a soft bed," she said to herself, tossing a silver coin into the air and catching it without looking.

At the entrance to the tavern, an old man sat begging for money. "Prithee, some coins for a starving soul?" he implored in a raspy voice as Halia approached.

She looked at the pouch and then back at the beggar. He was filthy, dressed in rags, and missing a leg. "If he truly is a cripple," thought Halia, "then I have found someone worse off than me." With a shrug, she dropped the pouch with the remaining coins into the beggar's lap before entering the tavern.

CHAPTER VI

HALIA'S DECEPTION

The first few rays of yellow sunlight peeked through the window in Halia's room but failed to rouse her. She slept straight through until late afternoon, awakening only when a pair of wharf dogs began barking and howling at the sight of a few fishing boats returning from their outings.

Startled by the noise, Halia leaped out of bed and spun around, spying the unfamiliar surroundings and trying to remember where she was. Having spent so much time on the raft, it took her a moment to shake off her disorientation and realize that she was safe in a boarding room above the pub. With a stretch and a yawn, Halia looked out the window at the loud dogs begging for scraps from the first of the boats to dock. Slowly, the events of the past few days flooded back into her mind: the seedy tavern where she ate and bought a bed for the night, the coins she stole, the raft on which she almost perished, and the crystal sphere she had found. "The sphere!" she exclaimed, quickly opening the pouch on her belt and hoping she hadn't been relieved of her prized possession during the night. Sleeping boarders were always an easy target for thieves or unscrupulous tavern owners. Fortunately, her treasure was still there. "I do seem to have lost half the day," she told the sphere, "but perhaps I can find someone who knows what you are before nightfall. You may yet bring me riches." She closed the pouch, firmly attached it to her belt, and trotted out of the room to the docks.

The numerous bait shops had already closed for the day, normally catering to the pre-dawn crowd, but Halia doubted they would have yielded any insights into her treasure. Instead, she began her search by talking to the sailors in town, careful to avoid any that looked the slightest bit suspicious. Most of them did their best to avoid her. Of the few who took the time to speak, none had any knowledge about the sphere. With her torn, dirty clothes and wearing an oversized, obviously stolen, cloak, she had a similarly difficult time getting any information from shopkeepers, who thought her to be a street urchin hoping to steal their goods.

"Before I do anything else," thought Halia, "I shall find a new set of clothes. Everyone must think of me as a noble, or at least a well-to-do trader from out of town. If I were a merchant, I would not welcome myself in these rags."

Within the hour, Halia found herself wearing a beautifully embroidered linen shirt; a soft wool hooded cloak, which fit her nicely; and a pair of deerskin boots. Unfortunately, she learned nothing more about the sphere other than the name of an expert jeweler in the wealthier part of town. She returned to the tavern frustrated and hungry but happy with her new outfit.

Halia woke early the next day, although it was still a good deal after sunrise, anxious to learn the value of the sphere and collect her gold. "The jeweler is bound to have answers for me," she thought excitedly, "but first I must make sure he knows I am wealthy." Halia spent a few minutes in her room practicing an elegant walk: holding her head up high, keeping her shoulders back, and taking long, balanced steps. During the rehearsal, she constantly reminded herself, "You must act like a lady today. One misstep and the city guards are likely to haul you away."

Brimming with confidence, Halia left the tavern and headed for the wealthy district of Seaton. She strolled westward, away from the ocean, until the smell of fish no longer lingered in the air. The houses grew larger, belonging to the nobles and more prosperous merchants, with manicured gardens and wrought-iron gates. The more she distanced herself from the docks, the fancier the people's attire became, until even her new outfit looked cheap. Halia was admiring a particularly elegant jerkin when she realized the person she was staring at had pale green skin. "I have never seen an Arboreal before," she thought, her eyes affixed to his slender features. "I did not realize they ever ventured forth from the deep forest."

Without a word, the Arboreal entered a perfume shop, letting out an exotic aroma of nectar tinged with cinnamon. Halia took a deep breath of the spicy scent and dreamed of the riches that soon would be hers. In a daze, she drifted down the street with her eyes closed until she passed a blacksmith. The ringing of a hammer against an anvil reminded her that she needed more of a weapon than her small knife, but she soon forgot about obtaining a sword when she arrived at the Silver Plum, purveyor of fine gems and jewelry.

Halia entered a shop that was dimly lit and devoid of any visible jewelry. There were many tables in the room, each covered with metal instruments: files, chisels, cloths, hammers, and tongs of all sizes. Several wooden cups held tiny wires of gold and silver, and a larger tray overflowed with dull stones of every color imaginable. In the center of it all, Sterm sat in a small chair surrounded by a set of oil lamps, working away on a nondescript red stone. Completely engrossed in his project, he didn't even notice when Halia entered the shop. She waltzed up to his chair and hovered over him as he filed the tiny gem. When her shadow floated over his workspace and interrupted his concentration, Sterm looked up. He placed both the tool and the stone on the table and curtly asked, "Do you wish to buy or sell?"

"Neither … or perhaps both," Halia replied as she removed the crystal sphere from her pouch and showed it to the jeweler. "What can you tell me about this sphere?"

He took the orb from her and examined it in detail. He held it close to an oil lamp and brought it to the open door to view it in the sunlight. Then he looked at it under a magnifying glass and weighed it against a pile of metal chips on a scale. Finally, he handed it back to her saying, "This is not a natural gem but expertly crafted glass. You may have its weight in gold."

Halia considered accepting the seemingly generous trade, but she didn't trust the jeweler. "The value of the sphere most likely far outweighs gold. How could you make such an offer without knowing its true nature?" she asked.

"That is precisely why I can do no more than an even swap for gold. The orb you carry displays superior craftsmanship. One would not go through the trouble of seeking such perfection if it were not an important relic." Sterm picked up his file and gem and continued smoothing the corners of the stone. "I suggest you ask Duma for his help. You will find him at the end of this street."

At least he was an honest man if somewhat callous on the outside. Almost forgetting her proper manners, Halia remembered to thank him just before stepping into the street. She continued down the block, passing a furrier and a cheese shop whose smell was overpowering, until she came to a building with a painting of a white mortar and pestle on a sign above the doorway: Duma's Elixirs and Sundries. "An alchemist," thought Halia, "I wonder how much gold he would offer me if this were a magical sphere?"

She entered the shop and received a warm greeting from Duma. "Good day to you, young lady."

With magic and riches on her mind, Halia marched straight up to the alchemist and handed him the crystal sphere. "Sterm, the jeweler, suggested you may be able to help me. Know you anything about this?"

The alchemist, noting her abrupt manner but thinking it to be the condescending attitude that many nobles displayed toward other folk, took the sphere from her without any further words and studied it closely. He rolled it around in the palms of his hands; submerged it in a beaker of a greenish liquid, which began glowing immediately; dried it off on his robe; and handed it back to Halia with a puzzled look.

"This orb has had a powerful incantation placed upon it, but I can tell you no more."

Disappointed that the alchemist hadn't showered her with gold, Halia managed to say, "Many good thanks," before turning toward the exit.

Duma stepped in front of her, blocking the way. "Perhaps you could leave the sphere with me for a few days? There are others in Seaton who would be able to examine it in greater detail, and—"

"Nay," she interrupted, pulling her hood over her head, "I could not bear to part with it." Duma must have thought her a fool to make such a suggestion. Halia knew she would never see the sphere again had she left it with him. She stepped around the alchemist, continued toward the door, and was just about to leave the shop when Thulin walked in, nearly colliding with her.

"Hail, young Thulin," Duma greeted the apprentice. "What brings you to my shop this fine morning?"

"I am on an errand for Minaras. Have you any fresh Nightshade Root?"

Halia perked up at those words, quickly forming a plan in her mind. She glanced briefly at Thulin, memorizing his features, before ducking out the door with a grin spreading across her face. "Only a wizard would use a poisonous Nightshade plant, and a wizard might be just the type of person to help me determine the true value of the sphere. Unfortunately, wizards could be tricky and powerful as well as knowledgeable. I must take great care in determining to whom I will reveal this magical object."

"Anything for my good friend Minaras," the alchemist replied as he passed through a door in the back of the room.

Thulin happily paced around the shop, fascinated by every little item. As he stood in front of the shelves filled with glassware, he ran his hands over the various pipettes, beakers, and flasks, some empty and others containing colored liquids. Most of the vials had labels written in delicate script, but Thulin already knew what they held, based on the liquid's color, consistency, and placement in the room.

In his frequent visits to the shop, he had memorized the complete layout. When he came to a flask filled with "Essence of Night," a swirling black substance, he suddenly remembered another request from his master. He shouted to Duma in the other room, "Bring me a few strands of Black Widow's Silk as well!"

The alchemist called back, "Are we learning necromancy today? Or has Minaras finally given up on the elements and begun a new specialty?"

"We study necromancy."

"I had hoped the latter," responded Dumas. "Alchemy is an underappreciated discipline and is not much different than necromancy. How do you fare with your studies?"

"The theory is simple enough, but I have had some difficulty creating Dark Whey. I shall complete the potion soon enough, once I manage to get the correct proportions."

Duma returned from the back room with a long, hairy root and a handful of silk strands so thin they were nearly invisible. He placed each in a separate glass tube sealed with a cork stopper. "When you add the bone powder, does your water remain cloudy?" he asked, handing Thulin the supplies.

The apprentice nodded.

"Thulin, try to let the magic flow from within you to the potion. Otherwise, the powder will not react with the water, and you will be left with a useless mixture."

Showing no appreciation for the advice Duma had offered, Thulin turned and said in a flat voice, "I shall try." He exited the shop and headed home, gaining an extra shadow after passing the Silver Plum. Halia trailed him from a distance.

Thulin led her straight to his master's house at the southeastern corner of the wealthy district. The three-story house, taller and older than any of the other surrounding buildings, had a spectacular view of both the ocean and the river. Halia spent a few moments on the steps straightening her cloak before knocking. Thulin, who had just arrived himself, opened the door and immediately became transfixed by

Halia's bright smile, staring at her as if he had never seen a woman before. She stood half a head taller than him, with long, dark hair draped over her back. He was sure he recognized her from somewhere, but, having seen her face only briefly under the hood at Duma's shop, couldn't remember where.

With barely a glance at the young apprentice, Halia stated, "I have need of a wizard."

Thulin beamed and responded, "I am a wizard, the elder apprentice to—"

Halia cut him off. "I asked not for an apprentice. Where is your master?"

"My master is at home, but let it be known that I shall complete my training soon—"

Minaras, who happened to be passing by on his way to the kitchen, interrupted him. "Thulin, who is at the door? I was not expecting any visitors today."

"'Tis a young woman who requests the aid of a wizard, Master. She looks familiar, but I do not seem to recall—"

Minaras stepped in front of his apprentice and addressed Halia directly. "Good morning, young lady, I am the elementalist, Minaras. What do you wish of me?"

Halia, continuing her act, put on a haughty air and asked, "Do you always conduct business from your doorstep?"

Her ruse didn't fool Minaras. He held back an urge to grin and stood aside, motioning for Halia to enter. "Please forgive my manners. You are welcome into my home."

She accepted his invitation, ignoring Thulin as she walked past him.

Minaras watched closely as Halia stepped into his house, trying to remain calm despite his curiosity. "Why would someone pretending to be a noble want to enter a wizard's home?" he wondered. "There are much easier targets if stealing gold is the answer." He led both Thulin and their guest into his study, pulled out a chair for her, and sat down while Thulin hopped into the seat beside Halia.

Minaras waved his hand around the room and said, "I trust these surroundings suit you better."

Halia spun about, taking note of the decor. "Are you a ship captain thinking he is a wizard or a wizard thinking he is a sailor?" she asked.

Thulin was shocked at her candor, but Minaras chuckled. Despite her charade, the wizard already liked her, which only deepened his interest. He leaned over and whispered in her ear, "I am as much a captain as you are a wealthy noble."

"I see," she purred, quietly reaching inside her pouch. Halia wondered briefly what had given her away, but she knew that Minaras was just the wizard to assist her. He had seen through her disguise and neither threw her out nor alerted his apprentice to the deception. She unfolded her fingers to reveal the crystal sphere.

Arwold, at his home in the distant town of Krof, sat down to sharpen his sword and polish his armor, following the same morning routine he performed every day of the year. First, he carefully laid out his equipment on a table. Then, with a piece of clean cloth, he took each item in turn and polished it meticulously. His armor would shine like new by the time he was done. When he got to the claymore, he honed the blade and cleaned it with extra care. His hand would frequently touch the sphere on the hilt of his family sword. Arwold smiled when he remembered the time his friend Calazar had tried to wield the claymore. The warrior, strong as he was, could do little more than drag it along the ground. The thought reminded Arwold that he was due to check on the progress of the mercenaries. With a final wipe of the cloth, Arwold returned the sword to the table and began packing for his short trip.

Upon viewing the sphere, Halia's eyes widened as she let out a roar of astonishment. "Never before have I seen such a color!"

She handed it to Minaras and pointed at a small purple dot glowing inside, about a quarter of the way in toward the center. The mysterious purple spot disappeared moments later.

Minaras took the sphere from Halia and inspected it from all angles. His brows furrowed at the puzzling object. He had neither seen nor heard of anything like it in all of his numerous travels. He was no expert in artifacts, but he liked to think he could at least identify most magical items.

"The jeweler and alchemist knew naught about it, though the alchemist determined it to be enchanted," Halia recounted.

"Whence came this sphere?" asked Minaras.

With a slight hesitation, Halia made up a lie. "'Tis an old family heirloom, passed down to me from my recently departed grandmother. Know you its worth?"

Minaras eyed her suspiciously. "I do not, but I certainly agree with Duma that it is magical in nature. I would like to study this further. Would you consider leaving it with me for a few days?"

Halia shook her head. "Nay, I shall find an answer to my question elsewhere." She stretched her arm toward Minaras to retrieve the sphere, but the wizard closed his hand, denying her the object for the moment.

"Thulin," he said, "find Oswynn and do a bit of research for me. Start with the *Sorcerer's Mineralogy*."

Minaras opened his hand and held the sphere up to the window. Even in the bright daylight, he couldn't detect a single flaw in the transparent orb. "With an heirloom such as this, you must come from a fine home, no doubt."

"No doubt," echoed Halia, her smile fading as she averted her eyes.

Once Thulin had left the study, Minaras turned to her with a direct look. "I should like to know where 'your family' is from. It may help me in deciphering the origin of this enchanted crystal."

Halia pointed outside. "They live up yonder river, not far from the village of Hillside."

Minaras walked to the window and peered at the Anxiar flowing into the ocean. Running along the southern edge of the human lands, there were relatively few habitations built along the river. Perhaps a trip upstream was in order. "Since you are a stranger in town, you will stay with me for a few days while my apprentices conduct the research." He placed the sphere in one of his empty pockets, giving Halia no choice other than to accept his invitation.

After offering Halia a quick bite of lunch, Minaras led her to the library on the top floor of his house. "I have been collecting books ever since I was an apprentice many years ago. In my youth, I traveled to the ends of the kingdoms, and from each place I visited I would bring home a score of texts."

Trying not to look bored, Halia said, "Your library is as impressive as the rest of your home. I do hope you can find some answers in here."

They approached the table in the center of the room where Thulin and Oswynn were diligently looking through a large pile of books. Minaras interrupted their research. "Halia is new in town and shall be staying with us for a while." He circled behind his students, peeked at the open pages, and asked, "Have you come across anything of interest?"

"Nay—" Thulin began.

"But find something we shall," Oswynn quickly cut in. The younger apprentice, smiling at Halia, stood and bowed his head to her. "I am Oswynn. If you want anything, Miss Halia, you need only ask, and I will do my best to help you."

Not to be quieted this time, Thulin glared at him and said, "Master, should Oswynn not be returning to his studies? He has fallen far behind in his reading."

"How can you think of such things when Halia needs our assistance? We have more research to complete. Just look at this stack we must get through, and there are many more to find back there." He waved his hand at the shelves full of books. Oswynn didn't want to return to his tedious studying, even though this task was much of the same. Moreover, he was hoping to impress their attractive new guest.

Thulin had a similar thought. "I was thinking not of my studies but of yours. I intend to continue seeking the information Halia desires and am better suited to do so."

Minaras stopped their bickering by dropping a few more books onto their already hefty piles. "Continue your research a bit more. Necromancy can wait a few days."

Each apprentice grabbed the next thick volume off his pile and continued looking for anything that might yield a clue about the crystal sphere.

CHAPTER VII

THE MISSING PAGE

Two days of research had brought the apprentices no closer to identifying Halia's mysterious orb. For Oswynn, the novelty of the request had worn off by the beginning of the second day, and he had reverted to his usual complaints about endless reading and studying. Thulin, on the other hand, had worked diligently both days and still found nothing of interest. Neither of the apprentices, to their dismay, had much time to spend with their guest other than an infrequent meal. On the morning of the third day, the library was a complete mess, with mounds of old tomes scattered about the floor and the table. Thulin spent two hours returning the books he had used to the shelves where they belonged. He left Oswynn, who disliked cleaning even more than research, to complete his portion of the chore.

With his two apprentices occupied upstairs, Minaras began preparing for another one of his short excursions, this time up the coast to a small fishing village where the town leader had asked him to assist in the building of a tidal barrier. He didn't expect it to take more than a couple of days, and selected a single robe to wear for the entire time. It was a deep sapphire in color, made from iridescent silk, given to him by his former partner after they had completed their final adventure together. The robe, a masterpiece of transmutation magic, was composed of the webs of one thousand orb weaver spiders. It had dozens of pockets filled with assorted spell components ranging from specially prepared powders and vials of every liquid imaginable to mundane items such as leaves, twigs, and clumps of dirt. Running his hands up and down the garment, he felt for missing items, a task that took him only seconds to finish, having done it countless times before.

Minaras pulled a leather sack off a shelf and filled it with a pile of books he had selected as gifts for the village elementalist. He was almost ready to leave when the door to his study crashed open and Thulin barged in, out of breath.

"Master … one of the locks … broken … make haste!" he gasped, before rushing back out of the room.

Minaras carefully placed the sack of books on his desk and leisurely followed his apprentice upstairs to the library. Oswynn, looking anxious, awaited the two of them near the back of the room. No longer was there a painting of a doomed ship on the wall. Instead, the younger apprentice stood next to an empty doorway. He had opened a secret panel in the wall, hoping to find some books about spell casting. Instead, what he had found behind the painting was even more thrilling to him—evidence that a thief had visited Minaras' private collection.

Upon entering the library, Minaras was immediately angered at the sight of the open doorway. He marched straight to Oswynn, frowning at the young boy. "Why has this door been opened? You know I have expressly forbidden anyone from entering my personal archives. Many of the older tomes are fragile and could be destroyed by the slightest disturbance and others are a bit too dangerous for the unskilled to handle."

Oswynn didn't know how to respond. Part of him was ashamed at breaking his master's rules, yet another part was excited about his discovery. He started, "I was … putting away some of these texts, when I noticed—"

Thulin jumped in, "He was looking through your private collection to find books about powerful spells. Master, he is unwilling to wait patiently for your proper guidance."

"No!" Oswynn began, but Minaras's stern gaze bothered him. He held his head down and admitted, "Yes, I did want to learn more, but I knew it was not allowed. I should not have—"

"Then why did you open the door?" Thulin asked, hoping to get Oswynn into more trouble. "We should consider ourselves lucky. Our master does not have many rules in this house. I have heard about other wizards who are quite strict with their apprentices. You should at least follow the few rules Minaras has set for us, even if you find your lessons boring."

Oswynn knew Thulin was right but would never admit it. At least the results had justified his action. "I could not stop myself once the idea was in my head. I should not have gone into the back room." His eyes lit up as he continued, "But is it not good that I have uncovered this treachery?"

Minaras quieted him with a simple, "I am disappointed, Oswynn."

The young boy felt terrible, as if he had betrayed his master, yet deep down he could still feel the exhilaration of his discovery.

The wizard and his two apprentices walked through the secret doorway into a dark, musty passage, with Thulin carrying a small oil lamp to light their way. On either side of the hall were two solid oak doors only five feet tall, secured by large iron handles and padlocks. Minaras stopped at the farthest door and sighed. The padlock had been broken and placed on the door to appear untouched. He removed the broken lock and dropped it into one of his few empty pockets.

"Wait here," he told his apprentices as he took the lamp from Thulin and opened the door to reveal a cozy room with a ceiling not much higher than the top of his head. Minaras ducked into the small, dry chamber, an annex to the main library containing his private collection of rare tomes and scrolls. Minaras quickly scanned the shelves and returned to the hallway with a bewildered look. Even though he had no method to his organization, he knew at a glance that all the items in the room were safely in their place.

"Nothing appears to be missing," he told his apprentices upon his return. "Oswynn, did you open this door?"

The younger apprentice shook his head and replied, "I did not. I found Thulin and told him to fetch you as soon as I saw the broken lock. Then I returned to the entrance and waited for you."

"It must have been Halia," thought Minaras, "but what was she looking for and how did she know about this secret annex?" He reached into a pocket and removed a few gold coins.

"Thulin, go to the locksmith and purchase a new padlock for me. Be sure it is a good one ... Terun if possible," he said as he handed the money to his apprentice. Then, gazing at the other doors in the hallway, he changed his mind. Minaras grabbed a few more coins and added, "You had best buy four new padlocks, and perhaps I should consider some type of enchantment as well. I must remember to call on your father one of these days. I know of no better conjurer in Seaton."

Thulin took the gold and hurried out of the house, hoping Minaras would use the time alone with Oswynn to dole out a severe punishment. Oswynn's behavior, however, was the last thing on the wizard's mind. He looked back, wondering why the thief had only entered one of the secret chambers and why nothing had been taken. It was impossible for her to have known what was in each room. "Oswynn, bring Halia to my study."

Minaras strolled out of the hallway, closed the door behind him, and stared at the painting for a moment. The sight of the water unleashing its fury on the tiny boat calmed him down. Then he extinguished the lamp and left it on the cluttered library table before walking back to his study. Within a few minutes, Oswynn showed up with their guest.

"Sit down, Halia," Minaras said in a grave voice as he pulled the padlock out of his pocket. "Oswynn, leave us."

Oswynn was about to protest, but Minaras shot him a sharp glance, putting a quick end to the thought. Sulking, he shuffled out of the room.

Standing across the table from Halia, Minaras stared at her as if trying to see directly into her mind. He knew from the beginning that she wasn't a wealthy trader, yet he still felt foolish to have fallen prey to her scheme, whatever it might have been. Oddly enough, she was staring right back at him. Someone with a guilty conscience would have tended to look away.

"I let you, a stranger, into my home. I agree to help you, and now I find this on the door to my personal library," Minaras said, slamming the broken padlock onto his desk. "Is this how you repay my generous hospitality?"

Being innocent of the charge, Halia didn't know what the wizard was talking about, but she did have a great deal of knowledge about locks. She picked up the padlock and ran her fingers over it. It was human-made, average quality, and quite old. Someone had cut through the shackle, using a thin file to open the padlock without destroying it. Removing the lock pick from her belt, she proceeded to pick the lock in no time at all. The piece of the shackle between the cut and the locking mechanism fell into her hand. Taking a closer look at the small piece of metal, she said, "I know nothing of your personal library. I can say only that I have no need to destroy a padlock if I wish to get past it." Halia threw both pieces of the padlock onto the desk. Sitting back in her chair, she added, "And from the look of the rust where the thief made the cut, this lock was breached many years ago."

Relieved that his initial perception of Halia was accurate, Minaras picked up the two pieces to have a second look. She was correct. The filed portion of the shackle sported the same fine layer of rust prevalent on all of the other metal pieces. He quickly admitted his mistake. "I am sorry for accusing you, Halia. I hope you understand the position I was in."

She accepted the apology with a sly grin. "If I were you, I, too, would not have trusted me. This time, however, I was innocent."

"But if not you, then who else would have been interested in those old books? It seems we have yet another mystery to solve."

Later that night, Minaras returned to his secret annex without the others. He spent hours combing through his entire collection and eventually discovered that one of the older tomes, an Arboreal history book, seemed to have less dust on it. Speaking a couple of mystical words, "*maete brond*," he lit a row of lanterns hanging from the walls. Then he gently picked up the history book, placed it on a stand in the middle of the room, and slowly began flipping through the pages.

The book was hundreds of years old, but the pages were surprisingly supple, a marked difference from ancient human tomes that became brittle after a century or so. It took him another hour, but about halfway through the book, Minaras found a particularly interesting page containing several drawings of a glass sphere. Holding the crystal sphere, he compared it to the pictures he had just found and thought to himself, "This may be an Arboreal artifact, which would explain my lack of knowledge. At least now, we will get some answers." He turned the page, expecting to find the information they had been seeking, and gasped, "'Tis gone!"

The next page had been ripped out of the book. Minaras quickly flipped through the rest of the tome looking for the missing page, but he couldn't find it. Whoever had broken into the annex had been looking for something very specific and evidently had been successful. Turning back to the missing page, Minaras fingered the torn parchment. He was positive the stolen page contained details about the mysterious crystal sphere he now had in his possession.

"Well, Halia," he muttered out loud, "it may be time for us to pay a visit to the Arboreals."

CHAPTER VIII

ASSAULT ON THE FORTRESS

Ahriman and Xarun plodded through increasing undergrowth on their way toward the Arboreal Forest. Their trek had begun so early in the morning that it was the first time in years Xarun had seen the rosy light of dawn. The warrior wore a suit of thick leather armor, boiled to make it extra tough, over a light cloth shirt and leggings. He augmented this outfit with a set of greaves, bracers, and pauldrons, each containing a row of sharp metal spikes. Strapped to his back was a large battle-axe, chipped in a couple of spots but still deadly. In addition to his armaments, he carried two packs laden with food and supplies. Behind him, Ahriman, wearing his brown robe and holding nothing but his staff, occasionally stole a peek inside one of his pockets when Xarun wasn't looking. Despite the hot weather, his early rise, and the heavy burden, Xarun never seemed to grow tired as they headed ever deeper into the dense forest.

As the two of them drew closer to the border of the Arboreal Forest, the vegetation became all but impenetrable. Xarun held both packs with one arm and used his axe to hack ceaselessly at the mounting obstructions. This added chore began to tire him out, but he knew their destination couldn't be far and continued to forge onward, slashing at any vine or branch in his way.

The nature of the forest changed as soon as the two crossed from human lands into Arboreal territory. Instead of a chaotic collection of vegetation, the entire wood seemed to become a single living organism with the trees its limbs, the abundant creeping vines its arteries, and the moist, sultry breeze its breath. It grew darker, too, as the sunlight had a more difficult time penetrating the dense clusters of leaves in the canopy. Even though the forest had become quite eerie, neither Xarun nor Ahriman displayed any fear, each one completely focused on his current task. As they walked, Xarun kept a constant lookout for any sign of the Arboreals, a hopeless gesture since in their home environment the Arboreals were virtually undetectable when they chose to remain hidden.

The two continued on a southwesterly course for about two hours after entering the Arboreal Forest. Xarun couldn't tell one direction from another, but Ahriman always seemed to know which way to go. Eventually, Xarun broke through some particularly heavy undergrowth and wound up in a small clearing. As soon as the wizard joined him, a large crow flew down from the sky and landed on a nearby branch. Ahriman leaned over and addressed the black bird. "Hafoc, what news do you bring me?" The crow jumped from the branch onto his shoulder and appeared to whisper in his ear.

"Do you speak with birds?" Xarun asked.

"Hafoc is not just any bird," replied Ahriman. "He is my familiar."

Xarun had heard of familiars before. Some wizards shared a special bond, a physical link, with an animal called their familiar. This bond allowed them to communicate with the creature through words, emotions, and sometimes thoughts alone. That same bond was also a liability since the death of the familiar would cause severe pain, both physical and psychological, to the wizard. Because of this trauma, wizards never kept more than one familiar at any time. Ahriman had lived with this particular familiar for many years, and he often sent Hafoc on scouting and reconnaissance missions, as was the case this time.

The wizard turned to Xarun and said, "We will use this spot for the summoning. The fortress lies one hundred paces due south. Clear away some of these plants, before the sun sinks too low."

Xarun stepped directly in front of Ahriman, scaring Hafoc. The bird hopped from the wizard's shoulder back to the relative safety of the tree. Smirking, the warrior folded his arms across his chest and stated, "I have had enough gardening."

"As have I, but still we must be ready by nightfall. If we delay any further, the Arboreals are certain to become aware of our presence. I would not be surprised if they are able to communicate directly with these trees."

Xarun didn't budge from his spot in front of the wizard, causing Ahriman to groan. There was no way he could force the warrior to assist with this manual chore, so he removed a small knife from one of his pockets and began enlarging the clearing. He started by cutting back some of the thinner vines. Xarun watched him briefly before realizing how long it would take to clear the area at the rate the wizard was working. He threw the two packs onto the ground and began using his axe on the larger vines and a few small trees.

"This fortress be close to humans," Xarun observed between swings. "Why did they build here?"

Ahriman put away his knife so he could haul some of Xarun's cuttings out of the clearing. "The Arboreals did not build this fortress. It was a human castle ages ago. Do you not remember the one we had spoken of in the tavern? The land you now stand upon could very well have been the home of some innocent family."

"Go to!" Xarun growled, smacking his axe into a tree trunk. The weapon bit deeply into the wood.

"I speak the truth, Xarun. In their expansion to the north, the Arboreals have taken over more than just this human settlement. Entire villages and towns have fallen to their slow migration. Do not believe their claims of peace."

Xarun squeezed the handle of his weapon, angered by this information. He let out his aggression with a few more strong chops, fell-ing the small tree. It always improved his mood to destroy something with his axe.

The pair continued their work without any further discourse until the sun began to set. Xarun then sat down for a small bite to eat while Ahriman removed the remaining debris from the center of the clearing. The wizard paced back and forth, tamping down the dirt to leave a completely flat area on which to perform his spell. Next, he uncorked a vial of bright red powder. Walking in a large circle, he carefully spilled the contents of the vial on the ground, leaving behind a uniform dusting. When the first circle was complete, he removed another vial from his robe and made a second circle adjacent to the first. Finally, he took a tube of black powder and inscribed a hexagram in the second circle, six lines stretching from one side of the circle to the other and ultimately forming the shape of a six-pointed star.

Xarun had finished his meal and was watching the wizard from his comfortable spot on the ground when Hafoc landed next to him and began pecking at some scraps. Xarun swatted at the bird, chasing it away. Determined to get some free food, the crow returned, but Xarun took his axe and thrust it at the bird. Hafoc screeched at Xarun, flying to the branches of the nearest tree as the warrior scooped up the crumbs and buried them in a shallow hole.

Meanwhile, Ahriman retrieved a well-padded bundle from the pack of supplies and gently removed the cloth wrapping. Inside the special package was a large obsidian egg about the size of a helmet. He placed the egg in the center of the plain circle before he took his staff and stepped into the hexagram, trying not to disturb any of the powder.

"Xarun, are you finished playing with Hafoc? We have but one chance at this summoning. Phoenix eggs are nearly impossible to find, and once I begin the spell I cannot stop or the egg will be lost."

"Why do you need me?" asked Xarun. "Demons be stronger than—"

"As I have told you before, it is not a demon that I summon. It is a magma spirit and, although quite powerful, the creature is no match for a full legion of Arboreals." He pointed his staff at the hexagram surrounding his feet. "The magma spirit is one of the few creatures able to withstand the will of their master after they have been summoned. I cannot leave the protection of this magic circle or I shall be at the mercy of the spirit. You must grab the vase while the Arboreals are occupied in battle, unless you can defeat the entire legion yourself."

Xarun stood up and stretched. "I be ready. Summon your demon," he said as he left the clearing and headed south.

"Be silent when you approach the fortress and wait until the sounds of fighting echo through the trees before you enter the building. You will not have much time to retrieve the vase as the Arboreals are sure to defeat the spirit within an hour."

Xarun glanced over his shoulder at Ahriman. "If your demon fails," he threatened, holding up his axe. "You shall answer to this." The warrior disappeared into the thick foliage.

Ahriman turned his attention to the black egg on the ground, clearing his mind for a moment before starting to chant, "*Bridd hieran, mara aweaxan, attor forstrang, scynscapa forealdian.*" At first, his words were almost inaudible. He continued the chant louder and louder, gesturing at the black object with his staff and never removing his unblinking eyes from the magic circle. Slowly, the egg began to grow, and as it grew, it changed shape. Small legs sprouted from the bottom, the sides of the egg elongated into wings, and a beaked head formed on the top. Next, a dull red glow appeared from within the egg and spread outward.

Ahriman increased the volume of his voice until he was practically yelling the words. The egg, now looking much like a large eagle, began to deform. Lava seemed to erupt from every part of the creature, smoothing out each angle on what was formerly a bird. It grew taller and fatter with each passing second. The legs puffed up into tree trunks and the feet swelled, consuming the claws in two mounds of magma as three pudgy toes appeared. The once feathery wings stretched out seven feet from the body. They became as smooth as volcanic glass and sharper than the finest metal blade. The creature was now the same height as the wizard and still growing. Ahriman's voice began to crack, but he continued to scream the chant. The beak disappeared into the huge globular head, replaced by a gaping maw. At a towering nine feet tall, the magma spirit was fully grown.

The hulking creature glowed like the embers of a recently extinguished fire. Its skin was in constant motion, flowing down its body, swallowed by its feet, and spit back out of its head. The spirit spread its wings, as if waking from a long slumber and glared at Ahriman with its dark, soulless eyes.

"You will perform a task for me," demanded Ahriman.

The spirit looked at the red circles on the ground, seeking some way to escape its mystical prison. Then, with a moaning, low-pitched voice, it rumbled, "Name thy task, half-breed."

Unperturbed by the denigration, Ahriman pointed his staff to the south. "Attack!" he yelled, "Wreak havoc on the Arboreals! Destroy their fortress and you will be free of my command!"

The spirit furiously beat its wings, blowing dirt everywhere, but curiously, the powdery circles and hexagram remained intact. It took more than a few powerful flaps before the enormous wings lifted the bulky creature off the ground and high into the air. It flew over the trees toward its avowed target, the Arboreal fortress. As soon as the creature was out of sight, Ahriman fell to the ground, utterly exhausted.

Xarun made his way through the undergrowth, attempting to travel as silently as possible, but the sounds of cracking twigs, rustling leaves, and occasional grumbles under the breath followed the big warrior through the woods. Any creature within fifty paces would have known he was coming. On top of the noise, he forgot to keep track of the distance he traveled and had no idea when to stop and wait for the signal. Xarun kept pushing his way forward. The fortress, well hidden beneath the vegetation, remained invisible to him as he came closer and closer to the building. Luckily, Xarun heard the wail of the magma spirit and stopped just in time. Soon enough a glowing shadow flew over the far wall of the castle, drawing shouts from atop the building. Xarun's eyes followed the sounds of the Arboreals, allowing him to detect the faint outline of the fortress through the trees.

Crouching down as low as he could, Xarun inched forward until he had an unobstructed view. Lush, green vines covered the entire building except for the entrance, which looked like the dark opening to a great emerald cave. A single Arboreal, guarding the entrance, had heard the noises coming from Xarun's direction and was about to investigate when he saw the magma spirit fly over the castle wall. Xarun took advantage of the distraction and ran toward the lone Arboreal, axe in hand. A swift blow to his head knocked out the guard before he had a chance to spin around and see his attacker.

"This be too easy," thought Xarun, "demon or not." He ducked into the fortress and found the interior of the building to be nothing like he had ever seen before. Plants covered every inch of the floor, walls, and ceiling. A fluffy green carpet of moss blanketed the floors, making it feel as if he was walking on a cloud. Yellow, phosphorescent lichen lined the ceiling, brightening when he was beneath and dimming when he moved on. Along the walls grew a variety of flowering plants, most with tiny colored petals that combined to form patterns as if the Arboreals had painted them by hand.

"The wizard lied to me," Xarun mumbled to himself, thinking it impossible for humans to have built this living structure. "He shall pay soon enough." Standing next to the wall, he used his axe to dig into the flowers and was surprised when the metal blade scraped the solid rock beneath the thin layer of foliage. Satisfied with the result, he continued deeper into the fortress.

As he sneaked through the hallways, the exquisite sights and smells overwhelmed Xarun, nearly causing him to forget his mission. Beautiful, living murals detailing the native animal life decorated the walls with vibrant colors, and the delicate scent of sweet nectar permeated the air. Even his anger toward the Arboreals had abated until he was shocked back to his senses when he reached the next intersection. A dozen Arboreals, armed for battle, rushed down the corridor in front of him, their footsteps no louder than the rustle of a single leaf in a gentle breeze. He hurriedly slid up against the nearest wall and waited for the group to pass before continuing down the long corridor, this time with no more distractions.

Ahriman had given him a detailed description of the layout of the fortress and the information, although outdated, was quite accurate. Xarun headed straight to a door on the far side of the building. His grip tightened around the axe as he stepped into a rather spacious chamber whose mural of flowering plants depicted a great war between three armies. Xarun ignored the diorama, focusing instead on a pair of Arboreals guarding the chamber. Regor, the taller of the two, hovered near the back wall, while Sindula sat on what appeared to be a tree stump.

The Arboreals sprang into action at the sight of the big warrior, each brandishing a slim rapier and wooden shield.

"Halt, intruder!" ordered Regor. "Drop your weapon and we will not harm you."

The two guards stepped forward, pointing their swords at the trespasser to block his way. Keeping the two weapons in his sight, Xarun glanced around the room until he saw a green vase atop a lone pedestal in the corner. He nodded at the vase. "Give that to me!" he ordered. "I shall spare your lives."

The guards paused in confusion at the overconfident remark. Passing a slight nod to Sindula that went completely undetected by Xarun, Regor responded, "You are quite arrogant, even by human standards. Let us see if your actions can live up to your words."

In a single coordinated move, they surrounded Xarun but hesitated ever so briefly before thrusting their swords forward. The big warrior used that short moment to feign an attack against Sindula, swiftly spin around, and swing his spiked bracer straight at the head of Regor. This trick had helped him out in the past, but the lithe

Arboreal avoided the danger, easily ducking out of the way. Sindula immediately unleashed several rapid jabs unsuccessfully at Xarun, who blocked the onslaught with slower but more powerful swings of his axe.

Both Xarun and the Arboreals now appreciated that it wouldn't be an easy victory. The two guards settled down into a more passive stance, knowing time was on their side. Either the intruder would tire out or more Arboreals would arrive and overwhelm him. Xarun also recognized the danger of his situation and wondered how much longer the magma spirit would last. Perforce, he came up with a new plan of attack. The Arboreals seemed more interested in disabling than killing him, and this detail was not lost on the seasoned warrior. Using his size advantage, Xarun ran straight for Sindula, the smaller of the two guards, and rammed his entire body into the Arboreal, flinging him back against the wall. The Arboreal hit his head against the hard stone, taking out a good section of the flower mural, and fell to the ground, dazed. With one adversary down, Xarun turned to face his remaining opponent. He pressed forward, hacking fiercely at Regor and soon demolished the Arboreal's shield.

Although Xarun had expected Sindula to be unconscious for the remainder of the fight, the downed Arboreal recovered quickly. He leaped up after a few seconds and sliced into the intruder with his sword. The sharp blade pierced Xarun's armor, biting into his flesh and inflicting a minor but painful wound on his side.

"You surprise me," Xarun remarked as he ran his hand over the bleeding gash. "A fight we shall have!"

The melee continued for some time with the speed and resilience of the Arboreals giving them a slight advantage. As the battle progressed, Xarun suffered several more cuts on his arms and legs. Quick when necessary, the Arboreals patiently danced around the human intruder, waiting for the best moments to spring forward with their rapid pinpoint attacks.

After Xarun had received a rather large gash on his leg, Regor offered him a truce. "I admit you are a decent fighter, but you will not last much longer. Throw down your weapon, and you will be treated fairly."

Realizing this might be a good chance to turn the tide of the battle with more trickery, Xarun agreed with a single nod and admitted, "You be a noble adversary."

He relaxed his fighting stance, but instead of dropping his weapon, he threw the axe straight at the feet of Regor. The Arboreal leaped up to avoid the weapon. In that instant, Xarun sprang forward and grabbed him out of the air. With a firm grip on Regor's shirt, Xarun threw his entire weight backward, pulling the guard down with him. Both fighters fell over, and in the midst of the fall, Xarun lifted the lighter Arboreal over his body and smashed him head first onto the stone floor.

Sindula promptly moved forward to attack the temporarily grounded warrior. Xarun was barely able to roll out of the way of the Arboreal's first thrust. He grabbed his axe and did well to avoid the next few attacks. Slowly, Xarun worked his way to his feet. He blocked most of the guard's lightning quick jabs but took a few more wounds in the process. One-on-one with the remaining guard, Xarun pressed forward, backing Sindula against the wall and leaving him no room to maneuver. After he had trapped the Arboreal, Xarun smiled. He moved even closer, pinned down his opponent's sword arm, and knocked him out with the flat of his axe.

"Stay down this time," he commanded the prone body.

Without stopping to rest or dress his wounds, Xarun walked straight to the pedestal in the corner of the room. Resting on top of the marble stand was a vase decorated with cabochon-cut emeralds and circular patterns of green and black lacquer. Inside the ornate container grew a strange plant with five branches and tiny odd-shaped leaves resembling a miniature weapons rack. Xarun quickly discarded the plant and tipped the vase over. A crystal sphere rolled into the palm of his hand. Xarun rubbed some dirt off and examined it. "'Tis a worthless trinket," he thought as he placed the sphere in a pouch on his belt and carried the vase out of the fortress.

Xarun returned to the clearing to find Ahriman resting on the ground within the hexagram, his staff positioned neatly across his legs. The warrior placed the green vase on the ground outside the red circle and said, "Here be thy vase, wizard."

Without looking up, Ahriman inquired, "Did you return the sphere?"

"You asked for this."

Ahriman wasn't amused. He shattered the vase with an angry swing of his staff. "Give the sphere to me now!" he demanded, lifting his head and looking Xarun straight in the eyes. "Do you think I would have risked this attack for something so mundane?"

They stared at each other for a moment before Xarun broke the silence. "Tell me more. I be interested."

A slight grin escaped the wizard's lips. Xarun would be a useful ally to have in this quest. Leaning heavily on his staff, Ahriman pushed himself up from the ground and limped over to Xarun, scattering some of the red powder. He reached into his robe and removed a small pouch. The warrior leaned closer as Ahriman emptied the contents of the pouch into his hand. It was a solid crystal sphere, identical to the one from the vase.

Xarun, surprised at the sight of the orb in Ahriman's hand, immediately checked the contents of his pouch. The sphere was still there. He took it out and held it in his open palm. A red dot glowed in the center of Xarun's sphere, and a green dot glowed in the center of Ahriman's sphere.

Ahriman explained, "These two spheres are part of an old key unlocking a great treasure. The glowing spots you see enable one to find the other spheres as long as someone is touching them. I have been waiting many years for a chance to find all five, and now it may be possible." He returned his sphere to its pouch, indicating with a nod that Xarun should do the same. "Another one lies to the north. It is likely to be a dangerous journey."

Xarun tucked his sphere away, looked Ahriman in the eye, and said, "Consider me your partner."

Chapter IX

Searching for Answers

On the morning after he had found the Arboreal history book with the stolen page, Minaras called Thulin, Oswynn, and Halia into his study. As they entered the room, each of the three had a different idea about why Minaras had summoned them. Thulin thought his master would be informing them of another one of his trips, Oswynn feared he would be asking them to continue their tedious research, and Halia hoped he had new knowledge about the sphere.

"Last night, I returned to my personal library thinking I must have overlooked something during my initial inspection." He placed the Arboreal tome on the table in front of the others and added, "My judgment proved to be true when I found a page missing from this book." He opened it and turned to the drawings he had found.

Halia instantly recognized the pictures and exclaimed, "'Tis my sphere!" She jumped up and leaned over the table for a better look, forcing both apprentices to rise from their chairs to get a clear view of the markings. The two squeezed closer to her on either side.

"What is this book and what page has been taken?" asked Oswynn. "I do not understand the writing."

"'Tis written in Arboreal," Thulin was quick to point out. "You should have recognized the symbols, Oswynn. It was the first language we studied together."

Minaras continued his explanation. "This is an old history book, penned more than six centuries ago. There are no other references to the orb, except here, perhaps." He turned to the missing page and ran his fingers over the torn parchment. "Someone else seems to have been interested in your sphere, Halia."

"Does the book offer any information to aid me in my quest?" she inquired.

"The size, shape, and weight of the crystal in the drawings match the dimensions of yours precisely. One can only guess what was to be found on the next page."

"A description of how to use the sphere no doubt," mumbled Oswynn, "but it is of little use to us now."

Excited by the prospect of uncovering more information, Thulin began, "There must be more books in your—"

"No, Thulin," Minaras cut him off. "Arboreal books are difficult to acquire, especially old ones. The Arboreals enjoy hoarding their literature as much as do I."

"What of human books? You have many—"

"I do, but the ones we humans have created rarely survive more than a couple of centuries, crumbling to dust as they age." Minaras thought for a moment before adding, "We really must learn how the Arboreals produce such enduring materials."

"If these types of books are rare, then they do exist," noted Halia, "and 'tis but a matter of finding them. We need only know where to begin looking."

"That is what I am about to suggest," Minaras responded. "It is time we did a bit of field research. Thulin, you and Halia will go to Zairn to meet an old friend who lives—"

"I should go with Halia," objected Oswynn, nudging even closer to her. "Thulin is behind in his experiments."

Not about to lose his chance of traveling alone with Halia, Thulin shot back, "Oswynn, you are too young for such a trip and cannot read Arboreal. How would you know if you are successful in your research?"

"Nevertheless, you have yet to create Dark Whey. Halia and I will return from Zairn long before you complete your first vial."

"I shall travel on my own," said Halia, taking a step away from the apprentices. She didn't relish the prospect of traveling with anyone else, even Minaras himself. "Either of you would only serve to slow me down."

The three continued arguing about who would make the trip to Zairn until Minaras slammed the book shut, drawing their immediate attention. He proceeded to give them clear and irrefutable instructions about the upcoming travel plans. "Oswynn and I will pay a visit to the Arboreals and ask to search through a portion of their archives. Thulin, you and Halia will travel to the Great Library in Zairn where you will speak with my old friend Sigmus. It is there you should have the best chance of finding the information we wish to uncover."

Thulin grinned smugly at Oswynn, who just shrugged it off. "Anything will be better than continuing these monotonous studies," thought the younger apprentice.

Halia disliked the wizard's decision. She would be much better off on her own; she always had been. At first, she decided to sneak off to Zairn alone, but soon realized that having a wizard as powerful as Minaras for a friend would be much better than as an enemy. Finally, she decided to put up with Thulin until they met with Sigmus, after which she would come up with a good excuse to continue on her own.

The two apprentices left the room to prepare for their journeys, but before Halia reached the door, Minaras stepped up to her and said, "Sigmus will need to see this if he is to be of any help to you and Thulin." He opened his hand revealing the crystal sphere. "Take good care of it. I believe this enigmatic little object may be of some importance."

Halia grabbed the orb from Minaras and tucked it securely away. As her hand touched his, she briefly wondered how her life would have been different if she had met him years ago. "I could have been a wizard by now, although I do not like the robes they wear." She quelled the stray thought as soon as she realized he was sending Thulin to keep a watchful eye on the sphere. "He is no different from everyone else, thinking only of himself." Halia tapped her pouch. "No one shall take you away from me again unless they part with a great deal of gold."

By the end of the day, Minaras and Oswynn were heading upstream on the Anxiar River while, against her wishes, Halia and Thulin had booked passage on a merchant ship bound for Zairn. She would have preferred traveling on foot or by horse, but there was no arguing that the boat would provide the fastest route to the big city and, as each day passed, her curiosity about the sphere grew stronger. Two days later, they found themselves entering the port of Zairn.

The city was an order of magnitude larger than Seaton. It was also much older than any other human dwelling in the land. The core of Zairn surrounded an ancient castle, which according to legends, had withstood the onslaught of an overwhelming enemy many ages ago. As the years went by, the various kings and governors built layer upon layer of roads, houses, shops, and walls around the castle in concentric circles, each called a ring of the city.

The first ring of Zairn, the castle itself, had been uninhabited for the better part of two centuries. The old walls of stone that had once signified strength and leadership in the past were beginning to show their age, even collapsing in a few spots. Very few people would dare enter the building now for fear of a cave in.

The city leaders and wealthiest nobles lived in the lavish second ring. Their fancy homes, built on lush, green landscapes complete with flower gardens and fishponds, each had a direct view of Castle Zairn. The third ring housed the city guard, partly as an honor to the duty of serving the city but more as protection for the inhabitants of the second ring. As an added bonus, their barracks were expansive and comfortable, the opposite of the confined quarters prevalent in most other cities and towns. The middle two rings of the city served as the center of commerce for the entire land. Merchants came from the farthest kingdoms to buy, sell, trade, and try their hand at bartering with the experts in Zairn, whose skill at haggling was legendary. Despite being out-negotiated every time, the foreign traders always came back to try again. Most of them considered leaving the city with a halfway decent deal a great sign of success.

Zairn had expanded so much throughout the centuries that the farmlands of the sixth and seventh rings actually swallowed several villages and even one small town. The outermost rings expanded deep into the interior of the continent but were broken up on their eastern sides by the coastline and Zairn's busy harbor.

Thulin stood on the upper deck as the merchant vessel entered the huge port of Zairn. The panoramic views of the great city captivated him as the ship approached its destination. Up and down the coastline, he noticed the differing architectures of the outer rings. The efficient brick walls, houses, and streets of the fifth ring contrasted sharply with the wooden barns and open fields of the sixth and seventh rings. Looking further inland he was able to make out parts of the inner rings, including the castle, slightly elevated from the rest of the city. In the harbor, he saw every type of boat imaginable, from small fishing skiffs to great warships. Too seasick to enjoy these views, Halia stayed below deck until the end of the journey and pounced onto the wharf as soon as the boat bumped into the dock.

"Are you unwell, Halia? You look somewhat pale," said Thulin as he joined her on the pier.

"That will be the last time I travel by boat," Halia declared firmly. "I shall return to Seaton on horseback."

"Perhaps we shall, but I enjoyed this trip. The sights and sounds of the ocean are a wonder to experience. If you had stayed in the fresh air for any amount of time you would have felt much better."

Halia shook her head. "I have had enough of rivers and oceans to last me a lifetime. Let us be done with this water and head inland."

Although she had no need of Minaras' directions, Halia pretended to be lost. Thulin led the way into the fourth ring of the city where they found the Great Library. The large stone structure rose high above its neighbors with four rectangular wards surrounding a beautiful courtyard of flower gardens and wooden benches. Thulin had never seen a building so large and stared wide-eyed as they climbed the set of seventeen stairs.

"Welcome to the library," an acolyte greeted them. "Are you—"

"We are looking for Sigmus," interrupted Halia. "Where can we find him?"

The acolyte bowed and waved them in. As Thulin crossed the threshold, he said, "You wear the garb of a priest."

"I see you have never been here before," the acolyte responded. "These walls once housed a monastery. The original priests gathered their collections of scrolls and manuscripts together to form the original library in the southern ward. As the years went by, however, the amount of literature grew until only the northern ward remains as lodging for us caretakers."

Thulin and Halia followed the acolyte to the top floor of the eastern ward where Sigmus was hard at work in his cramped study, interpreting and transcribing ancient texts. Piles of old tomes lined the floor, waiting their turn to undergo the scrutiny of the master archivist. His work was tedious and somewhat difficult, with many of the pages disintegrating at the slightest touch, but he was fascinated with history and loved every minute of it. He would continue to do his part to preserve the legacy of times gone by as long as he could hold a pen.

The acolyte pushed the door open and peeked around the corner, receiving a wave from the old sage to allow the visitors into the room. When Thulin and Halia entered the study, Sigmus lowered his quill and looked at them with a gleam in his eyes like a grandfather seeing his grandchildren for the first time. Born the same year as Minaras, but with gray, thinning hair, wrinkled skin, and a pronounced hunch to his posture, he looked as if he could have been the wizard's father.

"Greetings, young ones," he said cheerfully. "I am Sigmus. How may I help you?"

Thulin stepped forward, carefully avoiding contact with any of the books on the floor. "Good Sigmus, I am Thulin, apprentice to the wizard Minaras."

"Go to! Minaras is your teacher?" he asked in an incredulous tone.

Taking offense at the remark, Thulin replied, "Why do you mock me? Minaras is a great teacher!"

Sigmus gave Thulin a wink. "I have no doubt he could be the best in the land. Minaras had always excelled at whatever he set his mind to. When last we parted, he had settled down in Seaton. What brings the two of you so far from home?"

Halia squeezed in front of Thulin and accidentally knocked down one of the piles. Ignoring the scattered literature, she removed the crystal sphere from her pouch and held it out to Sigmus. "Know you anything about this sphere?"

Sigmus reached out to take the orb from Halia, but she held it back. Instead, he moved his head back and forth, closer and farther, examining it briefly.

"I do not recall an object such as this in any of my readings, but that does not mean your trip has been in vain. Follow me." Sigmus rose from his desk and led the two through his back door. "In the many years since I first came to Zairn, I have had the pleasure of transcribing only a small fraction of the library."

Thulin's eyes bulged as soon as he entered the spacious room. As with everything else in Zairn, the library dwarfed any in Seaton, including Minaras' own substantial collection. The young apprentice couldn't believe this was but one floor of a single ward. Rows upon rows of shelves and cabinets filled the room, each one completely packed with books, tomes, manuscripts, parchments, and scrolls. Unlike his master's library, Thulin noticed that the priests had organized the texts by category and, within each category, by age. It would be much easier for him to find what he was looking for, although the sheer quantity of materials promised to make it a time consuming project.

"Welcome to the Great Library!" Sigmus proudly exclaimed.

Halia yawned, hoping their stay wouldn't be long. Thulin smiled broadly and began immediately. He raced through the library selecting items here and there. Minutes later, he was sitting at a table with a large stack of books in front of him. Even though she was eagerly awaiting the results, Halia didn't share Thulin's enthusiasm for the actual research. She sat beside him, gazing deeply into her crystal sphere.

Not much changed throughout the rest of the day. Thulin remained glued to his seat, though the tall stack beside him slowly diminished in height. Halia eventually retired to a couple of hard chairs against the wall nearby. She placed one of them under her feet and the other under her head and proceeded to toss and turn in a futile attempt to find a comfortable position.

Sigmus, who had stopped by to check on Thulin, noticed Halia's discomfort and walked over to her. "Allow me to help," he said, motioning for her to step aside. She did so, standing behind him as he waved his arms and chanted, "*Faegrian bedd.*" The two chairs melded into a comfortable sofa, on which Sigmus sat and rested from the effort needed to cast the spell. After a moment, he stood up and said, "That should do for now, but you are welcome to sleep in our guest quarters until your research is complete."

Halia nodded her thanks and leaped onto the sofa, looking forward to some sleep on a stationary bed.

The transformation spell caught the attention of Thulin, who looked up from his reading and said, "You are a transmuter. Why settle to be a lowly scribe with such an ability at your command?"

Sigmus gave him another wink. "Wizardry is nothing more than a tool. It does not define who you are."

Thulin's research continued for days. While her companion buried his head in the books, Halia studied the glowing dot in the sphere each morning and wandered about the city until nightfall, careful to avoid any of her old haunts. When she happened upon a decent weaponsmith's shop, she used her last few coins to purchase an old sword, worn but sturdy.

On the morning of the fourth day, while the spot was still glowing, Halia interrupted Thulin. "Look inside the sphere," she said, handing it to him. "Each morn, the purple dot appears inside ... at the same time."

Thulin examined the glowing spot while Halia continued her observation. "The purple dot has been in the same position ever since we came to this city," she said, "but when we were in Seaton, it was closer to the side."

Thulin agreed, looking up at the ceiling, "Yes, I do remember." After a minute of thought, he pushed the remaining books to the side, clearing out a large area in front of him on the table. "Wait here," he told Halia with a sparkle in his eyes as he skipped to a section of the library containing large scrolls. Thulin picked out a detailed map of the known lands, brought it back, and unfolded it on the table. Halia drew closer.

"The sphere may be a type of compass," Thulin hypothesized. "Look at this map," he said as he pointed to Zairn. "We are here now, and the glowing spot points us in that direction. When we were in Seaton, it seemed to point us in this direction." He drew two lines on the map with his fingers. "If my theory is correct, the purple spot inside the sphere may be directing us to somewhere around the town of Krof, but I know not why."

Halia perked up. "Indeed! That could be so! Perhaps the answer we seek awaits us there." She pointed at the Sinewan River snaking its way through the countryside between Krof and Zairn. "We shall follow this river. It should take us but a few days to reach the town."

Thulin shook his head, "Nay, even by boat it would be more than a week of travel, and Minaras said naught about us going elsewhere. We were to conduct our research in Zairn and then return to him in Seaton."

With a sly smile, Halia said, "Worry not about Minaras."

Chapter X

Captured

"How much farther until we reach the Arboreal Forest?" asked Oswynn, not for the first time.

"We are close," replied Minaras, stopping for a moment to catch his breath.

While his master rested from their long hike, Oswynn flitted from one spot to the next, looking under leaves, flipping small stones, and examining each plant. "What is this called?" he asked upon finding a small, tubular sprout with a hairy stem.

"I do not know its name. Living things were never my specialty. Shall we continue?"

With a smile, Oswynn darted ahead, occasionally glancing backward to make sure he was on the right course. "This forest is quite different from the woods surrounding my farm. It must be the Arboreal—"

"You shall know when we have crossed the border," interrupted Minaras. "I was there once, many years ago, and although the details may have faded from memory, the experience will never be forgotten."

Oswynn knew immediately when they had entered the Arboreal Forest. The nature of the woods changed dramatically, yet subtly. He couldn't pinpoint any specific difference between the human side and the Arboreal side, but the two portions of the forest were different, nonetheless. Although he dared not admit it to Minaras, Oswynn became frightened, not of getting lost or of dangerous creatures lurking in the shadows, but of the forest itself. He felt like an intruder, as if he didn't belong and should immediately head back to the more familiar human lands. Instead of giving in to his fear, Oswynn let Minaras take the lead. He focused exclusively on the wizard's blue robe, following his master deeper into the realm of the Arboreals.

Minaras stayed on a southwesterly course for hours, cutting away at the dense undergrowth with a small ceremonial dagger. He purposefully had left his larger blades at home, hoping the Arboreals would look more favorably on them if they caused minimal harm to the foliage. The old wizard pulled a compass from his pocket to confirm their direction and said, "The fortress should be around here. Can you see anything?"

"Nothing," Oswynn replied quickly, not wanting to leave his master's side.

Within the next few steps, they broke through a heavy outcropping of vegetation and found themselves standing directly in front of the fortress. The lone guard at the entrance had been replaced by four archers and an experienced captain, who took no chances with strangers. The Arboreals had heard the two noisy humans approaching for some time and had already loaded their bows with poison-tipped arrows. As soon as Minaras and Oswynn were in sight, the captain of the guard yelled out, "Human intruders approach! Archers, fire!"

Thinking quickly, Minaras threw his arms forward and chanted, "*Lyft bord*," just as the archers released a flurry of arrows. Two arrows each came directly at their bodies, but a gust of wind blew out of nowhere and flung the projectiles backward onto the ground before they reached their targets.

As the archers prepared another round of arrows, Minaras called out to the captain, "Good Arboreal neighbors! Please halt your attack on us. We do not wish to fight, only to seek a bit of information."

The Arboreal captain held his hand up, signaling the archers to hold their fire but remain alert. He looked back and forth between Minaras and Oswynn and decided that the wizard likely spoke the truth. If it were a battle he wanted, then he would not have brought a child with him. "You may come closer," the captain said cautiously, "but try no magic or you will feel my wrath."

Minaras and Oswynn inched forward, staring at the Arboreals. The archers' bows remained focused on their targets, ready to loose a barrage of arrows at the slightest provocation. Oswynn, confident in his master's ability to defend against any attack, was less frightened now than he was when they were hiking through the forest. Instead, he felt an overwhelming curiosity about the fortress, never having seen more than a single Arboreal at any one time.

"That was a bit unfriendly," said Minaras when he was within two steps of the fortress. "What would bring about such an unprovoked attack? I thought humans and Arboreals were at peace with each other."

"Such a peace was broken by a recent encounter with a human intruder and a powerful spirit," explained the Arboreal captain. "We—"

"What type of spirit?" asked Oswynn, eliciting a frown from both Minaras and the guards. He quickly scurried behind his master's robe.

"We took heavy damage during the vicious battle but prevailed for the most part," continued the captain, ignoring the interruption. "Now, we must remain more vigilant than before."

"Vigilant I would understand, but sending a wall of arrows against two defenseless people was a hasty decision and one not befitting an Arboreal. We could have been killed."

"You are not defenseless," said the captain. Minaras gave a nod of acknowledgement as the Arboreal continued, "And the arrows would have rendered you unconscious, nothing more. It would not have been for me to determine your ultimate fate."

The captain turned and whispered to one of the archers who then retreated into the fortress. He reappeared soon after with two additional armed guards. "If you have come with goodwill, then please forgive us this unpleasant necessity. If you have not, then know you are unlikely to leave this fortress alive."

Minaras nodded slowly. "I understand your caution and reiterate our intention of seeking information only."

"You may follow me," the captain said as he led Minaras and Oswynn into the fortress followed by the two guards with swords drawn.

Oswynn gazed in awe at the interior of the fortress, his eyes glued to the strange plants that covered the hallway. His pace slowed while he ran his hands over the flower patterns on the walls. The two guards, wary but exhibiting the usual Arboreal courtesy, constantly gave him polite reminders to walk faster.

The captain stopped in front of an open door and held his arm out, motioning for Minaras and Oswynn to enter the small room. They did so, followed by the two guards. Kuril, the commander of the fortress, greeted the strangers with a serious stare. He was tall and lanky, displaying the typical greenish tint to his skin common to all Arboreals. A fresh scar ran down the side of his face from his right eye to his chin, marring an otherwise perfect face.

"You may be seated," he said, pointing at a pair of chairs, which looked like the overgrown roots of a tree. Oswynn, amazed at the chair, jumped into the seat while an apprehensive Minaras sat down more cautiously. He thought it possible that the Arboreal commander would cause the chair to bind his arms and legs, making it much more difficult to cast a spell, but, ultimately, he decided he had little choice in the matter. The guards positioned themselves behind the chairs, ready for the smallest sign of treachery.

Kuril paced back and forth, examining the strangers. A slim golden sword at his side swayed back and forth with each step. As the minutes passed, Oswynn became increasingly agitated and was about to speak up, but Minaras gave him a stern look. The apprentice settled into his wooden yet surprisingly comfortable seat and began to imagine what it would be like to live in the fortress.

Eventually, Kuril came to the same conclusion as the captain of the guard. "Forgive us this minor misunderstanding," he said. "We were recently attacked by a skilled human warrior and have been on high alert ever since."

"The captain noted as much." Minaras pointed at the scar on Kuril's face and asked, "Is that a reminder of your recent battle?"

The Arboreal ran a long, slender finger over the full length of the scar. "That it is, along with the loss of a score of my brethren." He paused a moment before continuing, "I have been told you wish to find information here. Of what nature would that be?"

Minaras reached into a large pocket at the bottom of his robe and produced the Arboreal tome. He turned to the page with the drawings of the sphere and handed the book to Kuril.

"As you can see, this is one of your old histories. I seem to have had a visit from a thief who tore the following page from this tome," Minaras explained.

Kuril took one glance at the page and knew this was no coincidence. The attack on the fortress was related to the theft of the page, and he would need to uncover the link to track down his enemies. He looked at the torn page for some time before handing the book back to Minaras. "The elders are expected here soon. You will stay as my guests until they arrive."

"Are we to be your guests or your prisoners?" asked Minaras.

Kuril answered him with a blank stare. "You will be treated as guests, but I would strongly urge you not to leave this fortress until the elders arrive. It seems we have something in common. A crystal sphere matching the description on that page was stolen during the recent attack on our fortress."

For the first time since Halia had stepped through his doorway, Minaras became worried. "Someone with the ability to steal an object from within an Arboreal stronghold is an extremely dangerous person," he thought. "If this thief should ever find Thulin and Halia, they will face great peril indeed."

Chapter XI

Following the Orb

On the second afternoon of her trip up the Sinewan River, Halia sat alone in the cargo hold of a small trading vessel, squeezed between a box of clove-scented incense and a large crate that leaked sand. Each time she tried to doze off, the ship would sway to one side, causing her to bump her head on the hard wood of one of the containers. "This is worse than the raft," she thought. "At least then, I was able to spread out and relax. I should never have broken my vow to avoid traveling by water!"

Halia looked around for Thulin but couldn't see him. "He must still be upset with me, and it was more than two days ago that we fought."

She thought back to when he had booked their passage to Krof. Full of joy, he sprinted the entire length of the docks to tell her the good news.

"Halia," he cried, excitement oozing from his voice, "I found a ship leaving for Krof this very day! It took all of my remaining gold to buy us a spot on the boat, but we leave in two hours and will reach Krof in no more than six days! Is this not a good omen?"

She gave him a lukewarm response, trying to eke out a grin. Halia secretly hoped they would have had no choice except to travel by foot or on horseback, despite her strong desire to solve the mystery of the sphere. "You certainly were lucky to find such a ship, Thulin. We shall worry about paying for our return to Seaton when the time comes."

"Why should there be any worries about returning home? Are you not from a wealthy family?"

Halia shook her head, "I am not, nor do I have a single gold coin to pay for food, lodging, or transportation."

"But what of the clothes you wear?" Thulin argued. "They bear the sign of nobility."

"I … traded for them with their former owner." Halia looked at her fancy outfit and wondered briefly if anyone had missed it. "Without his prior knowledge," she added.

"You stole them."

Halia looked away and sighed, "If you wish."

Thulin stood motionless with his mouth half open, looking as if she had slapped him in the face. He was unable to speak for quite some time. Then he whispered, "Why did you lie to us?"

"I thought Minaras would refuse me aid if he knew I was poor. What would a master wizard think of a street girl, forced to steal the clothes she wore?"

"And from whom did you steal the sphere?"

"'Tis mine by all rights," she stated, proud to be speaking the truth. "I found it deep within an abandoned castle in the middle of a deserted forest. I am not all bad, you know."

Thulin gave her a cold, unfeeling stare, which managed to cut straight through to her core and give Halia a rare pang of guilt. She knew he didn't believe her story about the sphere, and it bothered her.

"Minaras guessed the truth about me from the start," she admitted.

"Then he should have told me … you should have told me." Thulin turned away with angry tears in his eyes. He took it personally that neither his master nor Halia had confided in him.

The boat lurched to the side, giving Halia another bump on the shoulder. Trying to forget the uncomfortable ride, she pulled the sphere from her pouch, rolled it between her fingers, and felt its smooth exterior. "Are you leading us into danger?" she asked aloud. "Perhaps I should continue this quest on my own. I could jump off the boat and travel the rest of the way on foot. Thulin is too naive for this type of adventure. He will never be able to find his way home on his own. I should have sent him back to Seaton before he spent his gold on this boat. Now, it is my responsibility to protect him and bring him safely back to Minaras. This is yet another reason why I should have gone alone."

Halia stared deeply into the crystal sphere, trying to imagine where it was leading her. Would it ultimately bring her to a faraway land? Would there be a fabulous treasure involved? A bright light suddenly appeared inside the sphere. Her heart raced for a moment but calmed down when she realized it was only the sunlight pouring in through the entrance to the hold. Thulin had just opened the door and ducked into the room.

She put the sphere away and asked, "Are you still cross with me, Thulin?"

"I am not as angry with you as I am upset with my master. I cannot understand why Minaras did not trust enough to tell me the truth. Oswynn is still too young, but I am nearly an adult."

"Perhaps he thought you saw through my disguise as well? He already knew, as I quickly learned, that you are an extremely intelligent young man."

His cheeks turned red at the compliment. "Perhaps," said Thulin, his heart beating faster with the knowledge of Halia's admiration.

"I am sorry for the deception, Thulin. I shall try to be more honest with you in the future. If it helps at all, I told you the truth about the sphere."

From then on, Thulin was even more excited than before. He couldn't wait to find out where the crystal sphere would take them.

Halia wasn't happy with the extra burden of protecting Thulin, but at least they were on speaking terms again.

After another few days on the river, Halia and Thulin finally set foot in Krof, a good-sized town situated midway between Terun City and Zairn that served as a convenient port for merchants traveling between those two large cities. Some of the most extravagant and comfortable taverns in the land were built along the riverfront, each trying to outdo the next in an attempt to entice well-guarded gold away from the passing traders. One famous inn offered a personal lyrist to lull its guests to sleep with soft, relaxing music. Another boasted salted breads baked into any shape one could imagine.

Neither Halia nor Thulin cared about such luxuries; besides not having a single brass coin between them both, they were too engrossed in their own quest. As soon as they were on dry land, they headed past the lavish taverns toward the center of town. As usual, a small purple dot glowed inside the sphere each morning, but since they were near their destination, it was very close to the center.

"How do we know where to go?" Halia asked. "This town is larger than the map had led me to believe. If we are forced to search each building, we may never find an answer."

"Let me see the sphere," said Thulin, holding out his hand.

Halia resisted at first, then reluctantly allowed him take the sphere. Thulin studied it for a few minutes before noticing his fingers appeared larger when he stared at them through the crystal.

"I have an idea," he sang.

Using a strip of parchment, Thulin created a ruler with tick marks at regular intervals and wrapped it around the sphere to use as a guide. When the dot made its brief appearance the next morning, he was able to use the magnified ticks on the ruler to determine the approximate direction in which to walk. Each night the two set up camp in the woods outside of town, and each morning, they followed the spot until it stopped glowing. It was a slow process, but Halia and Thulin made their way to Arwold's front door on the morning of their fourth day in Krof.

Arwold was sitting at his table performing his usual morning routine when there was a knock at his front door. He finished polishing the sphere on his sword before putting down both the weapon and the cloth. Before he had a chance to stand up, he heard another, more urgent, rapping at the entrance to his house. With measured paces, he walked down the hallway and opened the door to find Halia and Thulin standing on his threshold. The impatient apprentice was just about to knock for the third time but instead lowered his hand as Arwold greeted them with a polite, "Right welcome are you."

Thulin held out the sphere and asked, "What do you know of this?"

"And greetings to you, young wizard," Arwold replied sarcastically, clearly appalled at the lack of manners displayed by the two on his doorstep. "Do please come in—" he paused, waiting for an introduction.

Halia stepped forward and offered one. "I am Halia, and this is Thulin, apprentice to the great wizard Minaras of Seaton. We have traveled a long way and hope you can offer us some assistance."

Arwold lifted her hand lightly and said, "It is a pleasure to meet you, Miss Halia. I am Arwold, son of Ardune, and you both are welcome in my home."

He stood aside to let the pair into his house. Thulin gave a frown as he squeezed between them. Arwold led them into the back room and walked over to his cleaning table.

"I know naught about the sphere you hold, but it looks quite similar to this one," said Arwold, lifting the claymore by its blade.

A blue dot glowed in the exact center of the orb attached to the hilt. When he gently cupped the sphere in the palm of his hand, a purple dot appeared in the center of the sphere Thulin was holding.

"My theory was correct!" Thulin yelled, nearly dropping the crystal sphere. "Look at the blue and purple spots! They glow in the center of each sphere."

With only a slight amount of interest, Arwold said, "Long have I wondered about those glowing lights. Have they any meaning?"

"They act as a compass, guiding one to the other sphere. Watch now."

Thulin placed the crystal on the table beside the suit of armor. As soon as he let go, the blue light inside Arwold's sphere disappeared. He gave an explanation with a great deal of pride in his voice: "When one releases the sphere, the spot in its companion disappears, but what happens next I know not. I doubt the sole purpose of the spheres is to find one another. It must have taken some powerful enchantments for these to remain bound to each other over great distances."

The sphere began to roll toward the edge of the table. Halia lunged forward, snatched it before it hit the ground, and tucked it away in her pouch. "Have you seen any other colors, Arwold?"

"Yes, I believe there have been several throughout the years."

"This could only mean there are more than two of these spheres! What other colors have you seen?" asked Thulin.

Arwold shrugged. "'Tis hard to remember them all. Red, blue, green, mayhap others."

Thulin laughed incredulously in Arwold's face. "Ha! Can you not remember something as simple as a few basic colors?" His voice carried a clearly degrading tone. "'Tis inconceivable to forget a set of colored lights shining within an otherwise plain crystal sphere. I doubt even the nobles of Zairn have access to such magic."

"Fancy colors do not aid me in battle. Why should I bother to remember them? Besides, I thought they were natural, like a rainbow or the sparkling of a—"

"Whence came the blade?" Thulin interjected.

"Diamond," the tall warrior completed his sentence with a slight frown. He stroked the weapon gently while he reflected on the history it represented. Then he held it blade side up and declared, "My father wielded this sword before me, and his father before him. It has been in my family for many generations, handed down from one warrior to the next. This sword has been a symbol of good and has struck down more enemies than you could count."

"'Tis a fine blade," said Thulin absently, all but ignoring Arwold's speech. "Your father or grandfather must have known something more about the sphere. Did they tell you naught about its history?"

"'Tis more than a fine blade," Arwold fumed, "but an important part of who I am: champion of Krof, protector of the people, and the son of Ardune." He eyed the sword tenderly before placing it back on the table.

Exasperated, Thulin whined, "This oaf is of no help to us, Halia! We are as lost now as we were before making the trip to Krof and we have spent all our gold!"

Arwold's patience with Thulin was running thin. He was about to chastise the young wizard when there was another resounding knock on his door. Taking a deep breath, he excused himself from his guests and opened the front door. A mercenary covered head to toe in armor stood on his doorstep. With a plumed helmet, chain mail, steel greaves, and a thin saber at his side, he appeared ready to take on the devil himself.

"What news do you bring me, Calazar?"

"Good Arwold, we have found the necromancer you so desperately seek," answered the mercenary, bringing an immediate lift to the warrior's spirits. "He frequents a graveyard in the town of Hidville."

"I am somewhat familiar with the village. Is it not a couple of days west of here?"

"Aye, but the men need some rest before the return trip. They have given an extraordinary effort in tracking down your quarry and are deserving of a short break."

"For the safety of Krof, I can wait no longer. You and I shall leave forthwith," commanded Arwold, spinning around and heading straight for his weapon. "The men may have their rest, but not the necromancer."

Thulin, who had been listening to their conversation, became frantic. Even though he had learned nothing new, Arwold was still his only link to solving the mystery. He jumped into the hallway and positioned himself between the warrior and the claymore. "Arwold, you cannot leave now!"

Arwold glared at him and shot back, "How dare you raise your voice to me in my own home? Stand aside, child."

The overwhelming size and ferocity of the warrior forced Thulin to shrink out of the way. From the side of the hall, he said in a much softer voice, "But, I must find out more about these spheres."

"And I must kill this evil wizard! Neither Hidville nor Krof itself are safe while this villain walks the earth."

He returned to the cleaning table, donned his breastplate, and sheathed his sword. Thulin wouldn't stop pleading with him. "Your friend seems a mighty warrior. Could he not go in your stead?"

"Nay, it was I who swore the oath, and it is I who must rid the world of this evil. Pester me no more!"

"Perhaps if we were to aid you in your quest, you could return the favor upon its completion," Halia chimed in. "What has this wizard done to deserve your ire?"

Arwold paused for a moment, seemingly stunned by the question. In a dead serious tone, he answered, "The wizard is a necromancer … he is evil."

"You have not yet answered me. What has he done to threaten the people of this fair town?"

Arwold still couldn't comprehend her question. It was known that all necromancers are evil. Rushing toward the door, he said sternly, "I can tarry here no longer."

Thulin, upset as he was, knew they couldn't afford to lose this lead. If, somehow, Arwold succumbed to the necromancer, they might never see the sword and sphere again. "Halia, if Arwold says the wizard is evil then evil he must be. Do you not trust him?"

Halia shook her head and admitted, "I trust but one person in this world."

"Arwold," Thulin begged, chasing after him, "When the necromancer has been defeated, would you—"

"When my oath has been fulfilled, I could be persuaded to learn the history of this sword."

"Then, be he evil or not, let us find this wizard and deal with him promptly," decided Halia, her curiosity once again winning over her better judgment as she and Thulin followed Arwold out the door.

CHAPTER XII

AHRIMAN'S SECRET

A smile lit up Ahriman's withered face when he noticed that the purple and blue spots had converged in his sphere. He turned to Xarun and said, "The fourth sphere seems to be on the move with the third. Our task will be much easier as long as they remain together."

He closed his pouch and warned, "You must remember not to touch the sphere. We do not want to let ourselves be known until we learn more about the others."

Xarun grunted his acknowledgement. "Do we still go north?"

"Yes, there is a small town not far from here where we will rest for the night."

"And eat," added Xarun. "I be starved."

"I am sure there will be enough food even for you," replied Ahriman.

Suddenly, the big warrior began twitching. He swatted at his arm several times, shook violently, and yelled in a thunderous voice, "Begone, filthy creature!"

Ahriman spun around, preparing for the worst. "What do you see? Have the Arboreals followed us?" The wizard beckoned his familiar to fly closer with a wave of his hand.

"A spider," Xarun spat, "on my arm."

Ahriman didn't even try to hide his amusement. "Why would a man as large as you be afraid of such a tiny creature?"

Xarun shrugged. "They crawl under my armor," was the only explanation he could think of at the time.

Hafoc swooped down and ate the spider before landing on his master's shoulder. It cocked its head briefly at Xarun as if acknowledging that it had finally received a free meal from the warrior. Ahriman whispered a few words to the crow and sent it back into the sky.

"Fear not," taunted the wizard, "the mighty Hafoc will protect you."

A faint, "Caw, caw," could be heard in the distance.

Xarun said nothing but did keep a close eye on Hafoc as it flew away. Although he was unable to speak the bird's language, he knew it was laughing at him.

The two continued their journey northward without any further incidents, arachnid or otherwise, until they approached an outlying hamlet, not far from town. Just when the trees began to thin out and they could see several small cottages in the distance, a peasant ran up to them, out of breath.

"Warrior … please help! Fracodians … attacking my family!"

Ahriman shooed the man away. "Your problem does not concern us. The Fracodians can have them and anyone else they want. Do they not have to eat as well?"

He was about to continue walking when Xarun grabbed his robe and lifted him into the air. He threw the wizard against the nearest tree, knocking the wind out of him. "Here be a better idea," barked Xarun. "I offer you to the beasts."

He let Ahriman drop to the ground and turned to the villager, who by now was almost as scared of this pair as the Fracodians. "I shall save your family," Xarun offered, removing the great axe from its sheath on his back. "In return for a meal."

Without thinking, the villager's head moved up and down.

"Where be the fight?"

The villager took off into the forest followed closely by the big warrior. Ahriman stood, brushed the dirt off his robe, and picked up his staff. "Very well," he called after Xarun, "will we at least make quick work of this distraction?"

Not far away, seven heavily armed Fracodians surrounded a log cabin in a small clearing. Each was dressed for battle, wielding a variety of hand-to-hand weapons, wearing heavy leather armor reinforced with metal studs, and sporting steel skullcaps adorned with a set of antlers. Three guards, armed with long glaives, were on lookout, posted at the southwestern corner of the cabin. The other four, including Fen, the leader of the group, stood near the door on the western side. Lying on the ground behind them was a slain villager, recently bludgeoned to death.

"Open door!" grunted Fen as he rammed his shoulder into the wooden structure with a thump. The solid door held.

Despite the forceful collision, the Fracodian leader came away completely uninjured. Even so, it wasn't something he desired to try again. He pointed at the dead villager and barked an order to two of his men who proceeded to lift the body and hold it prone between them. They charged forward and thrust the corpse into the door, head first, with a resounding thud that left behind a smear of blood. They were about to back up for another run when Xarun and Ahriman arrived at the edge of the clearing. The sight of the human battering ram infuriated the warrior, who immediately charged at the two Fracodians holding the body.

"Wretched beasts," he yelled, killing the nearest one with a mighty blow of his axe.

The villager's dead body dropped to the ground as the remaining three Fracodians surrounded him. They stabbed and pounded at him, but Xarun jumped backward to avoid their weapons. He matched their grunts of rage with his own growl of delight.

At the far corner of the cabin, the three lookouts dashed toward Ahriman, who had been rummaging through his robe at the edge of the clearing. As the large Fracodians came at him, glaives poised for a deadly strike, he calmly removed some white powder and a piece of a vine from one of his pockets. He covered the small plant clipping with the powder, rolled it into a ball, threw it to the ground, and chanted, "*Aweaxan bearu, aweaxan lim, aweaxan beam.*"

When the bundle hit the dirt, it split apart into three pieces, and each began growing at an incredible rate. Long strands formed and spread around the three approaching Fracodians, impeding their progress. They tried slicing at the vines with their weapons, but for each one they managed to cut, three more grew in its place.

Ahriman continued chanting the same line repeatedly, each time in a higher pitch. He pointed his staff at the vines, causing them to rise off the ground onto the bodies of the doomed Fracodians. The mass of writhing plants wound its way from their feet to their legs to their hips. The Fracodians struggled hopelessly, trying to free themselves. Within seconds, the vines had reached the arms and chest of each victim. Escape was now impossible since they could neither move nor wield their weapons effectively.

Ahriman didn't stop after the spell had rendered his opponents immobile. He increased his pitch further and watched as the vines continued creeping upward on their lethal journey. Finally, three thick strands reached the necks of the Fracodians, wrapped themselves twice around, and tightened with a vice-like grip. One at a time, the guards fell to the ground, unable to breathe.

By the entrance to the cabin, Fen waved his sword at Xarun and snarled, "You outnumbered. Surrender now!"

"I be outnumbered, yes," answered Xarun, spinning his axe from a two-handed grip to a right hand only grip and raising it above his head. "But not for long."

He tried the same trick as with the Arboreals in the fortress. Running toward Fen, he faked an attack with the axe, swung his left arm around, and killed a Fracodian, who had attempted to sneak up behind him, by slicing his throat with the spikes on his left bracer.

He wiped the blood off his wrist and grinned, "Beware, you be but two."

Only the leader and a Fracodian with a war hammer remained alive. More cautious than before, they attempted to keep the human between them, attacking simultaneously from both sides. This forced Xarun to move backward constantly to keep both of them in his sight at all times, giving him little chance to go on the offensive.

Fen, the more dangerous of the two, swung his weapon with faster and more accurate strokes. If Xarun could dispatch of him first, he was certain the other would pose no threat. He needed just a single opening, and it was only a matter of time before one of his impatient opponents would offer him just such a chance. The Fracodians lunged at Xarun and lashed out fiercely, but the warrior smoothly blocked their attacks, handling his large axe as if it were no heavier than a dagger.

"Die, human dog!" Fen shouted and lurched forward, slashing wildly with his sword.

The second Fracodian, taking the cue from his leader, pressed forward, boldly swinging his war hammer, but Xarun was now in control of the battle. He dodged under the slower hammer and blocked the sword with his axe. Then he slipped in front of Fen, brought his knee up, and jammed his spiked greave deep into the Fracodian's abdomen. Fen groaned in pain and tried one last thrust, but Xarun easily knocked the sword away from his mortally wounded opponent.

The sight of his leader beaten and the rest of his gang sprawled on the ground caused the final Fracodian to become berserk with rage. Instead of cowering in fear as Xarun had expected, he seemed to gain extra strength and speed with each violent swing of his hammer. Xarun blocked one attack after another. Each time the hammer and axe collided, the resulting impact jarred Xarun to the bone. The heavy blows took their toll on the big warrior, who was already fatigued from a full day of hiking with no food. Needing a swift conclusion to this battle, he went after his opponent's weapon arm. As soon as the Fracodian attacked, Xarun jumped aside and chopped downward, severing the limb. One last swing to the head put the battle to rest.

When he saw that all seven Fracodians had been defeated, the villager came out of hiding and dropped to the ground in front of Xarun. "We give you many thanks, great warrior. We shall repay you with a feast tonight." A tear escaped his eye when he saw the battered body of his brother. "But first … we must bury—"

"I shall wait," Xarun said coldly. "But not for long."

Ahriman sidled up to the two and said, "Xarun, you have done a good deed here. You must feast with the villagers alone while I take care of some business to the west. I will meet you at noon tomorrow in this same spot to continue our journey."

Xarun was so excited about the prospect of a large meal that he didn't wonder at all about Ahriman's business. He followed the villager into the cabin, thinking about cuts of meat, while two young men dealt with the multitude of dead bodies.

"This victory feast is quite serendipitous," thought Ahriman as he slipped into the woods. "It might have been difficult had I needed to sneak away at midnight." When he was out of sight of the cabin, the wizard summoned Hafoc to his shoulder and gave the bird a command. Ahriman watched his familiar fly off to the west before removing a seemingly empty glass vial from his robe. Clearing his mind, he uncorked the vial and chanted, "*Lyft gast lyft gast, beran min bodig faeste.*"

A strong breeze began to blow, spinning around his body and ruffling the bottom of his robe. This was no normal wind, however, but two invisible air spirits, which had materialized at Ahriman's request. The sorcerer continued singing the magic words as the spirits lifted his body off the ground and carried him high over the trees following the same path as his familiar. The spell required all of his concentration, but he had no worries about reaching his destination with Hafoc in the lead.

After four hours in the air, the spirits deposited Ahriman on the ground outside a large village and dissipated without a trace. The wizard dropped to his hands and knees, exhausted from the energy it took to keep the air spirits under control for so long. Few other wizards, if any, could ever hope to manage such an impressive feat. Ahriman crawled a few steps and collapsed by the trunk of a large tree. He had almost fallen asleep when two Ferfolk, dressed in the typical garb of farmers, approached him.

"We are to bring you straight to Argen," the first said in a raspy voice.

Ahriman tried to stand but was too tired.

"Carry him, and be careful."

The second Ferfolk lifted the wizard as easily as one would carry a child and followed the first into the center of town, setting him down on a stone wall beside the village leader. Argen was a particularly hefty Ferfolk, dressed similarly to the pair of farmer-turned-guards.

"We were expecting you," he said, pointing at a crow perched on a nearby rooftop. Hafoc flew onto the wall near Ahriman and nuzzled up to its master.

The leader continued, "You shall join us for a feast celebrating your return. We have just completed a most successful harvest of early vegetables."

"We have no time for a feast," panted Ahriman, "just some food and rest before I take my leave."

Argen nodded at the familiar. "Then why send Hafoc in advance of your arrival? We rushed to prepare some of your favorite—"

"Yes," interrupted Ahriman, "you will be preparing, but not for a feast. The time has come for our revenge."

The village leader displayed a look of surprise, which he forcefully converted into a smile. "You have found the weapons?"

"Not yet, but they will be uncovered soon. You must gather the army together now."

Argen was somewhat hesitant. "'Tis good news, yet—"

"Yet, what?" growled Ahriman. Gathering his strength, the wizard stood with the help of his staff.

"Some feel that we lead a good life here in the forest. They do not wish to fight."

Ahriman pointed his staff at the large Ferfolk, who backed away. "You will convince them otherwise."

With a nod at his crow, the bird disappeared into the darkness of the forest. "I will be watching you."

The village leader put his fists together, "As you wish, Lord Ahriman."

"Bring me some food!"

Argen signaled the two guards to comply with the wizard's request.

Ahriman returned to his seat on the wall. "Do our people not realize that all this land belongs to us? Why must we remain banished to a tiny farming village in the wilderness? The humans have grown weaker by the century and are complacent now. This is our greatest chance to avenge our ancestors and take back what is rightfully ours!"

Chapter XIII

The Knowledge of the Elders

Minaras stood beside a vine-encrusted window and peered out at the emerald sea of foliage surrounding the fortress. The songs of exotic birds mixed with the chattering of a troop of monkeys and drifted in through the window, lulling the wizard into a relaxing meditation. He took slow, deep breaths and cleared his mind. Although he preferred the sight of the ocean from his own study window back in Seaton, there was no arguing the overwhelming sense of tranquility here. Even the forest itself, which had previously appeared dark and menacing, seemed quite peaceful when viewed from within the confines of the converted castle.

Oswynn, on the other hand, disagreed with his master's perspective and found no comfort in their living prison. He was restless, constantly pacing around the room and talking to himself.

"If we had anything to do with the attack, why would we come back? And even if we did return, we would never have come knocking on their front door. Surely, the Arboreals must realize we are too smart to attempt such folly."

Oswynn frowned as he neared a wall.

"Halia and Thulin are certain to be having more fun than I am. Why could I not have gone to Zairn instead?"

He pulled a few leaves from the wall, turned, and dragged his feet back to the other side of the room.

"What do they plan for us? They must intend to torture us with boredom!"

The non-stop ramblings of his apprentice brought Minaras back to reality. The wizard smiled at Oswynn and suggested, "This is a magical place few humans have a chance to see. Take a bit of time to appreciate the Arboreals while you are here."

"I have already taken enough time. I could be learning spells now!"

"Do you not enjoy the company you keep? Perhaps you miss Thulin?"

Oswynn looked aghast. "I should say not!" he blurted out, even though there was some truth to the statement.

"Is it the hospitality of our hosts then? Do you dislike the food they serve us?"

"No, we have been treated well, but I cannot remain here watching these plants grow. If I had wished to learn about botany, I would never have left my farm." He pulled more leaves off the wall and dropped them onto the mossy floor.

Minaras merely stared at his young apprentice and remembered the days when he was just as impatient. There was nothing much different between the two of them other than their age.

"The elders have already been here two days! Why do they take so long to do anything?"

"Arboreals have a different perception of time than humans do. Days to them are like hours to us."

"Then they have been here two hours, and that is most definitely long enough to have met with us. I refuse to wait any longer!"

As if on cue, Kuril entered the room. "The elders have decided to grant you an audience," he said. "You may follow me."

Oswynn, instantaneously changing his mood, leaped beside the Arboreal, grinning from ear to ear. In the span of a second, his enemy had become his closest friend. Kuril, who had just heard the boy's diatribe from the hallway and didn't understand the fickle nature of children's emotions, remained as wary as ever about him. Without thinking, he put a finger to his scar while he waited by the doorway for Minaras.

Kuril led his two guests into the great hall, an enormous room with a vaulted ceiling in the center of the fortress. As with the rest of the building, plants covered the floor, walls, and ceiling, but, in here, an abundance of hanging vines grew from the ceiling and extended all the way to the floor, forming living curtains, which encircled the room. Kuril held a few vines aside to let Minaras and Oswynn through. Three Arboreals, sitting in the root chairs so common throughout the castle, awaited them at the far end of a long wooden table. They stared in unison as the two humans approached the table. Kuril stepped forward and made a slight bow to the elders.

"May I introduce the wizard Minaras and the human child … Oswynn," he said, before lifting his head.

Minaras followed Kuril's lead and bowed to the elders, bending down slightly more than the Arboreal. Oswynn simply stood and stared at the elders, out of sheer curiosity rather than disrespect, a fact lost to all but one of them. He had neither seen nor heard of an old Arboreal. As far as he was concerned, Arboreals were all the same age.

Kuril turned to Minaras and continued the introductions. "I present to you the Arboreal Elders … Druida," he said as the female elder nodded. She looked no older than Kuril. Thin, with long strands of hair draped over her shoulders, she reminded one of a willow tree. "Ulfen," he added as one of the male elders, a near replica of Kuril, gave a slight nod.

"And I am Falgoran," declared the final elder, withered and ancient looking. He motioned for the newcomers to sit, although there were no chairs in the spot to which he pointed.

"We most humbly appreciate this audience," Minaras said as two root chairs grew out of the floor beside the elders. A third one appeared at the far end of the table for Kuril.

After giving the visitors more than enough time to sit, Druida began, "Minaras, it seems an unlikely coincidence you would visit us seeking information about an object stolen only days before."

"We have granted you an audience because there are no such coincidences," added Ulfen. "In some way, those two events are related, and it is imperative we determine how."

Druida continued, "May we hear the entire story of how you came to be here? Please, take your time and do not skip any of the details. Even a seemingly insignificant fact can have a great effect when deciding the proper course of action."

Minaras sat back in the uncomfortable seat, reflecting on the events of the past fortnight. He then proceeded to give a full account of all that had transpired since Halia arrived on his doorstep. At the end of his story, the elders paused for some time to ponder the information. Only the restless squirming of the young apprentice broke the utter silence in the room. The Arboreals communicated with one another through nearly imperceptible facial movements for a few minutes before addressing the humans.

"Thank you for an interesting narrative, Minaras," said Ulfen, "but the story you tell is somewhat incomplete."

Oswynn jumped up and yelled, "It was not incomplete! My master left nothing out! We have waited patiently, and I have no doubt that you know more about these spheres than you let on!" He pointed an accusing finger at the elders.

There was a stunned silence as Oswynn drew the gaze of everyone at the table. He sat down slowly, feeling all ten eyes on him. Both shocked and amused by the outburst, Minaras wondered what the elders would think of this behavior. They might send him back to his room to contemplate his actions or even banish him from the forest for his lack of respect.

Falgoran's laugh, echoing through the great hall, answered the wizard's question. "I am sorry," he whispered in a soft, cracked voice. "We tend to forget how impetuous humans can be. Young Oswynn,

Ulfen was not commenting about your portion of the story, he merely noted there was more to be told."

The oldest of the Arboreals rose from the table and walked toward Oswynn. Taller than the others, he was also the only one who wore any type of jewelry, a silver pendant in the shape of a Z. With a wave of his hand, his chair disappeared from its spot next to Druida and grew out of the floor beside Oswynn.

"I myself know another piece of this story," Falgoran continued. "It took place many, many years ago when I was a young lad of only eighty springs. I can still remember the creation of the five crystal spheres as if it were last summer."

"There are five of them?" asked Oswynn.

Falgoran nodded as he recounted the origin of the spheres, an event that took place more than six hundred years ago. As he spun his tale, Oswynn hung on every word, mouth agape.

When the Arboreal finished speaking, Oswynn shouted, "We must stop them!"

Druida responded, in a gentle, calming voice, "Do not worry, young one, we shall. But first, we will take some time to plan our strategy."

"I must agree with Oswynn," Minaras declared. "It may be a bit dangerous to wait too long before acting."

Both Minaras and Oswynn tried arguing their case, but with the typical Arboreal attitude, the elders didn't see any urgency to the situation. There was no way a pair of humans could sway them to make a swift decision on the matter.

"We will consider our options until we can arrive at a proper decision," said Ulfen. "Even a human must understand it could be just as dangerous to act without a plan."

Minaras disagreed but gave up trying to persuade the elders. He knew delaying any longer could be disastrous. Getting up from the table, he declared, "Oswynn and I will travel north immediately. Discuss what you must, but I will use all of my power to protect this land from the weapons and the danger they represent!"

"Minaras, you face a long and perilous journey ahead of you, and he is but a child." Druida turned her head to the other elders, silently speaking with them. "You may leave young Oswynn under our protection until you return," she offered.

"I am not a child!" Oswynn argued. "I am ready for an adventure!" Falgoran laughed again.

"Besides, there will be much for me to learn," added Oswynn, glancing hopefully between the old Arboreal and Minaras.

His master agreed with a wink, "That there will be, my anxious apprentice."

Happy with the decision, Oswynn hopped out of his chair and followed Minaras toward the door, but when they reached the other end of the table, Kuril stood and blocked their way.

"Stand aside, Kuril," threatened Minaras. "We are leaving now."

"If I may, I will travel with you as well." He touched his scar and growled, "I have a score to settle."

Ulfen immediately disapproved of his rash decision. "Kuril! Do not forget you are the commander of this fortress," he protested.

"You have a responsibility to your men," added Druida.

Falgoran, however, gave a nearly imperceptible shake of his head, quieting them. "We will likely remain in this fortress debating our options until long after their quest has ended, either in success or failure. Kuril, it may do you well to travel with these humans, but before you embark on your journey, I have something that will prove most vital to your success. It is an old scroll on which is inscribed a powerful banishment spell. Please take Minaras and Oswynn to my library and search for a parchment partially scorched in the upper left corner. I am sorry, but I cannot recall precisely where I placed it so long ago."

Kuril bowed to the elders and brought the humans to the library. It was a disorganized jumble of books and scrolls, randomly scattered throughout the room. Minaras felt right at home in the mess and set to work immediately. Oswynn helped initially, but soon lost interest in the task and returned to pacing while the other two continued the search.

Most of the tomes in the room were Arboreal, but a few were human in origin. Surprisingly, even the oldest of the volumes had well preserved pages. Minaras wished that he could have discussed the matter with Kuril, but the Arboreal was rooted to a spot in the corner, methodically going through each volume. One after another, he flipped through the pages and tossed them aside.

Oswynn groaned, "Falgoran should know where the scroll is kept. We waste our time in here." He headed for the other side of the room, then came back and added, "Minaras, do you not know where every book in your library belongs? This room cannot be any less organized than yours."

Without the slightest pause in his activity, Kuril explained, "Young Oswynn, Falgoran has collected many interesting artifacts throughout the past six hundred years, and this is but one of his dozen libraries. You would do well to forgive him this small task we perform."

"One of his libraries?" moaned Oswynn. "What if the scroll lies elsewhere?"

"We will travel to every library in the entire Arboreal Forest if we must!" noted Minaras. He pushed aside several heavy books and added, "We would finish our search faster if you did more than pace around and complain."

"This task would be more tolerable if I knew how to read Arboreal."

"Then you should have paid more attention to your studies when we reviewed the language."

"And you should have paid more attention to teaching—"

"Enough!" Minaras thundered, pointing at a large stack of books. "On your next trip across the room, bring me yonder pile."

Oswynn wandered to the corner, picked up a half dozen large tomes, and brought them to Minaras. Each one, wrapped in what appeared to be a single brown leaf, which felt as sturdy as cured leather, felt lighter than it should have been. "Are you certain this scroll is necessary?" he asked as he dropped the books on the floor.

Before Minaras had a chance answer the question, Kuril said calmly, "I believe I have found the spell." He handed a partially charred scroll to the wizard.

Minaras gently took the page from Kuril and ran his eyes over the ancient runes inscribed on the parchment. "Yes, this is what Falgoran had described." He held the scroll up for Oswynn to see. "Without this banishment spell, our task would be a bit more complicated," he said and handed it back to Kuril.

The Arboreal tenderly rolled the parchment and placed it in a special waterproof scroll case attached to his belt. Without wasting another moment, much to Oswynn's relief, the three left the fortress and began their journey to the north.

It was a long hike through the Arboreal Forest, but with Kuril in the lead, Oswynn no longer felt an overwhelming fear of the woods. As the Arboreal glided effortlessly through the trees, the vegetation seemed to clear a path ahead of him. Oswynn, who had always been a fast runner, could barely match his speed. Bringing up the rear, Minaras moved as quickly as he could, gasping for air with every step.

"Slow down … Kuril," he panted, "I am not … as young … as I look."

Kuril, showing no sign of fatigue, stopped and waited for the others to catch up. He watched them trample small plants and snap numerous branches as they made their way toward him. Half under his breath he muttered, "Humans have always had a difficult time coexisting with the forest. You prefer to clear it away for your cities and farms."

As soft as the statement was, Oswynn heard it and shot back, "I grew up on a farm, and we treated our crops with great care. Plants are just as important to us humans as to you Arboreals."

The Arboreal shook his head. He would have spoken otherwise but didn't want to continue this argument with a child. "Humans are not only impulsive but also arrogant," he thought. "How could Oswynn possibly understand the relationship between Arboreals and the forest?"

"Would it not be faster to fly than to walk?" Oswynn suggested when Minaras had finally caught up with them. "With a strong enough wind we could take to the air."

The young apprentice then chanted, "*Lyft bord*" and moved his arms in circles over his head. A small breeze rustled the leaves in the trees above him. He looked at his master and beamed.

The magical wind caught Minaras completely by surprise. He was amazed that Oswynn could have learned the spell to generate wind on his own. He was still watching the swaying leaves when Oswynn asked, "How do I summon a stronger wind ... one to lift us into the air and carry us over the treetops?"

"Oswynn, you have done quite well summoning this small breeze, but there is more to the spell than the words and motions. To summon such a wind would require a great deal of energy."

"I have a great deal of energy ... show me how to use it."

"This is not a classroom," Kuril broke in, "we must continue on foot for now."

"That is true, Kuril," agreed Minaras. "We will finish this lesson when we return home." The wizard rubbed his sore legs. "Once we reach the border of the Arboreal forest, however, it will be faster for us to travel on horseback."

Kuril cringed at the thought of riding a horse. They were filthy animals. He liked neither their smell nor their attitude, although he had seen them only once before. On his sole excursion into a human village, a horse had sneezed on him when he walked by. Then it let out a whinny as if it were laughing at him. Kuril had been unable to rid himself of the offensive odor for three weeks. "If you must," he admitted, "there is a human town close by."

"Good," said Minaras. "We will be able to purchase some horses and get a bit of rest for these old bones."

CHAPTER XIV

THE HAUNTING OF THE NECROMANCER

The sun had just begun to dip under the horizon when Arwold, Halia, Thulin, and Calazar entered an old graveyard. They cut through a spiral pattern of flat, unmarked headstones, making their way toward the center of the well-kept grounds. As night drew closer, the lengthening shadows cast by the setting sun slowly engulfed each tombstone and were soon replaced by a gloomy darkness. Halia noticed that the earth on more than one of the plots had recently been agitated. "This is either a popular burial ground or someone is interested in digging up old bones," she thought.

"This looks to be a likely place for a necromancer," said Arwold.

Thulin, upon seeing a half-dug grave, remembered his necromancy lessons and wondered what was lying underground beneath his feet. Sometimes the dead were only sleeping. With proper motivation, a wizard could awaken them from their slumber to do his bidding. With more than a small amount of dread in his voice, he asked, "Could we not return in the morning?"

"I did not ask you to join me in this quest," Arwold swiftly responded. "You may stay in the village if you prefer, but I shall fulfill my oath this very night."

"Thulin, perhaps you should listen to Arwold and head back to town. You would be safer there," added Halia.

Thulin looked at the two of them and instantly became jealous. The thought of her alone with Arwold gave him a fleeting sense of courage. "No," he said. "I am a wizard! I am not afraid of the dead."

"This is good," whispered Calazar, "because we face them now."

He pointed ahead at a circular mausoleum. The large stone structure rose from the ground in the center of the headstone spiral. Four dirty skeletons stood frozen in front of the entrance, each of them holding a large bone club and small wooden buckler.

"They look like statues," said Thulin.

"But they are not," continued Arwold. "Do you see evil now, Halia?"

She shook her head and replied, "I have heard that skeletons obey their master, good or evil."

"Evil they are!" Arwold drew his sword, rushed forward, and yelled, "Attack these abominations! They mock life itself!"

The skeletons sprang into action at his voice, raising their shields, bringing their clubs back, and spreading their legs into a defensive position. They moved clumsily, as if they were about to fall apart with each step.

Calazar and Halia drew their weapons and followed Arwold into battle. Each of the three engaged one of the skeletons. Thulin held back about ten feet, took some powder out of his pocket, and attempted to cast a spell. He didn't notice the fourth skeleton breaking from the group and lumbering toward him.

Arwold swung heavily at his opponent. The skeleton blocked the claymore with its shield, but the force of the blow sent it crashing into the wall of the building. Many of its bones cracked on the hard stone, but the skeleton didn't fall. It raised its club over its head and limped forward, ready to attack. Arwold confidently closed in. He sliced downward, drove his sword through the bone club, and crushed the skull of the skeleton. With a few more slashes of his sword, Arwold reduced it to a jumble of broken bones.

The mercenary had a similarly easy time dismantling his opponent, although instead of blind power, he chose carefully aimed thrusts at the joints. Halia, however, was having some difficulty. The skeleton she fought kept swinging its femur-turned-club while she effortlessly dodged the blows. Between each attack, she stabbed at it with her small sword, doing nothing more than nicking a bone here or there. "I need either more strength or a blunt weapon to cause any real damage to this creature."

The fourth skeleton caught Thulin by surprise, clobbering him with the club before he could get his spell to function properly. Dazed, the young wizard fell over and hit the ground hard. Luckily, Halia saw him in time.

"Thulin!" she yelled, jumping between his body and the skeleton that was about to finish him off. "To me, you pile of bones!" she taunted, waving her sword.

The skeleton obliged and swung its club at her. Halia ducked out of the way and tried kicking one of its legs. Her foot collided with solid bone, causing the creature to wobble for a second before it steadied itself. Her initial opponent stepped forward and attempted to crush her with a sneaky downward blow. Halia leaped aside and jabbed back, smacking her sword into the skeleton's buckler. Fortunately, she was agile enough to hold her own against the two skeletons until Arwold and Calazar finished their fight and came to her aid. Soon, there was nothing left of the skeletons but a scattering of splintered bones.

Halia blushed at the embarrassment of needing assistance, but she knelt down to check on Thulin before either of the warriors noticed. The young apprentice was unconscious. She removed her cloak, rolled it into a ball, and placed it gently under his head.

Arwold looked down at the boy and said, "Other than an aching head, he will be fine in the morning. Let us finish off this necromancer before he can do any more evil."

The tall warrior approached the building, kicked some of the bones out of the way, and broke down the door. Then he strolled through the doorway as if he were entering his own house.

Inside the building was a single chamber with a domed ceiling. The flickering flames from dozens of candles, laid out in semi-circles, lit the room with a sparkling light, which was magnified by reflections off ten white marble coffins. Near the center of the candle and coffin formation, a figure in a long black robe stood holding a small vial of blue liquid. Arwold pointed his claymore at the wizard and declared, "Your evil ends now, necromancer. You cannot escape me."

The necromancer looked at Arwold, let out a sigh, and drank the potion. "I do not know why you pursue me, but you will not succeed in your unrelenting persecution."

Arwold rushed forward, cutting sideways with his claymore at the wizard's midsection. As soon as the sword touched the black robe, the necromancer and all of his clothing crumbled into a pile of dust. All that remained of the wizard was a single gold ring, which fell to the floor and bounced four times in a sequence of metallic dings.

Surprised, Arwold jumped back and yelled, "Why do you insist on hiding behind your evil magic? Come out and face me in righteous battle!" He looked around the room, rushed to the pile of dust, and sifted through it with the tip of his sword. Angered at losing the necromancer once again, Arwold spun around violently, knocked over a few candles, and headed for the door.

Calazar, who had been standing in the doorway, pointed beyond the tall warrior and yelled out a warning. "Look behind you!"

Arwold turned just in time to see the remains of the necromancer begin to swirl around, eventually turning into a small dust devil, which rose into the air like a miniature tornado. The top of the vortex fanned out and formed the shape of a human torso with two arms, a neck, and a head. Gradually, the spinning stopped and the dust faded away, leaving only an inky blackness to the creature. A pair of dim yellow eyes glowed within, and the specter let out a faint moan.

Arwold cringed at the sight of the shadowy being. "We cannot let this infernal creature survive. It must be destroyed!"

He and Calazar approached the specter cautiously, unsure of what to expect. The mercenary attacked first with a random swing of his saber. The weapon passed directly through the specter's arm without doing any apparent damage. Arwold had no better luck when his claymore sailed through the lower half of the creature.

With a low-pitched groan, which almost sounded like a muffled laugh, the specter dove for Arwold, who jumped aside just in time to avoid a collision. Having missed its primary target, the creature veered sideways, aiming for the center of Calazar's chest. The specter caught the mercenary off guard and thrust its head into his body. Calazar dropped his weapon, clutched his heart, and fell to his knees.

"No!" he screamed. "What is happening to me?"

A moment later, he collapsed face first on the ground as the specter retreated to the center of the chamber, ready to continue its battle with Arwold.

As soon as she heard the scream, Halia jumped up from Thulin's side and ran into the building. Her eyes darted from Calazar, lying on the ground, to Arwold, desperately trying to avoid contact with the ghostly image. "By my sword!" she exclaimed. "What manner of being is that?"

"An evil one, the spawn of an evil wizard," responded Arwold.

Halia thought it best to move the wounded mercenary out of the building before aiding Arwold. When she knelt down beside his body to check on him, he slowly pushed himself off the floor and lifted his head up. His face had withered as if he had spent years in a desert without water.

Halia gasped, "Your face … your hands … how can this be?"

The mercenary stared at her with completely white eyes and said nothing. He continued his slow rise from the floor—to his knees, to his feet, and then toward Halia. She reached out to help, but he suddenly attacked, clawing at her violently. In one swift motion, her sword was out and she was defending herself. Calazar, now a ghoul under control of the specter, came at her relentlessly, punching with both of its shriveled fists. Halia's sword was quicker, however, cutting deep into his parched flesh with every blow.

Within minutes, she had severely damaged the creature's left arm, although no blood came from any of the wounds. Halia focused her attacks on that limb and soon severed it from the body. The creature didn't seem to notice and connected an unexpectedly strong blow to her stomach with its right arm.

"Ugh," she moaned. "'Twill take more than a flesh wound to stop you."

Halia moved her attention to the creature's lower body. "Perhaps without legs you will no longer be a threat," she thought as she viciously hacked at the left leg, eventually weakening it enough until it could no longer support the creature's weight. Unfortunately, she didn't notice the severed arm making its way along the ground toward her. The arm grabbed her ankle at the same time the ghoul fell forward. In the confusion, Halia dropped her sword as both she and the ghoul fell to the floor. The body of the much heavier mercenary dropped on top of her, pinning her to the ground.

She tried unsuccessfully to squeeze out from under the body, but the ghoul was too heavy for her to lift. It continued its attack by taking a bite near her shoulder and tearing a chunk of material from her beautiful shirt. Halia clawed at its face, trying to keep the creature away from her neck. The cracked lips of the ghoul curled into a hideous grin, expecting to taste blood with its next bite, but before it could sink its teeth into her flesh, Thulin rushed into the room and pulled its head backward. Halia once again tried to wriggle out from beneath the heavy body, but this time, Thulin's aid had given her just enough room to escape. Once free, she rolled over and lifted her sword in defense, but the creature chose not to attack. Ignoring both her and Thulin, it turned its attention to the other battle where its master was in danger. It crawled toward Arwold, dragging its bad leg behind it.

Arwold lunged at the specter. "Die, foul beast!" he yelled, as the claymore passed through thin air once again, causing him to lose his balance. He steadied himself and spun around only to see the specter coming straight for him, eager to turn him into another ghastly slave. Without thinking, Arwold lifted his claymore in defense. The sword passed backward through one of the specter's eyes, causing the creature to howl with pain. Arwold let out a grin as he regained his balance. "Your weakness has been revealed."

He began slashing back and forth at the specter's two eyes in a motion resembling a figure eight and didn't even notice when the mercenary-ghoul grabbed his leg.

"This battle is won!" Arwold bellowed in triumph with one final reverse swing of his claymore. The specter let out a piercing shriek and then dissipated, vanishing without a trace. At the same time its master let out its death scream, the ghoul collapsed onto the floor. Arwold kicked the hideous creature onto its back and looked in horror at his former companion.

"'Twas almost me," he said disgustedly. He paused to catch his breath. "Calazar has sacrificed his life to make this world a safer place. We must give him a proper burial. Take his legs, Thulin!"

Arwold and Thulin lifted the body of the mercenary to carry him out of the building. As Halia turned to follow them, a glint of gold on the floor caught her eye. She walked over and picked up the necromancer's ring.

"Leave his ring!" Arwold ordered when saw her bending over.

"The necromancer needs this bauble no more." She fingered the hole in her shirt. "It should be just enough to pay a tailor for repairs."

"It goes with him to his grave! We did not come to steal from this wizard." He stopped and gave her a stern glance.

She stared back defiantly. "Nay, you came to take his life."

"I came to rid the world of a dangerous evil. You have aided me in my quest and for that I thank you, but you shall not loot this tomb!"

Thulin, quickly tiring from carrying the heavy body, tried mediating. "Halia, now that Arwold's quest is complete, we can continue on ours. Let us bury Calazar and be on our way. We may yet find innumerable treasures."

Arwold, still glaring at Halia, refused to move until she threw the ring onto the floor of the chamber. Then, with a look of victory, he pulled both Calazar's body and Thulin out the door. They buried the mercenary outside the mausoleum and spent a restful night in the neighboring village.

The next morning, Arwold offered more information about his family sword. "This blade was forged by the Teruns many ages ago. They might know something of the sphere."

"Then north we shall go ... to the Pensorean Mountains," said Halia.

Arwold led them to a nearby trade route that followed a winding path to the northwest. Although the road was smooth and the weather was pleasant, Arwold and Thulin annoyed each other constantly. At first, Halia acted as an intermediary, but eventually she left the two to work things out on their own, often regretting her decision not to travel alone.

One day, Arwold and Thulin began arguing about how to cook the evening meal, a young wild boar that they had captured. After building a fire, Arwold tore a leg from the animal and held it over the flames to cook. Halia carelessly mentioned she was tired of eating cured meat every day and was looking forward to a nice juicy piece of pork. Hearing those words, Thulin walked up to Arwold and ordered him to cook the entire beast over a spit. "By rotating the carcass," he said, "the meat will heat more evenly and taste better." Arwold responded by threatening to cook Thulin. Things proceeded downhill from there until Halia grabbed the partially cooked leg and left the campsite for some peace and quiet away from the arguing duo.

The three spent a couple more days on the trade route before reaching an important bend in the road. Arwold pointed toward a large swamp to the north and said, "There is a shortcut through yonder swamp. It will take a full day of hiking to reach the other side."

"And the road?" asked Thulin.

"This road curves south, out of our way. 'Tis a safer choice but would delay our journey."

Halia looked at Thulin and said, "What is a few more days when we have already spent weeks? We shall take the road."

Arwold agreed with a sly nod at the young apprentice.

Thulin frowned and ran his hand over the bump on his head. "Nay, let us take the shortcut. I am not afraid of the swamp."

"Thulin, 'tis not a question of your courage," explained Halia, "'tis a question of whether you would be able to protect yourself or not."

"Aye, Halia may be unable to save your life the next time you face danger."

Thulin felt a rush of blood flow into his cheeks. "I can take care of myself! I needed no help against the skeleton, Halia!"

Arwold laughed, "And what exactly was your plan of attack while you were lying unconscious on the ground?"

"I am a wizard to be feared, not a helpless child to be coddled! We shall travel through the swamp!" commanded Thulin as he stormed away from the others.

"Good now," accepted Arwold. "We shall camp here for the night and head north with the rise of the morning sun."

"So be it," murmured Halia with a shrug of her shoulders. She would have to live with a moody Thulin on the trade route or keep an extra eye on him in the swamp. "At least it shall only take a day to reach the other side. If we keep to the path, what could go wrong?" she wondered.

CHAPTER XV

DENIZENS OF THE SWAMP

At the first light of dawn, Arwold sat with his equipment and began his usual routine of polishing his armor and honing his sword. Halia, who had just awoken, brought her sword over and said, "Perhaps this could use a little work."

Arwold looked at the battered weapon, scratched and dulled by combat. "Your sword has seen its share of battles. You would do well to grind a new edge, but, for now, use this to smooth your blade." He handed her the honing stone and added, "You should treat your equipment with no less respect than you treat your body."

Halia took the gritty black stone and sat next to him. She placed her sword across her legs and hesitatingly ran the stone up and down along the blade. Arwold reached over, corrected the angle at which she held the stone, and suggested she slide it in one direction only, from the hilt of the sword to the tip. Halia did as he suggested and asked, "Like so?"

Arwold nodded and said, "A fast learner you are."

The commotion of the other two roused Thulin from his deep sleep. He stretched, felt the bump on his head, which had finally stopped aching, and walked over to Arwold. Looking disgruntled, he asked in a slightly groggy, yet patronizing voice, "Arwold, why do you polish your armor? It will only become muddy in the swamp. You waste your time when you could have been preparing our breakfast."

Arwold placed the cloth on the ground next to him and held up the steel breastplate, which gleamed brightly in the morning sunlight. "This armor belonged to my father and has saved my life on more than one occasion," he declared proudly. "Proper care of your equipment is essential."

Halia had finished honing and had begun polishing her sword. Thulin glanced at her with a look that cried, "Not you too!" She tilted the blade, allowing the sunlight to reflect off the metal, while she continued looking for blemishes to wipe away. "'Tis essential," she concurred.

"Essential or not," he said, "Let us be on our way." He grabbed the honing stone and polishing cloth from Halia and handed them back to Arwold.

"Thulin, do I detect a hint of jealousy in you?" asked Halia.

He turned his head away, blushing. Halia sheathed her sword, which now looked much better than when she had first acquired it, and led him away from Arwold. "You need not be jealous, Thulin, for you are like a brother to me."

"A brother am I?" Thulin asked disappointedly.

Halia gave him a warm smile and said, "I have never had a real family."

Thulin didn't feel any better. "I must prove to her that I am a skilled wizard," he thought, "or she will never think of me as anything more than a child."

The three finished off the last of the wild boar for breakfast before leaving the safety of the trade route. As they headed for the shortcut through the swamp, the environment gradually changed. The earth under their feet became softer and moister, the trees thinned out and grew shorter, and a thick fog formed, blanketing the ground. Strong sunlight filtered down through moss-covered branches casting eerie, dancing shadows on the ever-present mist.

Arwold, in the lead, tried to keep them on as dry a path as he could find, but they frequently found themselves walking through an inch or two of muck. He was glad he had only worn his breastplate to fight the necromancer. The weight of his full suit of armor would have caused him to sink even deeper. Other than the sloshing sounds of their footsteps, it was unusually quiet as they made their way toward the heart of the swamp.

Twice, Halia noticed a creature ducking behind a tree as they walked by, but she didn't say anything, worried about unnecessarily frightening Thulin. As long as she stayed alert, she was confident that no creature could gain the advantage of a surprise attack.

High above the treetops, Hafoc flew in circles. For nearly an hour, the crow hovered in the sky, when suddenly it made a beeline for the trade route. It dove straight for its master, landed on his shoulder, and gave him the bad news.

"Hafoc has found the others," said Ahriman. "There are three of them traveling through yonder swamp."

He nudged his familiar into the air to lead the way. "I believe they could be in for some trouble. If they lose possession of the spheres, it may be impossible for us to complete our quest."

"After them we must," urged Xarun, his pace quickening from a walk to a jog to a sprint as time ran out.

Back in the swamp, the mist grew heavier until the three could no longer see their feet. Luckily, it lay in a thin layer that only reached their knees or they would have been unable to continue walking, much less find their way out. The group slowed to a crawl. As they passed a particularly wide tree trunk, a pair of bulbous eyes peeked out from beneath the mist. Arwold turned suddenly, but the creature disappeared before he could see anything.

The tall warrior held up his hand, stopping the group. He pointed at the tree and whispered, "Something watches us from behind that thick trunk."

"I know," responded Halia softly. "It has been tracking us for a while."

Arwold cautiously moved toward the tree, quietly unsheathing his sword. A few steps later, Thulin shouted, "Someone approaches!" A humanoid figure scuttled into view and approached the group. Halia peered at the familiar body and admitted, "'Tis ... you, Thulin ... I think."

From a distance, the figure closely resembled Thulin with the same face, the same body, and even the same clothing, but each of his features seemed melted. Its face looked like a watercolor painting instead of an exact replica, and its clothes appeared to be an extension of its body instead of being separate items. Two more of the creatures appeared in the distance: one resembled Halia and the other, Arwold.

Halia seemed amused. "We each have a twin."

Thulin, however, was more worried. "Are they friendly, or do they intend to replace us?"

"They are doppelgängers!" Arwold spat out, focusing angrily on his likeness.

"Are you certain?" Thulin asked. "I thought doppelgängers to be an exact replica of the original. These appear to be poor imitations at best."

"I know what I see," responded Arwold. "The doppelgänger mimics your appearance to gain the advantage. Not many warriors enjoy slicing into their own bodies. If you succumb to their deception, however, you will be doomed. These beasts will feed on any living being, apprentices included."

More doppelgängers appeared in the distance, no longer amusing Halia. She drew her sword while thinking eerie or menacing would be a more accurate description of the creatures, which shambled through the mist making no sound at all. Thulin backed away, heading for a tree to provide some cover. He reached into his pouch and removed a pinch of bone powder. In a futile attempt to cast a spell, he began chanting *"Freorig bans"* repeatedly as he tossed the powder into the air, but nothing happened.

Arwold stepped forward and swung at the closest doppelgänger, his claymore cleaving into the amorphous creature. "Doppelgängers or not, we shall defeat these evil simulacra!"

He yanked his sword back, but it wouldn't budge. His weapon was stuck in the side of the creature, which didn't bleed a single drop of blood despite the deep wound. He gave a firm tug on the weapon and fell backward when the sword suddenly came free. As the blade flew out of its body, the doppelgänger melted into the mist on the ground. Arwold recovered in time to meet two more of his likenesses approaching.

Halia thrust her sword at her first opponent, burying it in the center of the creature's chest. She pulled but was unable to dislodge the blade. It was almost as if the creature were holding on to the weapon. "Return my sword!" she yelled as she danced around the doppelgänger. It tried punching her, but she dodged the blow and pulled at the sword again. It wouldn't move. While she attempted to retrieve her weapon, a second Halia doppelgänger closed in on her.

Meanwhile, Thulin, completely immersed in an attempt to cast his Frozen Bones spell, failed to see the two doppelgängers approaching him. The first one landed a strong blow to the side of his head. Despite its fluid appearance, its fist was as solid as granite when it connected. Thulin staggered and fell to the ground, while the second prepared to deliver a final blow. It joined its fists together, lifted them over its head, and was about to strike when, out of nowhere, an axe hewed the creature down the center of its body. The doppelgänger dissolved into the mist. Behind it, Xarun stood holding the axe. Another strong blow from the warrior destroyed the second creature.

Thulin rose from the ground, his robe covered in mud. "I thank you good warrior," he said, but Xarun didn't stay for the gratitude; he proceeded immediately to Halia's side.

"Xarun is not one for talking," Ahriman said as he joined Thulin by the tree. The apprentice watched as the more experienced wizard waved his hands at the ground in small circles and chanted, "*Genip cnapas, gegaerian abutan.*" The vapors near his feet swirled around and formed into a dozen tiny mist spirits, small white clouds with legs, arms, eyes, and naught else. With another wave of his arm, they scattered in all directions. While Thulin's eyes followed the tiny creatures, Ahriman took an empty vial out of a pocket and scooped up some of the remains of the nearest doppelgänger. He quickly corked the vial and slipped it back into his robe.

By the time Xarun had reached Halia, the two doppelgängers had grabbed her arms and started to pull. The big warrior rushed in and dislodged her sword, destroying one of the creatures with it. A single swing of his axe easily killed the other.

He flipped the sword in the air, caught it by the blade, and returned it to Halia. "Here be thy sword, maiden," he said with the air of a knight coming to the aid of a helpless woman.

Halia disliked the insinuation. She grabbed the sword and slapped his hand with the flat of the blade. "I did not ask for your help with those doppelgängers."

"We do not fight doppelgängers," Ahriman called out.

"Then pray tell, what were they?" asked Arwold.

Ahriman gazed around the swamp, clearly concerned over what was lurking out there. "Just be ready," he warned.

"For what shall we be ready?"

A deafening roar startled the group, but Ahriman didn't flinch as he answered, "A battle."

In the direction of the loud noise, a very large marsh dragon rose from the mist. It bore a strong resemblance to the doppelgängers, looking more like a great watercolor serpent than an actual dragon. From the tip of its long, thick tail to its heavily fanged mouth, it was at least forty feet in length. The dragon stomped on the ground, dispelling the annoying mist spirits that had found and surrounded it. When the last of the bothersome little pests were gone, the dragon whipped its head around and leered at the group of humans. Within a heartbeat, it charged at them, flowing over the misty ground like a stream of water.

Arwold, surprised at the sight of this beast, exclaimed, "A dragon in a swamp? This cannot be! They live in the mountains!"

"The marsh dragon is not a true dragon, yet you will find it almost as dangerous," responded Ahriman. "And beware of its tail."

Arwold and Xarun positioned themselves between the dragon and the rest of the group. Halia jumped behind a nearby tree, thinking a surprise attack might be a more appropriate action for her than a frontal assault. She only hoped the creature didn't notice or didn't care about her departure from the others.

The dragon was upon the two warriors quicker than they had hoped. It reared up and snapped at Arwold before he had a chance to move into a defensive position. The beast's head slammed into his armor, surprisingly without a sound. The incredible force of the blow threw Arwold backward, skidding through the mud. Simultaneously, the creature lashed out at Xarun with its long tail. The appendage extended ever longer as it stretched through the air toward the warrior's lower body. Xarun was about to take a swipe at the dragon's head when the tail wrapped around his feet and pulled him to the ground.

"That would be the tail, Xarun!" yelled Ahriman, shaking his head.

Before the dragon could inflict any further damage on the warriors, Halia slipped out from behind the tree and stabbed it in the leg. The sword barely managed to pierce its translucent hide, and had she not recently sharpened the blade, it would have done no damage at all. As she withdrew her weapon, a clear, gooey liquid oozed from the wound. The dragon reared up with another great roar sounding more angered than in pain. Halia rushed back to the safety of her hiding spot when she noticed that the wound had already healed itself. The dragon poked its head around the trees searching for its attacker, but Halia stayed absolutely steady and quiet, out of its immediate sight. Xarun and Arwold used those few moments to regroup.

Thulin, having recovered from his minor injury, prepared another attempt at his spell. He pulled out more bone powder and chanted the magic words. Ahriman, who immediately realized the young boy wasn't yet a real wizard, smirked and said, "Even if you were the most powerful necromancer in the land, it would be impossible to freeze the bones of a creature that has none. Stand back, child."

The sorcerer gathered an armful of leaves and twigs from the ground, threw the entire bundle into the air, and chanted, "*Holt mann, hieran min hatan*." As the debris fell, it spun round and round, coalescing into a humanoid shape, about half the height of a man. Ahriman stared at the newly summoned forest spirit, pointed at the dragon, and yelled, "Attack!" The spirit shuffled toward the battle, growing larger with each step as it consumed more debris from the ground. Ahriman leaned against a tree for support, recovering the energy he had lost while casting the two spells.

The marsh dragon, in a deadlock with Xarun and Arwold, snapped back and forth between the two, keeping them constantly on guard. Arwold, with the longer reach, found an opening and thrust the claymore forward. The sword bounced off the creature, surprising the warrior.

"It has skin like a rock!" he exclaimed.

"Only when it sees your attack," Ahriman called from the ground. "It can strengthen or expand its body at will."

"Halia!" yelled Arwold. "Try finding the dragon's heart while we distract it!"

She jumped out of hiding and was nearly lashed by the creature's tail, which effectively held her at bay.

"What be that?" shouted Xarun when the forest spirit appeared, now slightly taller than Arwold, and positioned itself between the two warriors.

The spirit threw its arms forward, causing debris to fly from its hands toward the dragon's head. The creature wailed in pain as a plethora of small twigs stung its eyes. In a fit of fury, the dragon lunged at the spirit, swallowing it in one enormous gulp and choking on the inedible kindling now lodged in its throat.

Xarun let fly a huge swing of his axe, making a deep gash in the dragon's neck. Halia also took advantage of the moment and, avoiding its tail, sliced into its back leg. The dragon let out a great hacking yelp, twisted around, and, knowing its life was in danger, dived into the swampy mist. As the creature fled, it flattened its body, disappearing into the thin layer of fog hugging the ground.

"Where does the foul dragon hide?" yelled Arwold.

"It seems to have had enough fighting for the day," Halia replied.

"Tarry not! We must find and destroy the vile beast!"

"Leave it be, Arwold," Thulin said as he joined the others. "'Tis probably looking for an easier meal."

"'Tis evil … it must be killed!"

Ahriman, still resting against the tree, said, "Evil or not, shall we consider ourselves lucky to escape unharmed? I have never heard of anyone defeating a marsh dragon without a considerable amount of fire at his disposal."

Halia nodded, "I agree with the wizard. Let us be out of this nasty place."

The five proceeded quickly and quietly through the marsh. By evening, they had made it to solid ground and lit a nice crackling fire to dry themselves off. Ahriman began the introductions. "I am Ahriman, the sorcerer."

He removed the sphere from his pouch to show the others. "Xarun and I have been tracking a pair of crystal spheres, nearly identical to this one, for some time. When I noticed the two had converged several days ago, we made haste to catch them before they went their separate ways once more. Dare I say you were lucky we did so?"

Xarun removed his sphere from his pouch, as did Halia. Arwold lifted his sword and held the sphere in his hand. Blue, purple, green, and red spots glowed in the center of each sphere in combinations of three colors each.

Halia asked, "Know you anything about these four spheres?"

"And are there more?" Thulin added.

Ahriman graciously gave them a partial explanation. "This sphere has been in my family for many generations. I have been told they are part of a key that will unleash a great treasure once we have found the final sphere."

"A key to a treasure," said Thulin. "I thought as much."

"You thought no such thing!" barked Arwold. "Did you not call yourself lost when you were in my house?"

"I may have said those words in anger, but for what other purpose could these spheres have been created? Powerful magic was used to enchant these crystals."

Halia's face brightened at the thought of gold. "A treasure this well hidden shall be worth a fortune."

Xarun also was excited, but for a different reason. Grinning, he added, "And guarded by terrible creatures."

"Are we agreed?" asked Ahriman. "Shall we seek the treasure together?"

"We must each receive an equal share," said Halia.

"Why would it be otherwise?" Ahriman looked around the fire. Halia, Thulin, and Xarun all nodded in agreement. "And you, Arwold?" he asked.

The tall warrior responded, "As I have already told the others, I would learn the history of this sword. I have no interest in finding gold."

Ahriman lifted his sphere into the air and said, "The treasure we shall find!"

Halia and Xarun lifted their spheres as they and Thulin shouted, "The treasure!"

Arwold brought them back from their elation with a sobering point. "Before you can uncover the treasure, you must find another sphere."

"'Tis true," admitted Ahriman. "I have read that the fifth and final sphere resides in a castle lying at the foot of the Pensorean Mountains, not far from here."

"What do you think the treasure shall be?" Halia wondered aloud. "Coins? Rare jewels? A diamond-studded crown befitting a king?"

"Nay," hoped the big warrior. "It be a magical weapon."

Thulin agreed with Xarun. "Magic it must be ... long lost secrets of ancient wizards."

"Arwold, what do think the treasure might be?" asked Halia.

"Whatever it is, you must try to find the rightful owner before claiming it as your own."

Thulin laughed. "Prate not, Arwold. The treasure has been buried for centuries."

Halia agreed, "We keep what we find."

"'Tis not right to keep that which belongs to others," argued Arwold.

"You speak nonsense," said Thulin. "Knowledge of this treasure, and its owners, has been lost, even to the great libraries of Minaras and Sigmus."

At the sound of Minaras' name, Ahriman tensed up, casting a wary eye on Thulin. "Does this young pseudo-wizard know more than he admits? Perhaps this is a trap."

"What do you know of Minaras?" the sorcerer asked slyly.

"I am his apprentice," responded Thulin proudly.

Ahriman relaxed a bit. "I know him as well. I was his first ... student."

Thulin immediately became suspicious. "Did you study at his home in Seaton?"

"I did, but found it to be lacking in space."

The young apprentice frowned, thinking this couldn't be a coincidence. "Do you know anything of his personal library?"

"I might be able to help you ... what exactly do you wish to learn?"

Thulin jumped up. "I believe I already have my answer. You are the one who stole the page from the old Arboreal tome!"

Arwold murmured, "Thieves," and reached for his sword.

"Do I look like a lowly thief?" asked Ahriman. "I admit that I took some pages from Minaras, but I was merely borrowing them."

Incredulous, Thulin exclaimed, "You stole more than one page?"

"I stole nothing. The pages were from old histories rarely, if ever, used, and I planned to restore them once I had found the treasure. I am surprised the old wizard even noticed they were missing."

Arwold stood, drawing his sword from its scabbard. He would bring these thieves to justice. Feeling threatened, Xarun grabbed his axe and rose to meet the other warrior. "Shall we have at it?" he asked, smiling at the prospect of another battle before bed.

Ahriman attempted to defuse the situation. "Please, Arwold … Xarun … have we any reason to fight among ourselves?"

"You do not deny that you stole. 'Tis wrong even if you planned to return the items," replied Arwold.

"Whatever his reasons for—", Halia began.

Arwold didn't let her finish. "There is no excuse for thievery! You will accompany me to Krof or I shall bring you there by force!"

Xarun laughed. "That be easier said than done." He flexed his muscles and tightened his grip on his axe. His display of might was impressive, but Arwold refused to back down.

Thulin bravely stepped between the two large men. "As his apprentice, I shall speak for Minaras now. Ahriman may face my master when we return with the treasure. Would this satisfy your need for immediate justice, Arwold?"

The tall warrior hesitated. "For now," he reluctantly agreed, placing his sword on the ground. Xarun did the same with his weapon, looking somewhat disappointed.

Thulin turned to the sorcerer. "Ahriman, you must tell us everything you know or admit being a thief."

"Xarun had guessed the truth with his wish for a magic weapon. When the five spheres are held at the same time, they will guide us to five magical weapons of great power, forged many centuries ago."

"Those weapons have been hidden many years," Arwold said. "Maybe we should not disturb them."

Thulin laughed at him, garnering another angry look. "Again, you speak nonsense. The weapons remain hidden only because no one has found them yet."

"Or because no one should find them," persisted Arwold.

"Then why would anyone have created these spheres to be used as a map?"

Arwold shrugged, "I have no answer."

"Go to!" Thulin laughed again.

Arwold frowned, clenching his fist.

Halia shot an angry look at the apprentice. "Goad him no more, Thulin. We know only that the weapons remain hidden and naught else."

Ahriman added, "And we have yet to recover the final sphere."

CHAPTER XVI

DANGER IN THE WOODS

Minaras pushed his mount hard, racing through open fields, meadows, and farmlands on his way to the northern coast of the continent. The beautiful summer weather, with its warm, dry days and cool nights, offered perfect traveling conditions, allowing him to go for many hours at a stretch without taking a break, which tired the riders nearly as much as the horses. Whenever possible, he avoided any heavily wooded areas between the towns and villages, worried more about losing time maneuvering through the trees than getting lost. Oswynn and Kuril, together on the second horse, followed closely behind Minaras. The Arboreal, however, was more than a little uneasy on horseback, forcing Oswynn to hold back on the full speed of their mount.

As they galloped over uneven ground, Kuril wobbled to one side of the horse and clutched its mane tighter. The rhythmic pounding of the horse's hooves against the ground didn't alter in the slightest, even as the Arboreal hung from its neck.

"Might I … travel … by foot?" he inquired, slowly pulling himself to an upright position.

"You are a swift runner, faster than anyone I have seen, but still you cannot match the speed of this horse," Oswynn replied. "Minaras seems unlikely to slow down. Look! We lose ground even now." He urged the horse forward, trying to catch up to his master.

Kuril fell to the other side, but, this time, he couldn't regain his balance. Oswynn reached out and helped pull him up. The Arboreal grimaced, distraught at being forced to receive assistance from a human, let alone a child, but he accepted the aid nonetheless.

"You are none too steady on horseback," commented Oswynn.

"We do not ... see many ... horses ... in the deep forest ... and besides ... they are too ... domesticated," Kuril replied, his words broken by the jarring ride. "Are you not ... very young ... to be so ... skilled a horseman?"

"Nor do you see many humans in the forest," Oswynn said, laughing. "I have been riding horses ever since I can remember and most likely before that as well. Hold yourself ... it looks as if we will need to pick up our pace."

Once again, they were falling behind Minaras, so Oswynn leaned forward and prodded their steed to an even faster gallop. Then, to further show off his skills, Oswynn made their horse leap over a small stream. When its hooves collided with the hard ground on the other side of the stream, Kuril nearly bounced off its back, but the young human held him firmly in place. Kuril winced at the indignity of his situation. For enduring this torture, he now had even more reason to exact his vengeance.

"We should never have bought these beasts from the farmer," Kuril grumbled.

"This is true," agreed Oswynn. "The price was too steep. After Minaras helped him with his irrigation, he should have paid us to take the horses. My master's skills should not come cheaply."

"It is all based on necessity," said Kuril, clinging tightly to the horse's mane.

The sun had sunk low in the sky and turned a dark shade of orange when the riders entered a lightly forested area. The sight of the wilderness made Kuril feel more comfortable, and his tension eased further when the horses slowed to a trot. Soon, they approached a wide lake, spanning the horizon. Minaras and Oswynn stopped their horses beside each other at the shoreline. Kuril immediately slid off the back of his mount, guessing that the humans would want to rest for the night. He rejoiced silently when his feet touched the solid, unmoving ground.

Oswynn gazed across the large body of water. "This lake appears to be quite deep in the center," he said. "We must find a way around or swim the horses through it."

"Perhaps neither," Minaras responded enigmatically as he dismounted, "but it is getting a bit late and we should give the horses a break. Let us set up camp for the night."

Oswynn allowed the horses a long drink before tying them up while Minaras gathered some wild berries to augment the dried meats they had recently purchased. Kuril, anxious to spend some time away from the humans, disappeared into the woods to find his own meal.

By nightfall, Minaras and Oswynn had finished eating their dinner beside a small campfire. It was an idyllic, crystal-clear night with a myriad of stars twinkling in the sky. Minaras was beginning to reminisce about the times he used to travel with Sigmus when he first heard the howling. It started out as a faint echo from afar and grew louder and closer by the minute. Oswynn turned his head in the direction of the noise, looking quite worried.

"It is only a pack of wolves, Oswynn. They will not come near us, especially with this fire in the middle of our campsite."

Oswynn looked at his master and shook his head. "That would be true if they were gray wolves, Minaras, but this howling is from a pack of blaeculfs," he countered. "My father taught me long ago how to tell the difference between the two, and he warned me to head for shelter when blaeculfs are on the prowl. They are very aggressive and, unlike wolves, would dare to attack a group of armed men. Their hide is thick and their jaws are strong."

"If you are correct, then we must prepare ourselves. A bit of magic should protect us." Minaras had no reason to doubt Oswynn, having seen his aptitude with wizardry. "The gray wolf is an intelligent beast, and I assume that is no less true for these distant cousins."

"Even more so," Oswynn confirmed.

"We will use their intelligence against them, preying upon the fear of the unknown that is common to all beings who can think." Minaras promptly walked over to the lake and cast a spell on the calm water. Returning, he declared, "We should be safe if we remain between the lake and the fire until the blaeculfs leave the area."

"What spell did you cast?"

Minaras grinned, knowing his apprentice had really asked, "Would you teach me the spell?"

"I have animated the water with an extremely complicated incantation," responded the wizard. "You must wait until we study the elements to understand its casting."

"But I already know how to summon a wind."

Oswynn gave a hopeful look, but his master said nothing more. The young apprentice sighed briefly, stopping only when the thought of Kuril interrupted his dejection. "Kuril is in danger with the blaeculfs roaming the area," he said, worryingly. "We should warn him."

Minaras shook his head. "In the forest, an Arboreal is invisible if he so chooses. As long as there are trees around, Kuril will be far safer than we could ever hope to be."

They didn't have to wait much longer before the blaeculfs appeared. Although it was impossible to see their dark bodies hidden against the shadows of the night, the reflection of the campfire sparkled in their eyes, making them appear like a gathering of large fireflies hovering near the ground. Minaras removed a small tinderbox from a pocket and placed it in his lap, just in case.

The first one approached cautiously, fixing its eyes on the smaller human. As it stepped into the light of the fire, its large, muscular body came into view. It was twice the size of a gray wolf, with a coat of thin black fur. It held its ears back against its head and ruffled the fur on its shoulders. A row of sharp teeth, perfect for rending flesh, lined its salivating mouth. The predator had detected the scent of its prey, and it was ready to eat after a quick kill. Another blaeculf broke from the pack, following just behind the leader. The two beasts crept closer when, suddenly, a thin tendril of water rose from the lake and struck the face of the first one, stinging its nose and eyes. Surprised and soaked, it yelped and backed off. The same happened to the second creature after it took another step toward its intended meal.

The lead blaeculf barked at the water and tried one last time, but the unnatural activity of the lake spooked the animal. It retreated into the woods, followed by the rest of the pack. Minutes later, they reappeared on the other side of the fire, but the animated water continued to thwart their attempts at an easy meal. Drenched, they sulked back into the forest and faded into the darkness as quickly as they had appeared.

Soon thereafter, Kuril surprised Minaras and Oswynn by leaping down from a tree branch directly in front of them. They hadn't heard the slightest sound to give the Arboreal away even as his feet hit the ground.

"I am glad to see you respect the creatures of the forest, Minaras. It would have been just as easy for you to attack them with the fire instead of the water."

"That is not entirely true, Kuril. I am a bit stronger with water enchantments than with fire, and as such can use more subtlety in my spells." Minaras quickly pocketed the tinderbox before the Arboreal noticed. "A deadly assault with flames seemed inappropriate since I felt they were only looking for food."

"That they were," Kuril agreed. "The pack has gone elsewhere to hunt and will not likely return for the rest of the night. You and Oswynn should try to sleep now while I keep watch until dawn."

"Were you above us this whole time, waiting to see how we handled ourselves?" asked Oswynn.

"Only while the blaeculfs were near," admitted Kuril.

"Why did you do nothing to help? Did you intend to let them attack us?"

"There is not much a lone Arboreal can do against a pack of hungry blaeculfs, but I would have aided you had Minaras been unable to ward them off."

Kuril leaped back into the tree branches and disappeared, his voice trailing off "And what was the chance of such a thing?"

Oswynn smiled; the Arboreal was correct. Minaras versus a few oversized wolves would have been no match at all. There would have to be a much bigger threat to tax the skills of his master. He and Minaras then took Kuril's advice and slept peacefully until the rising sun woke them the next morning.

After a quick bite of a pair of fresh catfish that the lake had offered them for breakfast, Oswynn again asked if they would be finding a path around the water or swimming through it.

"We will do neither," proclaimed his master, leading his horse to the edge of the lake. Minaras paused a moment, breathing in the earthy smell of the shoreline. It wasn't as invigorating as the briny scent of the ocean, but a decided improvement over the musky fields and farmlands he had passed through. He raised his arms and chanted, "*Brim bricg, scieppan foldweg.*"

Directly in front of him, a thin strip of the water began churning. It started at the edge of the lake by his feet and traveled through the center all the way to the far shore. Minaras continued the chant as the roiling, bubbling water began to solidify into a path just wide enough for a horse. Oswynn knelt down to feel the solid water. It looked like ice and was just as hard, but it was neither cold nor slippery to the touch.

Minaras mounted his horse and walked it onto the newly formed water bridge. At first, the creature was hesitant to step onto the path. It would have preferred to wade through the cold water, but on hearing the wizard's gentle words, it slowly took a few steps forward. When it felt the strangely solid water holding its weight, the horse continued toward the other side at its normal stride.

Oswynn held out his hand to help Kuril onto the horse, but the Arboreal shied away and said, "Oswynn, this does not seem a good idea to me. If I may, I will cross the lake on foot."

"Do you not trust Minaras?"

"I trust the wizard, but the horse worries me. I will join you when we reach the other side."

"As you wish," said Oswynn, trotting his horse behind Minaras while Kuril followed on foot. The young apprentice pointed to the water bridge and asked, "When will I learn spells … powerful spells … like this one?"

"A spell such as this is but a few lessons down the road for one of your talents," Minaras replied.

Oswynn sighed impatiently, wondering how much further it would be.

CHAPTER XVII

THE CASTLE IN THE MOUNTAIN

Halia, Thulin, Arwold, Ahriman, and Xarun followed the trade route north for a few days until they saw the majestic Pensorean Mountains rise up from the horizon. The mountain range formed a great wall lining the entire northern coast of the continent, which separated the harsh Cold Ocean from the fertile human lands. When the tall peaks were in sight, Ahriman led the others into the foothills until they came to a dry riverbed, marking the location of the Castle in the Mountain. Appropriately named, it looked as if a hungry mountain had eaten the castle in the distant past. Only the two front turrets of the building remained exposed, the rest buried under rocks and dirt. The group wasted no time crossing the riverbed.

"I think this castle was built too close to the cliff," Halia noted sarcastically, "and the prior residents of the mountain were none too happy."

"Who be the prior residents?" Xarun wondered aloud.

Thulin ventured a guess. "Giants are rumored to live in these mountains, or perhaps it was the Teruns. I believe Terun City lies close to here."

Grumbling, Arwold argued, "The Teruns are a good people. They have been our allies for many ages and would have had no reason to destroy one of our castles."

"Teruns or otherwise, Arwold, 'tis through one's actions that makes one good or evil," said Thulin.

"And Teruns would never commit such an atrocious act! It must have been a giant."

Ahriman, growing tired of their banter, was more pragmatic. "If Teruns were the cause of this destruction, the entire castle would have been buried underground and put to use. If it were giants, nothing would have remained standing. Would you not agree the answer to this mystery has been lost to the cruel passage of time?"

His rhetorical question drew a look of general agreement from the others.

"Then let us find what we came for," said Ahriman. "Since I do not wish to be ambushed when we enter the building, shall we attempt to confirm it is deserted? Fracodians have been known to frequent these parts."

"Fracodians be welcome," said Xarun, gripping his axe and heading to the eastern side of the castle.

Arwold went the opposite direction while Ahriman and Halia scouted the entrance. The two, working independently, concluded that the lack of water was a good indication they were alone in the area.

"The collapse of the mountain must have shifted the course of the river," said Halia.

"Or blocked the water completely," added Ahriman. "There might well be a dam upstream."

Halia shook her head. "If that were so, the farmlands could have been saved. Unblocking the dam would not have been too difficult, especially to save one's home."

"She is both smart and observant," thought Ahriman, "a dangerous combination."

To the west, Arwold found the remains of an enormous rockslide, which had buried most of the building. The dry, rocky ground held nothing more than a scattering of dead wood, some of it charred. The tall warrior crept around the mounds of rubble, searching for makeshift shelters or other signs of human life. Finding nothing, he returned to the entrance.

Thulin followed Xarun past large chunks of rock that had cleaved from the mountainside and crushed huge portions of the castle. The debris convinced Xarun about the cause of the destruction. "'Twas giants did this," he concluded.

The young apprentice couldn't argue with him. It was difficult to imagine any lesser creature causing this much damage. It didn't occur to him that it might have been the result of a natural disaster.

Xarun, using his axe to prod between the boulders, scared out a family of four badgers. The two larger ones crouched low and hissed at him. He laughed and slashed at them with his weapon.

"Leave them be," said Thulin. "Halia and the others are already gathering over there."

When the warrior ignored him, he added, "You can always come back and play with your friends later."

Kicking the dirt, Xarun sheathed his axe and stomped back, arriving just as Halia was about to enter the castle. She led the group through the open gateway while keeping a sharp eye out for traps. She realized if there were any, the collapse of the building would have long since sprung them, but she still preferred to be cautious.

A dusty darkness met the five adventurers as soon as they were inside. The windows, buried under tons of rock and dirt, failed to allow a single ray of the bright sun through, and the light streaming through the doorway faded quickly in the musty interior. The barren hallway welcomed them with a subdued mocking of their footsteps. Nothing remained in the castle but dust, cobwebs, and scattered debris.

"Is there not some spell you could cast to light the way?" asked Halia. "I cannot even see the end of my sword."

"I am no elementalist," scoffed Ahriman. "Could we not use some torches instead?"

"I found a few good pieces of wood to the east. Thulin, go and fetch some of it to use as torches," ordered Arwold.

The apprentice glared at him. "I shall take no orders from you—" he started, but Halia shot him a frown and convinced him to comply with Arwold's request. Thulin reluctantly strolled outside and returned with five thick branches. Ahriman wrapped them with some rags, doused them with lamp oil, and lit the new torches. The five then split up to search each of the unburied rooms.

"There is nothing here. 'Tis another dead end," yelled Thulin after a frustrating hour, his voice echoing throughout the empty halls.

Having made a cursory pass through the entire ground level, Xarun agreed with him. "Even the doors be gone."

Ahriman, still inching along the first room he had entered, called back, "Shall we not make a more careful inspection? You are much too eager to give up hope when we may yet find a secret passage. Do you think an object as important as the sphere would have been left in the open?"

"No," replied Thulin. "'Tis likely buried beneath a mountain of earth. We shall need some Terun diggers to wrest it from this tomb."

Xarun, giving in to boredom, continued his inspection of the empty rooms. The warrior ran his fingers across a wall, barely paying attention as he walked back toward the castle entrance. When he stepped through the next doorway, a low-pitched sound rumbled through the halls. Xarun whirled around, checking to see if he had caused the sound.

Halia's faint voice rose from the ground beneath his feet. "I have found a secret door on the lower level! Come quick!"

The rumbling stopped while the rest of the group rushed downstairs to join Halia by the door she had opened. They froze beside her, staring at an enormous chamber full of treasures, unable to comprehend the unbelievable vision in front of their eyes. Mounds of gold coins covered the floor of the room at least two feet deep. A dozen large treasure chests, overflowing with gems of every color and magnificent pieces of jewelry, stood like rainbow islands in a great yellow sea. Lit torches lined the walls, making the abundant jewels sparkle brightly. This was a treasure unlike any other, the fabulous wealth of an entire kingdom, and it all belonged to them.

"We need not find the fifth piece of the key," remarked an elated Halia. "There is more than enough gold here to last a lifetime!" With a huge smile, she pranced into the room. To her dismay, however, as soon as she set foot in the chamber, the entire treasure vanished. Not so much as a single lonely coin remained in the dark room. She held her torch out, its feeble light barely managing to illuminate the large, empty chamber.

"What happened to the treasure?" Halia spun around and found nobody there. "Thulin?" she called. "Arwold? Where have you gone?" There was no answer; she was alone.

"They could not have gone far," she thought as she charged out of the room and bounded up the stairs. The castle was as vacant as before, minus her four missing companions. Halia put a hand to her pouch and found that it, too, was empty. "My sphere is gone!" she gasped, realizing then that the others had only been interested in her sphere. "I should never have trusted them!"

Meanwhile, Xarun received an entirely different experience when he entered the chamber. As soon as he crossed the threshold, a dark shape moved in the corner of the empty room. Having already forgotten about the treasure, he drew his axe and prepared for battle with a grin. The shape moved closer. It was black and hairy, twice the size of Xarun, with eight eyes, eight legs, and two powerful fangs dripping with venom.

"Ugh! A spider!" he shuddered.

The giant spider closed in for the attack, creeping steadily toward the big warrior. Xarun, facing the only creature he had ever feared, could not move. The spider lifted its upper body into the air and kicked out with its two front legs. Instinctively, Xarun raised his axe and blocked one of the legs, but he received a deep gash on his face from the other limb. Blood ran down his cheek and dripped onto the floor while the big warrior remained motionless.

Three more giant spiders crept toward him from the other corners of the room. He watched them converge toward him, neither able to defend himself nor run away. Visions of death ran through his mind. He imagined becoming their dinner, wrapped in a silky cocoon and having his blood drained while his life slowly ebbed. Then he pictured the same thing happening to Halia and his other companions. The thought of them in danger broke through his paralyzing fear. He would never let such a hideous fate befall them.

"You shall never get past me!" he roared while he began swinging his axe. One by one, he carved up the spiders, but as soon as he killed each spider, a new one took its place. They kept coming at him, and he kept fighting them off. He was determined not to let any of them through, and he enjoyed doing it.

When Thulin stepped into the treasure chamber, an old man limped toward him using a crooked walking stick for support. In the dim light, it was difficult to see any of the man's features other than his gray hair and stooped posture.

"Who goes there?" Thulin asked, squinting to get a better look at the stranger.

The old man responded with a question of his own, "Who do you think I am?" He stepped closer to the apprentice but remained covered by shadows.

Thulin ventured a guess. "Are you a guardian of the sphere?"

"A guardian I am of sorts, but not of the sphere."

The old man stepped into the torchlight. His face resembled a much older Thulin.

"You look familiar to me," Thulin said.

"'Tis well I should."

Thulin stared at the old man for a while before a look of recognition spread over his face. "You are me when I have aged," he said.

The old man gave him a slight nod. "You have never lacked intelligence."

138   *The Legacy of Ogma*

Thulin became concerned with the man's attire; most notably, he was missing the traditional robe of a mage, instead dressed in the plain linen garb of a scholar. "Are you a wizard?" he asked worriedly.

"I am not," the older Thulin replied. "Give up thy dream of pursuing magic, young Thulin, before 'tis too late."

Blood rushed to Thulin's cheeks. "You lie to me! You are nothing but an apparition sent here to haunt me, to scare me from completing my quest." He waved his hand at the old man and yelled, "Depart this room, evil spirit, and trouble me no more."

The elder Thulin stepped directly in front of the younger and said, "Although you may choose to deceive yourself, I would do no such thing. Heed my warning, young one. I am your future, and wizardry has no part in it."

"Prate not!" Thulin raged, overflowing with anger. "Can you not see I am already a wizard?"

The old man remained unconvinced and said, "You must give up your pursuit of magic, Thulin."

"I will listen to your deceitful words no longer!" shouted Thulin, leaping at his older counterpart and throwing him to the floor.

"You are not a wizard," he continued from the ground, oblivious that Thulin had just physically assaulted him.

Thulin leaned over the old man, grabbed him by the shoulders, and shook with all his might but could not get him to desist in his ranting.

"You do not have the gift of magic," he continued in a calm voice, which further enraged his younger self.

Thulin's hands reached for the old man's throat.

"I," Thulin started squeezing. "Am," he banged the old man's head on the floor. "A," he squeezed harder. "Wizard!" he finished, releasing his grip. The old body remained silent and motionless on the floor. Thulin had killed him.

Arwold strolled into the treasure chamber where an armored knight wielding a large sword greeted him. The knight, slightly shorter than Arwold, wore a full suit of well-maintained armor. A steel helmet covered his face, but even so, Arwold recognized the familiar figure.

"Is it you, father?" he asked.

The knight raised his sword, complete with a crystal sphere on the pommel. "You mock our family name, Arwold. You are evil!" he accused.

"You speak falsely, father," said Arwold as he drew his own claymore, a duplicate of the one the knight held. "I am sworn to fight evil! Through my heroic deeds, countless people have been protected from the wicked and unjust."

The knight groaned. "I have failed to teach you the true meanings of good and evil," he lamented. "Your damnable actions must continue no longer, and now I shall ensure they do not." The knight took a step closer and thrust his sword at Arwold with considerable skill.

The warrior backed out of the way of the weapon. "Father, you are mistaken," he pleaded. "Do you not see that you attack your own son, Arwold, Defender of Krof?"

"Mistaken I am not," the knight said, bringing his sword back for another swing.

Arwold, resigned to do battle with his father, defended himself with his claymore. The two large blades clanged against each other as they began to battle, evenly matched in both skill and strength.

As soon as Ahriman entered the room, he fell to his knees and held his head. "No! It cannot be!" he screamed, pulling at his hair. The sorcerer, however, was not so easily deceived by the enchanted treasure chamber. After a brief moment of frustration, he lifted his head and looked around the empty room.

"It is nothing but an illusion," he thought, "and quite a powerful one to have such an effect on me." He walked in front of the other four. Each one stood motionless just inside the chamber door, staring blankly into space. Ahriman shook each one in turn and shouted, "Wake up! All you see is an illusion. Nothing in here is real!"

Thulin was the first of the others to wake from their trances. He dropped to the ground and immediately began searching the floor. "Where is he? Where has the old man gone?"

"It was all in your mind, child," Ahriman explained, "an illusion to protect the sphere. Help me to wake the others."

Thulin stood slowly, disoriented, but was soon able to assist Ahriman in rousing the rest of their group: first Halia, then Arwold, and finally Xarun. As soon as she awoke, Halia touched her pouch and breathed a sigh of relief when she felt the orb safely tucked away. Each of the four chose not to discuss the details of their visions with their companions, preferring instead to search the chamber in silence. They found nothing but a hole in the far corner of the room.

Arwold laughed and said, "A spell to guard an empty chamber!"

"Empty now," noted Thulin, "but whoever made yonder hole must have taken the fifth sphere."

CHAPTER XVIII

TERUN UNDERCITY

The hole in the corner of the treasure chamber was precisely five feet high and six feet wide. Each of the adventurers crouched down to enter the tunnel beyond the hole, and for the tallest two, Xarun and Arwold, it was an uncomfortable fit. After they squeezed through the opening, they spent nearly an hour hunched over, shuffling along a small tunnel that had been hewn through solid rock by a small army of Teruns. Amazingly, the tunnel kept precise measurements for its entire length.

With no light reaching the passageway from the outside, only their torches provided any illumination. "Should we not conserve our source of light?" Ahriman was quick to ask. "We may have a long way to travel before we see the sun again."

"Aye," agreed Arwold, snuffing out his torch on the wall of the tunnel. "We must keep no more than one lit at a time."

Thulin, Xarun, and Halia quickly extinguished their torches, and Ahriman took the lead until his flame began to fade. It was a rough hike through the Terun tunnel. Those in front had difficulty breathing with the smoke from the burning torch filling their lungs, while those in back could barely see in the dwindling light.

After their first cramped hour, however, they received a slight reprieve when the passageway gradually widened to more than ten feet in diameter and began to take on a more natural appearance. The expertly chiseled, utterly smooth walls became rough and uneven, stalactites appeared on the ceiling, and water began gathering in small puddles, filling every indentation in the floor. The adventurers continued walking for another three hours before coming to a fork.

"Where do we go?" Xarun demanded, tired of the dank underground trek.

"We should split up to cover more ground and meet back here," said Halia.

Xarun was quick to accept her suggestion. "You and I go right," he said with a smile. "They go left."

"Nay, I shall go with Halia," objected Thulin with a quick peek at her. Even in the darkness, he marveled at her beauty.

"If we were to wander about aimlessly, might we not lose each other?" asked Ahriman.

"Not with the spheres to guide us," replied Arwold.

"Knowing which direction to go," sneered Ahriman, "does not mean we would be able to navigate an underground maze. We have been lucky to encounter so few side passages, but these tunnels could easily branch out."

A strange noise suddenly drifted in from the left. Thulin jerked his head to the side and peered down the passageway. "And we do not know what creatures live down here," he whispered.

Arwold suppressed a laugh and said, in a patronizing voice, "Worry not, young Thulin. Halia is here to protect you from any subterranean beasts lurking about." Then he pointed to the right. "I believe this is the way to Terun City."

Thulin, steamed at Arwold for embarrassing him, silently thanked his fortune that the darkness hid his face. "How could you know where each of these tunnels lead?" he asked. "With no landmarks to reference and no stars in view, there is no way to determine in which direction we have been traveling. We may easily have been walking in a circle."

"I have always had a good sense of direction and require no land-marks or stars to aid me."

"I should hope so, or—"

The tall warrior stepped directly in front of Thulin, towering over the young apprentice. In the flickering torchlight, he had a distinctly menacing appearance. "Or what?" he thundered, his harsh voice echoing through the tunnels.

Thulin shrank away and responded meekly, "Or lost we shall be."

Arwold confidently marched into the tunnel, followed by the other four. As they walked, the passageway merged with scores of smaller side tunnels and eventually became a well-used underground road leading straight into Terun Undercity. Arwold didn't gloat when his judgment proved correct, relieved to have reached the end of their monotonous hike.

The Undercity was an enormous subterranean city carved from an even larger natural cavern beneath a mountain called The Tooth of the Gods or just The Tooth by some. The Undercity was the lower half of Terun City with the remainder of the town built above ground on the side of the mountain. Teruns lived either above or below ground based on their family profession. Merchants and traders maintained houses on the mountainside, while blacksmiths, miners, and farmers resided in the Undercity. Although human visitors to Terun City were impressed by the grand stone houses of the traders with their spectacular views of the mountain range, it was more prestigious for a Terun to work with the earth, and those of the Undercity had a more respected position in the community.

Created by the undisputed masters of stone and metal, the Undercity was a wonder to behold. House on top of house, carved into the cavern walls, reached from the ground to the roof of the cave. Deep mineshafts and sprawling subterranean farms littered the floor of the cavern. During the day, sunlight streamed down through numerous ventilation shafts in the ceiling, and at night, the walls glowed with the faint green tint of phosphorescent fungus, grown by many of the Terun farmers.

Most of the Teruns were involved in the extraction and manipulation of various metals from the tons of ore retrieved from the mines. They handled the digging, smelting, and smithing without any interaction with the outside world. The Teruns preferred to send only finished products above ground for trading with the humans. Occasionally, they received special orders for raw materials, but it was rare for them to grant such requests.

The five adventurers reached the Undercity in the middle of the night. They heard only the faint sounds of chisels, picks, and shovels from the perpetually staffed mineshafts while the rest of the city slept in stone cold silence.

"Does this not imply it was the Teruns who destroyed the castle?" Thulin asked mischievously.

"It does not," responded Arwold in a huff. "Who is to say the Teruns dug those tunnels before the rockslide? Their work could have followed the destruction of the castle by generations."

"That may be so, but was it not a Terun thief who stole the crystal from the treasure chamber?" continued Thulin.

"Do you two still disagree about the Castle in the Mountain," interrupted Ahriman, "when we must find some clues about the final sphere? Forget about your argument and let us search for someone who can aid us."

"We should each take a different section of the city," Halia suggested, not wanting to let the others know of her past with the Teruns.

"Nay," Arwold began, "we should—"

"'Tis a good idea Halia," interrupted Thulin, "otherwise, we could be searching for days."

"Days be too long," said Xarun with a sigh.

With a frown, Arwold acquiesced. "Then let us rest until morning. Other than those in the mines, the Teruns sleep now as well. Tomorrow, we shall scour the city and return to this spot when the last rays of sunlight disappear."

After a few hours of restless sleep, they divided the city into separate sections. Halia went above ground; Thulin, Arwold, and Ahriman combed the Undercity mines, smiths, and farms respectively; and Xarun looked for a good meal. The adventurers spent an entire day speaking to countless Teruns and hopelessly searching for clues. As the cavern grew darker at sunset, they began to gather by the underground road.

Thulin, who had returned first, met Ahriman by the tunnel. "Did you bag any information?" he asked.

The sorcerer, paying no attention to the implication, answered, "There was none to be had."

"I do hope we have not come to a dead end in our quest. What if the final sphere has been destroyed?"

"Then the weapons would be lost forever," said Ahriman matter-of-factly. "But I would not be concerned with that possibility." He removed the sphere from his pouch and threw it onto the rocky ground.

Thulin winced but heard no sound of shattering. He picked it up and inspected it, unable to find the slightest scratch on its surface. He felt more confident than before as he handed the sphere back to Ahriman.

"These beautiful works of art were created by a master wizard," explained the sorcerer. "One who would never have wasted such magic on something as fragile as unenchanted glass."

Soon, Xarun joined the two, shaking his head as he approached. At least he had a full stomach. Arwold similarly came up with nothing. "I have found naught," he said.

"Did you find naught about the sphere … or naught about the rightful owner of the treasure?" asked Thulin.

Arwold scowled at him, but kept quiet. Just then, Halia joined the group with a triumphant smile. "I may have found a Terun with knowledge of the sphere … a legendary trader who is rumored to have the largest collection of crystals in the world. Follow me!"

Halia led the others out of the Undercity toward one of the larger homes on the lower tier of the mountainside. The house stood out from its neighbors, its front decorated with numerous colorful gems, most of which were uncut and unpolished. Above the doorway, a large quartz crystal adorned the wall, angled ever so slightly toward the ground. Halia stepped up to the door, but before she had a chance to knock, a Terun servant, dressed in rugged yet delicately stitched clothing, opened it. He was just shy of five feet tall with a muscular body, chiseled face, and short, thick fingers. Rings of gold and silver adorned each of his well-calloused digits, a sign that he had formerly worked the mines.

"What do you want?" he asked so quickly that it seemed like a single word.

Halia responded, "We have come to speak with Derst."

"Do you come to trade?"

"Nay, but we would pay well for some information."

The servant shook his head. "Derst needs none of your coins. Leave now!" He began to shut the door when Xarun pushed him aside.

"Stand aside, little man," barked the big warrior, barging into the house. "I shall fetch this Derst myself."

Halia, Thulin, and Ahriman followed Xarun, but Arwold stopped at the entrance and addressed the servant. "Prithee pardon their manners, but we would appreciate an audience with your master. We promise not to take much of his precious time."

As soon as the group stepped into his house, Derst intercepted them. He appeared out of nowhere with a loud, "I am Derst," causing Thulin to jump. The trader's appearance was similar to his servant's but the rings he wore shone with sparkling jewels.

"We shall drink some ale and then you may ask what you need."

Derst snapped his fingers at his servant, who limped to the sitting room door and let them in. He watched each of the adventurers enter the room and gave a slight bow only to Arwold as the tall warrior crossed through the doorway.

With a wave of his manicured hand, Derst offered the group seats in the cozy room, cozy at least for a Terun. Glowing egg-shaped rocks, stacked neatly in a hole in the wall near the floor, illuminated the small room with a soft, yellow light. Six chairs carved directly from the stone floor formed a semi-circle facing the hole. Throughout the entire room, an odd collection of crystals, multi-colored polished gems, and carved rocks sat in small cubbyholes cut into the walls at regular intervals.

Each of the five, along with Derst, took a seat, the humans squirming in the uncomfortably hard chairs. The servant then offered them large tankards of Terun Fungal Ale. Arwold was the only one who didn't accept one of the delectable drinks. Xarun polished off his ale in one swig and took the tankard intended for Arwold.

"What do you wish to know?" Derst inquired, gulping down a mouthful of the tangy beverage.

Arwold drew his sword and presented it hilt first to the Terun. "We wish to know more about this sphere. Know you of its origin?"

"And have you seen any other ones like it?" added Thulin.

"I know naught of the sphere on your fine sword, but I do own one just like it."

Halia's face lit up. "Truly, you have another?"

"They could be twins," replied Derst. "An old friend from the mines gave it to me for a rare black pearl."

"Might we purchase the sphere from you?" Ahriman asked, removing the sack of coins originally intended for Xarun from his robe. "We would pay handsomely for it."

"Nay, I do not want your gold, but I would like to trade."

Ahriman held up his arms. "We have nothing but what you see."

"That will do," said the Terun as an evil grin crossed his lips. "I need help with a small task, and for that you may have the sphere."

Ahriman nodded. "Name the task, Derst, and we will do our best to succeed."

"I have lost a small ring," Derst moaned. "'Tis in the shape of a snake carved from a blue gem. You must find it for me."

"No more searching," whined Xarun. "I be bored already!"

"Let us hear his request. We may be forced to retrieve the ring from someone who wishes to keep it for himself," Halia said with a wink.

The big warrior smiled at the thought.

Derst walked to a shelf carved from the wall above the glowing stones, much like the mantel of a fireplace, and picked up a glass wand with a large emerald on the end. He faced the five adventurers and pointed the glass wand at the group.

Thulin grew nervous, knowing how dangerous magical wands could be. "Maybe we should speak further about this before allowing him to—"

"You are too late." Derst laughed as he shouted, "*Fors. Wel. Gan!*"

A flash of bright green light sprang from the emerald on the tip of the wand and enveloped the five adventurers. In the next instant, they were gone.

CHAPTER XIX

LOST IN A BARREN WORLD

The landscape was a surreal, colorless parody of a desert. A dirty-white ground met a gray, cloudless sky at the distant horizon. Occasional leafless trees dotted the drab landscape, their brittle limbs clawing at bone-dry air. Everywhere the five adventurers turned, they saw a world devoid of any color other than their own clothing and skin. Besides themselves and the trees, not another living thing was in sight, and the state of the trees was questionable. There were no animals, no birds, and not even a single insect. There was no wind, no sounds, and no indication of where they might be.

Under their feet, a path of small gray pebbles, about three feet wide, led forever in either direction. A few steps away, a second path intersected the first at a right angle and continued ad infinitum into the distance.

"What be this place?" puzzled Xarun as he finished his ale and threw the tankard aside. The last remaining drop of liquid evaporated instantly when it hit the ground.

"I do not know where we are," said Halia, "but others must have been here before us. Someone spent a considerable amount of time building these paths."

"I agree," said Thulin, "this path is clearly not a natural part of the landscape."

"Can anything here be called natural?" asked Arwold.

Xarun looked around and said, "No." Then he kicked the top layer of stones off the path, exposing the white ground underneath.

"I see no reason for us to stand here," Ahriman said. "Shall we select one of these trails to follow? Perhaps from another spot we would be better able to determine where we are and how to find the Terun's ring."

Xarun shrugged his shoulders, chose one of the paths, and began walking. The rest of the group followed him. As they traveled along the artificial path, the scenery around them didn't change. The sky remained a constant shade of gray, leafless trees were scattered about, and there was still a noticeable absence of living creatures. Were it not for the intersection receding in the distance, it would have seemed as though they were walking in place. Soon, they could no longer see the intersection behind them and found it hard to believe they were making any progress at all.

After many tedious hours on the path, the group finally saw another intersection ahead of them. Their pace quickened and their excitement surged, but as they came nearer, Halia noticed Xarun's tankard on the ground beside the gray stones he had kicked off the path. In a fit of disappointment, she cried, "How could this be? We have walked in a straight line for hours and returned to where we began!"

"The path must have curved around and brought us back here," said Thulin.

"Do my eyes deceive me?" said Arwold in disbelief. "Does this trail not appear to be a straight line as far as the eye can see? Has it not looked that way for our entire trip?"

"Yes, it has," agreed Thulin, "but we must have traveled in a circle. There is no other way for us to have returned here."

The group stood confused around the intersection, looking back and forth along the path they had just taken.

"I be not tired," Xarun noted.

"Nor am I," added Halia, "and we have been walking for hours."

"Are we dead?" asked Thulin. "I cannot remember the last time I ate, yet I am not hungry."

"This is not the netherworld," responded Arwold.

Ahriman lifted Xarun's tankard from the ground, examined it, and threw it back. "We still live, and we still must find the missing ring. Shall we try the other path?"

Arwold sighed before saying, "And walk in another great circle? I would prefer to stay put and await your return."

Thulin glanced around with a furrowed brow. "There must be an explanation to all of this," he said to himself. "We started in the Terun's sitting room, Derst pointed the wand at us, and—"

Suddenly his face brightened. "We are inside the wand," he stated confidently.

Arwold laughed at him. "That cannot be. You are the one who prates now, young Thulin."

"Are you sure? What do you think happened when Derst cast the spell upon us?"

Arwold answered him with silence.

"He transported us into the wand to retrieve his ring. I do not know how his ring came to be in the wand, but I should guess a thief attempted to steal the ring from him. Derst caught him in the act and trapped him here as well."

"If what you say is true, then the ring has always been within his grasp but forever out of his reach," said Halia.

"It is an interesting theory," said Ahriman, staring upward, "and I can think of no other possibilities. I agree with Thulin. We must be inside the Terun's wand."

"During our walk along the path," continued the apprentice, "we traveled in a straight line and took no turns, yet we returned to where we started. We must have walked in a circle around a cross-section of the wand."

Halia understood, Arwold was unable to follow his logic, and Xarun didn't care. Whether they were in the wand or elsewhere, he remained quite bored.

"Ahriman, may I use your staff?" Thulin asked the wizard.

Understanding what Thulin had in mind, Ahriman handed him his staff. Thulin said, "Imagine an ant walking like so." He let his fingers travel in a straight line around the circumference of the staff. Upon completing one rotation, they were back to where they had started.

A look of comprehension crossed Arwold's face. "Then the other path should lead us to the ends of the wand," he surmised.

Thulin and Ahriman nodded together.

"But do we go to the left or right?" asked Arwold.

"It matters not," said Thulin. "Even with your sense of direction, there is no way to tell the difference."

By the time Thulin had finished his lecture, Xarun had already left the group. To him, it didn't matter if they were in the wand or not, if they were traveling forward or backward. It was time for action.

The journey along the second path began as monotonously as the first. After two more hours of walking, however, a new sight greeted them. A man, wearing the trappings of a warrior, stood in the middle of a crossroad, leaning on a long sword as if it were a walking stick. He was gaunt, looking as though he hadn't eaten in weeks and stared leisurely at the approaching group through a set of bloodshot eyes.

"I see some guests we have for our dinner party," said the lone warrior, speaking to no one in particular.

"Who be you?" Xarun demanded.

The man continued his phantom conversation. "We have had no guests for many a week. Is it not a happy day, my brothers?"

"Good sir, do you know how we might escape from this land?" asked Arwold.

Thulin snickered and said, "If he knew how to escape, why would he still be stuck in the wand?"

"He may know the way but be unable to leave himself."

Thulin stopped laughing; he hadn't thought of that possibility.

"If you do know the way out," offered Arwold, "we shall take you with us."

The pale man ignored Arwold's generous offer and walked closer to the group, gazing up and down at each person. He stood in front of Xarun, shook his head, and said, "Too big."

Xarun gave him a fierce look and snapped, "Stand back, knave!"

The warrior then walked up to Thulin and said, "Too young."

"You are mad," said Halia, keeping a close eye on him. Her hand hovered near the hilt of her sword as he stepped closer.

The warrior stared at Halia, fair skin weathered by years of hardship, thin yet well curved. "Just right," he said, as he brought his sword up to poke her midsection.

Xarun slapped the blade out of his hand before Halia had a chance to draw her weapon.

"You wish a fight?" the lone warrior fumed at Xarun. "We shall see about that. No one has ever bested us in combat."

He bent over to pick up the fallen sword, and as he reached down, a thin silver necklace fell out from beneath his shirt. A beautiful sapphire ring, in the shape of a serpent, dangled from the bottom of the chain. The warrior retrieved the sword and began swinging it erratically at Xarun, who only laughed at his incompetence with the weapon.

Halia, noticing the object of their quest, shouted with excitement, "The serpent ring hangs from his necklace!"

Immediately, Xarun jumped forward and attempted to grab the insane warrior, but the man stepped back and kept swinging his sword. Xarun's mood changed from one of amusement to one of anger.

"Be still!" he growled, moving forward again.

"To arms! To arms!" shouted the warrior, taking another step back, just out of reach.

Xarun kept walking forward, but the man kept moving backward until, finally, Xarun broke out into a full run. The warrior turned and rushed down the path, outdistancing the slower Xarun with each stride.

Halia, Thulin, and Arwold chased after the pair, but Ahriman held back, reaching for a small vial in his robe. He uncorked it and chanted, "*Lyft gast betraeppan beorn,*" but nothing happened. He tried again, with the same result. Ahriman sniffed the empty glass tube and threw it to the ground where it shattered. "I am unable to summon spirits from within this wand," he thought as he hurried after the rest of the group. "I wonder what other surprises await us?"

The lone warrior led the five adventurers off the path toward a small grove. As soon as he passed the first few trees, he stopped and spun around to face his pursuers. Four very pale ogres jumped out from behind their hiding spots and stood beside him. At least eight feet tall with rock-hard muscles and gruff faces, the ogres grinned hungrily.

"Beware!" warned Xarun. "It be an ambush!"

The heroes came to an immediate halt. Ahriman caught up to Thulin and handed him a long knife. "I am unable to cast spells, and it is unlikely you would fare any better. We must rely on brute force instead of magic until we find our way out of the wand."

The insane warrior pointed at the five adventurers and shouted to the ogres, "Look, my friends, I have brought dinner guests. We shall feast well tonight!"

The starving ogres advanced toward the group, licking their dry lips with sticky green tongues. Xarun and Arwold stepped forward to meet their attack, weapons ready.

The first ogre rushed forward and took a big swing at Arwold with a hammer nearly the size of a full-grown Terun and just as heavy. Arwold jumped aside as the huge hammer smashed into the ground, causing the entire terrain to shake. A second ogre, using a bulky tree branch as a club, swung at Arwold's head. He ducked and quickly jabbed the ogre in the side with his claymore, but the ogre's thick hide deflected the imprecise blow.

Arwold continued to parry attacks from both ogres, holding his ground against the much larger opponents even though the strong blows came closer to breaking his arm each time the hammer met the claymore. While the two ogres desperately tried to overpower Arwold, Ahriman slipped behind the creatures. Just as he was about to stab one of them, the second ogre noticed him and spun around with a swiftness that belied its size. The sorcerer hastily retreated to avoid a crushing death by the oversized wooden club. When the ogre took a step after the wizard, Arwold came up with a plan. He stood behind his distracted opponent, waved at the other ogre, and yelled, "Evil beast! I am here!"

The first ogre took a great swing at him with its hammer, but Arwold jumped aside at the last moment. The huge weapon smashed into the second ogre, crushing its arm. The unwitting victim screamed in agony and reflexively swung its branch club at the source of its pain. While the two brutes argued, Arwold threw his entire weight behind his claymore and drove it straight through the back of the first ogre and out its chest. The creature fell to the ground, nearly yanking the weapon from Arwold's grip. He pulled the blade free just in time to protect himself from the second ogre who had swung its club at his head. Ahriman returned to the battle and sliced the back of the ogre's thigh while Arwold attacked it from the front. Against the two of them, the creature had no chance; it was down within seconds.

Xarun didn't wait for the two ogres to attack him. He let out a battle cry and charged at them with his axe in the air. His aggressive behavior surprised the ogres, who were used to enemies who fled from them in fear, giving Xarun a brief advantage. He lunged directly at the first ogre, chopping down with his axe. The ogre easily blocked the attack with a heavy stone club, but it failed to notice Xarun's spiked greave simultaneously heading for its groin. The ogre fell to the ground in bloody spasms of severe pain. The one remaining ogre proved to be no match for Xarun, and the fight lasted only moments before the big warrior was victorious.

While Xarun was trading blows with his soon-to-be defeated opponent, Thulin crept close to the ogre writhing on the ground and slit its throat with his dagger. He smiled, enjoying his power over the life of another living being. Thulin then looked over to where Halia was fighting the insane warrior. Perhaps she would welcome his assistance.

Halia, having no problem sparring with the lone warrior, toyed with him, easily dodging his clumsy attacks and calling out taunts constantly.

"You shall have to do much better than that," she teased and danced around his body. "Do you not know how to wield a sword?"

The warrior didn't seem to notice her insults, nor did his effectiveness with the sword improve during the course of the melee. Eventually, Halia saw an opening. First, she lashed out with her blade and sliced one of his arms, and then she did the same to the other. His weapon fell from his hand as he dropped to the ground holding the pair of wounds. Thulin slipped behind the fighter and raised the freshly bloodied dagger, preparing for another kill. He was about to end the warrior's life when Halia grabbed the dagger out of his hand. She continued the motion he had started, thrusting the weapon at her opponent's head, cutting the necklace, and pocketing the ring. Halia scowled at Thulin as she threw the dagger to the ground.

The five heroes regrouped at the second crossroad where Halia held up the blue ring triumphantly and said, "We have the serpent ring."

"Now, we must find a way out of this wand," added Thulin.

With no other ideas for escape, they continued down the same path. After what seemed to be an eternity, the scenery finally began to change. "I see green up ahead!" Halia shouted. "What a splendid display of color!"

The others felt the same emotion when they saw a faint green glow far in the distance.

"Was there not an emerald on the Terun's wand?" asked Ahriman.

"Aye, a large gem," said Thulin, "we must be nearing the tip of the wand."

Eager to escape their dreary prison, the five adventurers sprinted the remaining distance until they reached the end of the road. Fifty paces away, a mountainous emerald extended from deep underground to high in the sky, bathing the ground in a brilliant green light. Hundreds and hundreds of bones, both human and otherwise, lay on the ground in front of the gigantic gem. Scattered among the bones were all manner of weapons and armor.

Xarun drew his axe and yelled, "Let us break our way out!" as he started for the emerald.

Halia screamed, "Abide, Xarun! Go no further!"

He froze on her command. Halia took measured steps toward him, keeping a close eye on her surroundings. She put her hand on his shoulder and asked, "Do you wish to end up like them?"

The warrior took one look at the mass of bones and shook his head. "I wish to keep my flesh."

"Then remain here until I can determine what killed our predecessors. These piles of bones look quite suspicious."

The others watched while Halia stepped forward slowly. As she neared the emerald, she dropped to her hands and knees and crawled around the bones, trying to disturb them as little as possible. She moved in a random pattern around the debris before she focused on one spot and began clawing at the dirt. Halia dug one foot down into the whitish soil. Then, satisfied with her discovery, she stood and walked carefully to the emerald. She inspected it from all angles and touched it lightly here and there before returning to the group.

"Those creatures were poisoned when they attempted to break the emerald." Halia pointed to the hole she had made. "The gas comes out of the ground through a tube buried in yonder hole. There are likely to be more of these traps where the bones are most numerous."

Ahriman walked to the hole and removed some pieces of cloth and a vial of water from pockets in his robe. He soaked the cloth in the water and stuffed it into the tube recently uncovered by Halia. "This should block the gas ... at least temporarily."

Halia joined him and together they found and plugged up two more poison tubes.

"We should be safe from the gas for a while," Ahriman stated. "Who will lend their weight against the emerald?"

There was no response. Even Halia was reluctant and started backing away. Ahriman sighed and walked up to the emerald. He put his hands on the gem and pushed as hard as he could. It wouldn't budge.

"This is too heavy for me to move by myself," he called out. "Do you wish to remain stuck in this wand forever?"

Xarun groaned, "I do not," and strolled up to the emerald next to Ahriman. They both pushed against the green wall. Xarun strained, his face tightened, and the muscles in his neck, shoulders, and legs bulged. The emerald trembled as a faint hiss escaped from the ground.

Xarun turned to the others and demanded, "Come hither and push! Make haste or feel my axe!"

The remaining three joined Xarun at the emerald and pushed as hard as they could. The emerald moved slightly as the hissing increased and small wisps of green gas began to escape the plugged tubes.

"We must push harder!" Xarun yelled.

The five adventurers all planted their shoulders against the gem, dug their feet into the soil, and shoved with all their might. They saw the poisonous gas wafting from the ground when, suddenly, the emerald fell away from them.

Seconds after Derst zapped the group with the magical wand, the glass shattered in his hand. The five adventurers appeared in front of him along with some of the bones, weapons, and armor that were closest to the emerald. The poison gas, so deadly within the wand, seeped out as a miniscule puff of green mist, which disappeared within seconds.

"By the gods!" exclaimed Derst, removing some bits of broken glass from his palm. "You broke my wand!"

"You fool!" shouted an angered Ahriman. "Did you expect us to remain trapped in there forever?"

Xarun raised his axe and stepped forward. "I shall teach you to—"

Halia swiftly leaped between him and the Terun. "Lower your weapon, Xarun." She removed the blue serpent ring from her pouch and showed it to Derst. "Here is your ring, Terun. Will you keep your end of the bargain or shall I let Xarun have his way? He does seem to be most upset with you."

Derst smiled and grabbed the ring from her. "A trade is a trade. I shall fetch the sphere at once!" He ran into the next room and reappeared almost immediately, holding the fifth and final crystal sphere.

When he offered it to Halia, she nodded at Thulin. Still giggling, Derst handed the sphere to the apprentice. With a smile, Thulin gripped it tightly, finally believing he was part of their group.

The others each took out their spheres. The colored dots appeared in the exact center of each orb, but were soon replaced by a single white light glowing slightly off center.

"These white spots must guide us to the treasure," Thulin guessed.

"They point us toward the Cold Ocean," added Ahriman.

"In that case," said Halia, "we must header deeper into the Pensorean Mountains."

CHAPTER XX

A YOUNG WIZARD'S CURIOSITY

After several days on horseback, the tedium of the long journey was beginning to surpass Oswynn's limited patience. He rode behind Kuril, guiding their horse through a monotony of grasslands and light forest, but as they traveled, his eyes began to wander toward the bone scroll case attached to the Arboreal's belt. The spell inscribed on the parchment was ancient and powerful. The young apprentice wondered what it looked like, what it sounded like. Even though he might not be able to understand the magical symbols, the scroll beckoned him to read it.

Donning a mischievous grin, Oswynn dug his heels into the horse, urging it into a faster gallop. The new speed forced Kuril, still an unsteady rider, to tighten his grip or risk losing his balance and falling off the horse. With the Arboreal's mind occupied, Oswynn reached for the scroll case, carefully opened the lid, and removed the parchment. He quickly tucked it into his shirt, his grin broadening into a full smile.

"I will look at the spell tonight and return it to Kuril while we are riding tomorrow," he thought. "No one will ever know I have stolen a peek."

That night, after a tasty dinner of rabbit and wild onions, Oswynn turned in early, although he didn't intend to fall asleep. With his eyes half closed, he watched Kuril disappear into the trees to the south. He knew it would be about two hours before the Arboreal returned to the branches above the campsite to stand guard in a half-sleep state of rest. Arboreals never truly fell asleep the way humans did; instead, they stayed in a meditative trance for about four hours every night. Oswynn would have to make it back to the campsite before Kuril returned, which would leave him plenty of time if Minaras didn't stay awake for too long.

His master complied with his wish, soon drifting off to sleep, but Oswynn waited a few more minutes to be certain he was alone. Then he got up, crept lightly past the sleeping Minaras, removed one of the lit branches from the fire to use as a torch, and headed to the north.

Strange sounds echoed through the dark forest, but Oswynn was too excited about this little adventure to be scared. He wound his way through the trees, failing to notice the fresh tracks on the ground, recently made by a large group of humanoid creatures. When he believed himself to be sufficiently far from the campsite, he built a small fire and sat down to study the scroll. Oswynn pulled the parchment out from under his shirt and held it near the bright flames. As he had expected, he couldn't understand the Arboreal symbols, which appeared to him as a jumble of random pictures, but at least he had paid enough attention during his lessons to sound out the words.

He hesitantly began reading the scroll one symbol at a time. After he had completed the first line, Oswynn thought the writing seemed lighter there than on the rest of the page. "Perhaps it was that way from the start, and I had not noticed the difference." He read a few more symbols and became concerned when the ink faded slightly as he mumbled each word.

Oswynn began to wonder if the writing would ever become darker again, but was distracted when a twig snapped close by. He listened for the sound of footsteps on the forest floor, expecting that Minaras had awoken and noticed he was gone. Instead, he heard the crackling of leaves. "It must be a raccoon or opossum," he thought as he looked around, "but it is much too dark to see anything, even with this fire."

By the time he returned to reading the spell, one third of the scroll had faded. Oswynn decided he should stop before the entire spell disappeared, allowing good judgment to rule his actions for once.

He carefully rolled up the parchment and was about to hide it under his shirt when a pair of unkempt Fracodians grabbed him. The first one covered his mouth with a sweaty hand and wrapped its large, hairy arm around his upper body. The other lifted him by the legs, and they carried him off before he was able to let out a scream. In the confusion, Oswynn dropped the scroll beside the fire.

The Fracodians handled the young boy roughly. During the long trip to the Fracodian encampment, his captors treated him no better than a trapped animal, practically dragging him along the ground. Branches scraped his arms and legs, thorns pricked his entire body, and bushes snagged his hair. Oswynn received an equally rough welcome when they reached their destination. The Fracodians tied his hands and feet tightly in scratchy twine and threw him chest first onto the ground with a thud, winding him for a moment. At least his mouth was free. He coughed and spit, trying to rid himself of the vile taste of the filthy hand that had been covering his face. Then he looked around and saw a dozen hungry Fracodians staring back at him.

"Help! Minaras! Kuril!" he shouted as loud as he could.

Kerr, the leader of the band of Fracodians, walked up to Oswynn and hovered over his body. "No help," he growled, lifting a rusty sword over Oswynn's head, "No yell!"

Oswynn understood this gesture; the leader would skewer him if he yelled again. Having no choice but to comply, he rolled onto his back and sat up with some difficulty. Then he stood and looked up into Kerr's weathered face. "I am a wizard," he stated boldly. "Release me or you and your friends will suffer my wrath."

The young apprentice was so confident in himself that, were it not for his short stature, he could have convinced the most obstinate skeptic.

The grizzled leader just laughed at the child and lowered his sword. "You dinner," he said in an emotionless voice, motioning for the others to prepare a spit over the campfire. Immediately, two of the Fracodians began setting up their stove while two others added some wood to enlarge the campfire.

Oswynn shuddered at the thought of becoming their dinner, but he couldn't think of any way to escape. Now, more than ever, he wished his master had taken the time to teach him a few powerful spells. A transmutation spell to loosen his bindings, a fire spell to use as a weapon and incinerate the entire band of Fracodians, even a thaumaturgic spell to call for divine aid would have been useful. At least he knew one incantation that might help. Oswynn stared at the flames of the campfire and hoped it would work properly without the use of his hands. Concentrating as hard as he could on the air around the fire, he chanted, "*Lyft bord.*"

At first, there was no effect, but as he continued reciting the magic words, a gust of wind sprang up and fanned the flames directly at the two Fracodians working on the spit. Their hair and clothing ignited, causing them to scream in both pain and surprise. Oswynn couldn't help but laugh. If his master had taught him more spells like this, he would have already been free of this mess and on his way back to the campsite.

"Release me now!" he commanded, "or you will pay dearly for your actions!"

Kerr wasn't about to let this tender morsel escape, nor did he want any further distractions. He raised his sword to silence the young boy permanently. Although Fracodians enjoyed listening to the dying screams of their victims, this one was too much of a nuisance to cook alive. Oswynn cringed and looked away. The Fracodian started his downswing when Kuril leaped out of the nearest tree and soared directly onto his chest. Kerr flew backward and smashed into the ground as Kuril landed deftly on his feet and drew his sword. With a flick of his wrist, he sliced the twine around Oswynn and then turned to face the Fracodians.

Oswynn wiggled free of his bindings. With his back to a cluster of trees and the Fracodians forming a semi-circle around him, however, he had nowhere to run. For now, he would have to wait and see how the Arboreal handled the rest of the group.

Kuril danced on the balls of his feet between Oswynn and the Fracodians, his eyes pinned to the enemy. "If you allow us to leave this place in peace, no more of you shall be harmed," he offered.

Together, they broke out in a fit of laughter and collectively drooled, "More food." Drawing their weapons, they advanced on the lone Arboreal.

As each one came forward, Kuril stepped up to meet him, sword ready. Faster than Oswynn could see, the Arboreal disarmed the Fracodians and dug his blade into their bodies. Two dropped immediately to the ground, and another pair staggered backward for a moment before keeling over. The remainder of the group stood back, waiting for their chance against the intruder.

Meanwhile, Kerr recovered from his collision with Kuril, retrieved his old sword from the ground, and staggered next to Oswynn.

"Nasty whelp," he muttered, intending to rid himself of this irritation.

"Kuril!" yelled Oswynn, luckily dodging under the sword of the livid Fracodian.

The Arboreal spun around and engaged the Fracodian leader, one on one. Kerr displayed considerable skill with his sword, proving why he was the leader of this band. His strength advantage over the much slimmer Arboreal made him even more dangerous, but Kerr was unable to match the speed and agility of Kuril. The Arboreal parried or ducked each powerful attack and frequently countered with quick jabs and slices. Slowly, Kuril carved up the Fracodian. As the battle progressed, Kerr became increasingly desperate in his attacks, but Kuril kept his patience, dodging each blow and countering only when he found a safe opening.

"Surrender now and I shall allow you to retreat with the others," offered Kuril, his sword dripping red with blood.

The Fracodians laughed once again, this time with much less conviction. Even though their leader was half-dead, they still viewed the Arboreal as a weaker opponent.

"Kerr win!" they growled in a show of support.

Their leader knew otherwise. He wiped some sweat off his brow, replacing it with a streak of blood from a cut on his arm. "Kill both!" he yelled, pointing at Kuril and Oswynn.

At the same moment he called out the order, the campfire exploded. An enormous blast sent smoke, flames, and burning embers flying through the air. Low-lying branches caught on fire, nearby tree trunks instantly became charred, and the Fracodians ran for cover. Even Kuril had to leap out of the way to avoid a red-hot log from scorching the left side of his face. Kerr, miraculously spared from the burst of flames, dove at him with his sword extended. He was sure this would be the end of the Arboreal, but Kuril was too fast for the Fracodian. He stepped aside and drove his sword down through the back of his opponent.

"We must leave before the Fracodians return," said Kuril. "There may be more of them in the area, and it would be difficult for me to protect you, even with the speed of my blade."

Oswynn looked around. There were a few small fires in the vicinity, remnants of the blast, but no sign of his master, who had no doubt caused the explosion. "Where is Minaras?" he wondered aloud.

"I am certain he will be safe. Now, we must take our leave."

Oswynn nodded and followed Kuril back to their campsite, where the older wizard awaited their arrival with the two horses ready for travel.

"Why did you return without us?" asked Oswynn. "Did you not care if I was unable to escape before the Fracodians came with reinforcements?"

"I could not leave the horses unprotected for long, Oswynn. The Fracodians might have captured or killed them, and we cannot afford to lose the time to replace these fine beasts. Besides, Kuril would have been able to handle a few more Fracodians." Minaras mounted his horse and motioned for Oswynn and Kuril to do likewise. "This is not a good spot for us to rest. We will continue riding to the north until we have left Fracodian territory."

Minaras was about to head out when Oswynn remembered the lost scroll. "The banishment spell!" he blurted out. "I took the scroll from Kuril earlier today, and now it is gone."

Kuril opened the bone scroll case on his belt and found the parchment to be missing. "It is not easy to get past my guard, Oswynn," he said stiffly. The Arboreal was both angered and embarrassed, but he did gain a tiny amount of respect for the young human.

"I would never have been able to take the scroll were you not so uncomfortable on horseback. You were concentrating so hard on your balance that I could have taken your shirt as well. Perhaps you would be willing to exchange a lesson in Arboreal magic for a few riding pointers?"

"Perhaps," said Kuril, still upset with the boy, "when the time is more appropriate."

"Oswynn," Minaras said firmly, "clear your mind of learning for now. We must concentrate solely on finding Falgoran's scroll. Where was it last within your possession?"

Oswynn recounted the events of the night leading up to the present. "After Kuril slipped into the forest and you fell asleep, I took the scroll and walked north. About two hundred paces away, I built a small fire and began reading the spell." He looked up at Minaras and stated, "It must have dropped when the Fracodians grabbed me. Once we find the fire, we should be able to find the parchment close by."

"Kuril, would you please—" began Minaras, but the Arboreal had already sprinted off in search of the missing scroll.

"The banishment spell is vital to our quest, Oswynn. You should have known better than to play with it. Even if there were no Fracodians in the area, you could have been in danger. Many scrolls have enchantments placed on them as a protection against theft."

"Could one of those enchantments cause the symbols to fade after they have been read?"

"Yes, I suppose so." His master glowered at him, guessing what had happened and hoping the spell remained intact.

"Please forgive me," begged Oswynn. "I promise never to do anything so irresponsible again."

"I should hope not. You were lucky to have escaped alive and unhurt tonight."

"I would have needed no luck had I known a few powerful spells. I could have easily overcome those Fracodians and returned before you knew I was gone."

"Powerful spells are never easy to cast!" boomed Minaras. "It takes many years of training and practice to master the art of spell casting. I have always been impressed with your ability, Oswynn, but you must take your time to learn the proper methods or you will risk putting yourself and those around you in danger."

Oswynn understood what Minaras was trying to tell him, yet he still felt the urge to learn faster. At least he had the sense to drop the subject, as his master seemed to be more agitated than usual. The young apprentice mounted his horse and trotted behind Minaras. They had barely left the campsite when Kuril reappeared holding the partially charred parchment.

"I found the scroll just where Oswynn thought it would be," said Kuril, "and the spell seems to be complete." He replaced the parchment in its container and joined Oswynn on the horse.

"Your luck has held out once again, my young apprentice," Minaras said without a single backward glance. "Tempt it no more."

CHAPTER XXI

THE SECRET COVE

"I be hungry!" exclaimed Xarun, stopping midway up a small slope. He leaned against the trunk of a white pine and crossed his arms.

"I could use some dinner as well," agreed Halia. "We have been hiking since daybreak without a proper meal."

"Ahriman!" Xarun shouted. "We eat now!"

The sorcerer, far ahead of the group, turned back with a shrug. "Shall we at least continue to level ground?' he asked when close enough to speak without shouting.

The others grudgingly agreed and followed him up the hill, where the trees thinned out and gave them a grand view of the surrounding mountains. Most ended below the tree line, but several taller ones still held a white cap of snow. As Thulin looked up at the peaks, Halia stepped behind him and said, "Be glad we were not sent to the Dagger Mountains. Our climb is much easier to the east of Terun City."

"We should have purchased food and supplies from the Teruns," said Thulin. "Now, we are forced to scavenge."

"Or hunt," said Arwold. "Come, Halia. We are sure to find a goat or other small animal around here."

Thulin inserted himself between the two of them.

"Do not get lost," warned Ahriman. "We left the trail hours ago."

"Just have a fire ready for the meat when we return," replied Arwold.

Ahriman looked at Xarun, still resting against the tree, and began to gather firewood on his own.

"There were so many trails leading out of Terun City," said Thulin as the three set off on their hunt, "but they have become quite scarce of late."

"Terun City is the center of commerce for their entire society," Halia explained. "The Teruns trade with humans, Arboreals, and even Fracodians, who live among these rocky cliffs. The further we get from the city, the fewer trails there will be. You should have guessed as much, Thulin."

The young apprentice blushed and responded, "Perhaps I am just hungry."

"Perhaps," echoed Halia, "but I have been wondering why Ahriman always seems able to find a new trail for us."

"'Tis nothing but blind luck," said Arwold. "We could easily have been forging our own way through the mountains."

"Nay," countered Thulin. "Ahriman still hides something from us. We must not let him into our trust."

Halia stopped suddenly and put a finger to her lips. "We shall have meat for dinner tonight," she whispered and directed the others to surround their prey, a surly buck looking to defend its territory.

Well before midnight, Halia awoke to some flapping noises. Knowing that most night birds flew silently, the sound of wings beating against the darkness sparked her interest. She listened closely and could have sworn she heard a human voice coming from the same direction. The two noises together prompted her to rise softly from the ground and glance around the campsite. Halia immediately noticed Ahriman was absent. She tiptoed quietly away from her sleeping companions and crept around the corner, following the peculiar noises.

Not twenty paces ahead, Ahriman stood on a small ledge talking to Hafoc, who had just landed on his shoulder. After they had exchanged a few words, the crow flew into the night, invisible against the black sky.

Suspicious, Halia approached him and whispered, "What were you doing with that bird?"

"Was I doing anything?" he responded, as if nothing out of the ordinary had happened.

"You were talking to a crow." She stepped closer to Ahriman and looked him straight in the eyes. "And I do recall seeing that very same bird when you joined us in the swamp." It was difficult to see his face in the pale moonlight, but Halia could feel his anxiety building.

The wizard stared back at her without flinching. "You have good eyesight, Halia … and a good memory. The bird you saw is my familiar," he said honestly. Then he lied. "Hafoc was merely … keeping me informed of the surroundings. A view from above often can be invaluable." He wondered if Halia had heard his instructions to Hafoc. If so, he would have to silence her, leaving only the four of them to search for the treasure. With five spheres, however, they might need five sets of hands to retrieve the weapons. Should he attempt to take the four spheres from the others by force and return with his Ferfolk brethren to unlock the treasure? Would he even be able to? He held his breath and awaited her response.

"And what has this bird informed you?" Halia inquired.

Ahriman was relieved, but hid his emotion while he silently let out his breath. "Hafoc said we should reach the coastline by sunset tomorrow. I suggest you get some rest, for we will soon see the end of our quest." In less than a few hours, the Staff of Ogma would be his, and it wouldn't matter what the others knew of his plans.

Halia yawned, stared after the crow for a moment, and yawned again. She agreed with Thulin that Ahriman was hiding something, but decided to deal with it after a restful night of sleep. Ahriman took his own advice and followed her back to the campsite.

By the time the sun rose the next morning, a dense carpet of fog had rolled in. It lay heavily on the ground, turning the beautiful colors of dawn to a murky gray. The group continued their hike over a small crest and eventually found another trail, wider than any they had been on before. With a tangy yet distinctively salty smell to the air, the adventurers knew the ocean couldn't be far off, despite the thick vapors obscuring their vision.

As they pressed onward, the trail sloped gently downward. Their pace quickened in anticipation of the completion to their long quest. Halia, however, slowed. In the rapidly fading morning mist, she saw a few pebbles trickling down the mountainside, smelled the faint odor of wet wool, and heard something that sounded like a hiss.

"Soft," she cautioned, "something follows us."

"Could it be another marsh dragon hiding in this fog?" asked Arwold.

Thulin giggled, "Does this look like a marsh to you? Perhaps this one is a true dragon."

"Hah!" spewed Arwold. "There has not been a dragon in the eastern mountains for centuries."

Xarun drew his axe and smiled. "Either way, I be ready."

Halia, on the alert for their new stalker, spotted a faint shadow on the ground. She stopped the group just in time as a blast of black, sticky acid splashed in front of Xarun. It hit the ground and splattered onto him, corroding some of the leather on his left boot. Immediately, the adventurers split up, ducking under the nearest rock outcroppings. Halia pointed upward and shouted, "Yonder, I see the beast!"

A large black and white creature loomed over them on a ledge. It had the body and legs of a gigantic goat, complete with wide, padded feet for mountain climbing. Two long, snake-like heads, covered in dirty white fur instead of scales, grew out of its extremely broad shoulders. Both heads moved independently of each other, as if they belonged to two separate beings. The beast jumped from the ledge, shaking the ground when its heavy frame landed on the trail.

Arwold and Halia drew their weapons and joined Xarun, who was already advancing on the creature. Moving cautiously, the heroes kept a close watch on each of the serpentine heads, in case one decided to spit acid again. They knew a direct hit to the face or neck would mean instant death. Xarun and Arwold each went after one of the heads while Halia sneaked around to attack its body from the side.

The creature had a lumbering, bulky appearance, lulling the two warriors into a false sense of security. As they thrust their weapons at the beast, the long agile necks easily avoided their attacks, swaying back and forth almost as if they were playing. Xarun and Arwold were too close to attempt a full swing of their respective weapons, which added to their difficulty in overcoming the beast.

Halia had more luck from her position. She stabbed at the body, causing the creature to let out a yelp. A thin red trickle of blood flowed from the wound. Halia sliced at it again, but the creature jumped out of her reach, just before her sword had a chance to nick its flesh. Both heads then rose straight into the air and made eerie barking sounds.

"Never have I heard a noise such as that come from a snake!" exclaimed Arwold.

Thulin, hidden safely behind a boulder, shouted, "It may be calling for help. Prepare yourselves in case there are others around."

No sooner had he finished his warning than two more of the beasts leaped down from the ledge, one in front of the group and the other behind. Ahriman pulled out his last vial of pure air and uncorked it. He swirled his hands around and chanted his favorite summoning spell. Instantly, an air spirit materialized next to him. He commanded it to assist Halia against the original beast while Arwold faced the one in back and Xarun the one in front.

Fighting the largest of the three creatures, Xarun tried to hack one of its necks, but as before, it twisted out of the way to avoid any contact with the sharp metal blade. The other head, meanwhile, slipped around the side of the warrior and bit him on the shoulder, its fangs piercing his leather armor but falling just short of his skin.

"May the devil take you!" he roared, slapping the creature's mouth off his body. The first head then reared back and let fly a thin stream of sticky acid at him. Xarun ducked just in time. The gooey liquid flew over his head and splashed harmlessly against the rocky mountainside.

"Thulin," snapped Xarun, "distract one of the heads!"

The young apprentice peeked out from his hiding place. "You wish me to come near that beast?" he inquired with a shaky voice.

"Yes, make haste, boy!"

Thulin stood and looked around. At first, he hesitated, unsure of what to do. Then he took out the dagger Ahriman had given him and slowly approached the beast. He crept closer when, suddenly, one of the heads jerked around and hissed at him. Startled, Thulin jumped backward and tripped on a small stone, dropping the dagger.

"Stop your playing!" Xarun bellowed.

Thulin retrieved the dagger and rose from the ground, resolved to prove he could be useful in a battle. He took a deep breath and began running around the creature, waving his dagger back and forth. "To me, snake beast!" he shouted and kicked dirt at its body.

His antics eventually drew the creature's attention. One of the heads began following his movements closely, watching and waiting. As soon as the apprentice was in range, the head lunged at him. Oblivious to what might have happened to Thulin, Xarun focused entirely on the other head. He closed in, feigned a few swings with his axe, and then grabbed the neck with his free hand. Once it was firmly in his grasp, he sliced the head off with one swift chop. Wasting no further time, Xarun promptly repeated this successful method of attack against the remaining head before it had a chance to cause any harm to Thulin. With the creature defeated, Xarun turned to the young apprentice and said, "Many good thanks."

Thulin, exhilarated, stood proudly over the dead body.

Arwold quickly realized his large sword was much too slow to wound either of the second beast's two nimble heads. He would have to find its weakness rather than execute a simple frontal assault. His first attempt was to stab the body of the beast, but the long blade of the claymore fell just short. The set of dangerous fangs on the first head kept him well out of reach, and the second nearly blasted his face full of the corrosive acid. While he paused briefly to consider his next plan of attack, the two heads dove at him, aiming straight for his chest. Their noses clanged against his metal breastplate and bounced off. Arwold smiled, "You cannot pierce my armor, evil beast. This battle has been won!"

Protecting his face as best he could, Arwold lifted the claymore, pointed it at the creature, and charged forward. The two heads lunged at him. Without his armor, they would have stopped him dead in his tracks, but instead, Arwold barged through and plunged the sword deep into its body. The blade pierced its lungs, cutting short its dying yelp. Arwold withdrew his weapon from the corpse and wiped the blade on the white fur, staining it a deep red.

Halia and the air spirit teamed up against the third beast. Although unable to cause any significant damage, the air spirit was enough of an annoyance to distract the creature from its real threat. The spirit constantly circled around one of the necks, diverting its gaze away from Halia, who concentrated her attacks on the other head. Using swift strokes and pinpoint precision, she was able to slice the neck with her sharp blade. She inflicted wound upon wound on the long appendage, eventually causing the entire head to fall limp. With half the threat abolished, it was a simple matter for Halia to complete the job. Ahriman, directing the spirit from afar, kept an eye on Halia for the duration of the battle.

When the fog had dissipated, a direct view of the ocean in the distance greeted the adventurers. The faint sound of waves crashing against rock reached their ears and infused them with a burst of renewed energy. They practically sprinted the remaining distance to a small cliff overlooking a white-sand crescent beach. Below them, they saw a hidden cove, surrounded on three sides by the mountains and on the fourth by the Cold Ocean. Aside from the ever-present shore birds and tiny sand crabs, not one living creature had set foot on the beach for more than six hundred years.

"A buried treasure," sighed Halia, "and we brought no shovels with which to dig."

"I see no signs of where the treasure might have been hidden," remarked Thulin after a quick scan of the area.

Xarun grumbled, "There be naught here but sand."

They looked at Ahriman, but the uninspiring view confused him as well. "Shall we take a closer look?" he asked.

The heroes climbed down from the mountain and combed the beach. Xarun used his axe to dig several holes in the sand, but after hours of frustration, he leaned his weapon against the rocks of the cliff and sat down to watch the others.

"Perhaps your stolen information was mistaken, Ahriman," said Arwold.

"The pages I borrowed have so far proved accurate. I see no reason why the weapons would not be here somewhere."

"There is nothing here but a deserted beach," said Arwold. "Do what you want with your spheres. I have been away from Krof for too long and plan to return home promptly."

Thulin thought otherwise. "Do not be too hasty in your judgment, Arwold. Let us take another look at our spheres together ... we may not yet have reached the end of our travels."

They all gathered around Thulin and held out their spheres. Inside each one, as Thulin had guessed, the white spot remained slightly off-center.

The apprentice pulled the parchment ruler out of his pocket and wrapped it around the sphere. "The white dots in our spheres are not in the center. They direct us to travel yonder," Thulin noted, pointing a finger toward the dark blue water.

Arwold said, "'Tis the ocean."

"You have remarkable powers of observation," Thulin blurted out sarcastically, eliciting a small chuckle from Halia and a frown from Arwold.

Thulin strolled to the shoreline, removed his boots, and waded into the cold water up to his knees. He began walking eastward when he tripped and fell face first without a splash. Even though the water covered his entire body, his skin and clothing remained completely dry. Puzzled by this paradox, Thulin sat for a moment and then reached back to find whatever it was he tripped on. There was something hard and invisible separating the regular ocean water from the dry water. "I have found something!" he called out. "Or, perhaps I have found nothing!"

The other four approached cautiously, stopping just where the waves lapped at the sand. Thulin motioned for them to step forward into the ocean. "Come closer," he said, standing up.

"What is there, Thulin? I see naught but water," Arwold commented.

"Are you not curious why my robe remains dry?" he asked.

Halia was. She stuck her hand into the water near Thulin and pulled it back with a start. "'Tis not wet water but watery air!" she exclaimed.

Ahriman ran his hands around Thulin and nodded his head. "It is an illusion of water … nearly impossible to detect and evidently many centuries old. Even guided by the spheres, this could easily be missed."

Thulin quickly found a second invisible wall holding back the seawater, about eight feet from the first. Between the two barriers, a detailed illusion exactly matched the random pattern of incoming waves to disguise a dry passageway leading far into the ocean. Thulin grabbed his boots and followed the path into the deep water, his head disappearing beneath the illusory waves. Moments later, and still completely dry, he ran back to the group. "You must see these sights! Follow me!"

He led the others into the magical passageway, which formed a cylindrical tube eight feet in diameter to hold the water at bay. Small silver fish swam around and, once everyone was deeper than eight feet, above the group. On the sea floor were spectacular views of sea-weed gardens, anemones, and all manner of crustaceans and snails.

Thulin, Xarun, Arwold, and Halia gazed in awe at the aquatic wonders. They had never seen such strange sights before. Only a few feet from the barrier, a horseshoe crab buried itself in the sand, exposing only a pair of eyes to watch for a possible mate. Sea anemones swayed in the ocean currents, keeping to the rhythm of the passing waves. A lobster pulled a large snail out of its shell and feasted on the soft body of the animal. Ahriman ignored all of these incredible sights and forged ahead, his eyes focused on nothing but the path in front of him.

"It seems as if we are a part of the sea," said Arwold, reaching for the side of the passage.

"Abide!" Thulin warned. "Keep your hands away from the wall!"

"Why can I not touch the side?" asked Arwold. "You did trip over it and naught happened."

Ahriman stopped suddenly and turned to them. "Take care! Do you not realize what would happen if this magic were to be dispelled?"

The sorcerer continued hurriedly down the passageway. The rest of the group looked at the water surrounding them and shivered. When they saw how far ahead Ahriman was, they scrambled to follow him.

With less sunlight able to reach this deep in the ocean, it became darker and colder as they progressed. It was nearly an hour before they reached the end of the undersea corridor. Not having torches with them, they could barely see two steps ahead for the last quarter of their journey, but eventually a soft green glow lit their way. It emanated from strange symbols covering the perimeter of a large hemispherical chamber at the end of the passageway.

"We have arrived," said Ahriman.

CHAPTER XXII

ANGERING THE GIANT HERDSMAN

"I found the entrance!" shouted Oswynn. He beamed as he stood at the bottom of a sheer cliff, pointing at a small mark on the wall of solid stone. The drawing looked like a holly leaf with five needlelike points, one at the tip and two on each side.

Minaras approached his apprentice and examined the ancient etching. Well preserved by magic, it had remained untouched by the rough hand of erosion for six centuries. "Good work, Oswynn," he complimented. "Now, stand aside while I open the door."

Oswynn was curious about the spell Minaras would cast to open the sealed door and what they would find beneath the mountain. He gave his master a questioning glance to which Minaras replied, "Even I cannot foretell what will happen when I invoke this enchantment." With a sigh, Oswynn fell back a few paces as Minaras put his hands on the rock around the drawing and chanted, "*Grund astyrian.*"

When he had completed the mystical phrase, he stepped away from the mountainside and watched as the etching began to elongate. The base of the leaf, originally at eye level, stretched downward until it hit the ground. Then, the four points on the sides of the leaf spread outward and pulled the wall of rock apart with a low grumble. The newly created opening formed an inverted 'V' in the side of the mountain, exposing a hidden cave.

Minaras removed an unlit torch from a pack on his horse and chanted, "*Maete brond.*" Flames instantly appeared on the end of the torch as he led his horse through the opening. Oswynn followed with the second horse, and Kuril took up the rear. It was dark, but by concentrating on his spell, Minaras was able to increase the intensity of the fire, and thus provide more light than usual without consuming the torch any faster. It took most of his energy to keep the spell in effect while they traveled beneath the mountain, but having a better view of where they were heading was worth the additional effort.

The cave was not only dark but also quiet. As they made their way through the narrow passage, the only sounds they heard were their footsteps echoing against the damp walls. On and on they plodded through the dreary tunnel without speaking a word. Eventually, Oswynn grew bored. Deciding to try his hand at another spell, he moved closer to Minaras' horse, reached forward into its pack, and pulled out a second torch. Quietly, he chanted, "*Maete brond,*" to no effect. Confident he would ultimately be successful, he tried a few more times, and, on his fourth attempt, a small flame danced from the end of his torch. Minaras looked back briefly, smiled, and continued onward. Oswynn, however, wasn't yet satisfied with his work. A lit torch was good, but he wished to have a lantern instead, and that would require the proper transmutation spell. He sang out "*holt awendan,*" "*hwierfan holt,*" and various combinations thereof with no luck until his seventh try, when four tines grew from the middle of the torch and the handle began shrinking. Within moments, the tines had surrounded the flames and caught fire, and the handle had completely disappeared. The intense heat near his hand forced Oswynn to let go. The torch-lantern hit the ground and went up in flames.

"Transmutation is one of the most difficult schools of magic to learn," Minaras cautioned. "Even the most basic spells take years to master, let alone ones that convert wood to metal." He stopped suddenly, and Oswynn, still wondering what had gone wrong with his spell, walked right into the rump of his master's horse. "This appears to be the end of the passageway," noted the old wizard.

"I will be glad to see daylight once again," said Kuril. "I would sooner live on a horse than underground."

"I agree with you," said Oswynn. "There is nothing of interest below these mountains. How do we get out of here?"

In front of them, the cave ended beside an apparently solid wall of rock, but Minaras felt a slight breeze on his cheeks. He reached out and his hand passed through the stone.

"This illusion marks the end of our underground journey," said Minaras, unimpressed with the quality of the wizardry. "The coast should not be far from here."

"Let us hope we find the hidden cove before the others," Kuril added. "Are you certain you will be able to disrupt such ancient and powerful magic?"

"I can say only that water has always been my strongest element, and I am not an unskilled wizard. I shall do my best to bury the weapons out of reach for the rest of eternity, but should I fail, we always have Falgoran's scroll. It will make things a bit more dangerous for us, but we must prevail at any cost."

The Arboreal involuntarily put a hand to the scroll case on his belt, hoping it wouldn't be necessary to use the banishment spell. He wondered if the five spheres would still guide the treasure hunters to the secret cove once Minaras had dispelled the magic. If not, it would make his quest for revenge more difficult, forcing him to go on a hunt for the warrior-thief who breached his fortress.

Minaras stepped forward, but his horse wouldn't budge. It took some prodding, but eventually he and Oswynn were able to urge their horses through the illusion. Once out of the cave, they had an easy hike for a half day through a hidden valley. Other than the dwindling sunlight and lack of a roof above their heads, it wasn't much different from their trek through the underground passage. They walked along a rocky path with solid walls of stone on either side. Occasionally, a tree sprouted from the side of the cliff and turned upward toward the sunlight. Kuril noticed the trees grew at regular intervals but kept the observation to himself.

As they came nearer to the coastline, the sounds of the ocean in the distance brightened Minaras' mood. He began to anticipate a trouble-free end to their quest. In his mind, he had already collapsed the undersea treasure chamber and was on his way home to Seaton, when they saw a large figure ahead, blocking their way. The enormous humanoid, a sour-faced mountain giant, was at least twenty feet tall and stood in the center of the trail. Its head, neck, and body were bloated to the point of bursting, making the giant appear even larger than it already was. The giant, clearly upset, gazed into the distance, slowly turning its head from one side to the other.

"What is he looking for?" asked Oswynn.

Neither Minaras nor Kuril ventured a guess.

"The object of his search does not matter," noted the Arboreal. "The more important question is how to get past him. He does not seem to be in a particularly good mood."

The rock walls on either side of the valley were fifteen feet high with barely a handhold in sight. Minaras shook his head. "I might be able to create a staircase, but even if we could scale these walls, the secret cove is well hidden. We could easily become lost in the mountains if we circled too far around and lost sight of this valley."

"Would it not then be a matter of finding the water and following the coastline until we happened upon the cove?" Oswynn asked.

"Do not forget we have little time left before the weapons are uncovered," replied Minaras. "Perhaps we can reason with him to let us pass."

"I have heard giants can be more stubborn than humans," warned Kuril, "but I have never seen one before."

As soon as the giant laid its eyes on them, it began taking huge strides in their direction, its large feet booming on the ground with each step.

"Oswynn, take the horses and stay behind us," Minaras said, concerned this might not turn out to be a peaceful meeting. He and Kuril stepped forward cautiously, preparing for the worst.

Even though his legs and feet moved slowly, the enormous length of his gait brought him within range faster than a wave crashing on the sand. In a deep voice, the giant bellowed, "Little people no pass."

"Please let us through," Minaras pleaded, looking straight up into his face. "We have no quarrel with you."

"Little people kill pets."

Minaras glanced at Kuril, but he, too, didn't understand what had angered the giant so. "Someone or something must have recently killed an animal belonging to him," thought Minaras, fearing it might have been the ones seeking the weapons. "That could only mean they already had reached their goal."

"We have seen no creature in these mountains other than you. Please allow us to continue along this trail," begged Minaras, growing more concerned with each passing second. "We have little time to spare."

The giant raised an enormous stone club twice the size of a grown man.

"I think he may not wish to speak with us further," noted Kuril.

They jumped aside as the club crashed into the ground, causing a clap of thunder to rumble through the hills. "Little people suffer!" the giant roared.

Minaras tried to convince the giant of their innocence one last time. "We are not the ones you seek! Please stay your weapon and listen to me. Perhaps we can aid you in your search after we complete one small task."

The giant answered by lifting his club high into the air. Kuril drew his sword and rushed forward, a seedling in the shadow of a towering tree. The giant swung his club, but the swift Arboreal leaped aside with time to spare and darted between his legs, jabbing with his sword as he passed through. The weapon did no more damage than a tiny mosquito feasting on a speck of blood from a human limb.

Meanwhile, Minaras grabbed his small tinderbox, pointed his outstretched hands at the giant, and chanted, "*Micel maete mara lig.*" Flames darted from his fingertips, hitting the giant's chest and causing his clothing to ignite. The wizard's spell proved as ineffective as Kuril's sword. The giant merely chortled and tapped out the small flames with his thumb.

After securing the horses to a small boulder, Oswynn moved closer to get a better view of the action. "You must try something else!" he yelled to Minaras when the Fingers of Fire spell failed to cause any damage.

"This I can see," his master replied. "If I were not so tired from the underground hike, I could have tried a Wall of Flame, one of the most powerful spells at my disposal, but now I must think of something less demanding."

Kuril, standing behind the giant, knew that attacking the creature's legs or lower body would be futile. He needed to find a more vulnerable area, preferably somewhere near the head or neck. The Arboreal sheathed his sword and began climbing the side of the mountain while the giant was distracted with Minaras, his nimble fingers finding small cracks in the rock wall to hold.

"Pets gone!" the giant wailed. "You gone!" He placed both hands on his club, took a single step toward Minaras, and made a fierce sideways swing at the wizard. Minaras dropped to the ground, barely avoiding a crushing death. The club smashed into the side of the mountain and caused a rockslide.

Kuril clung tightly to the tiny handholds and called out, "Minaras! Beware of the falling rocks!"

The wizard, however, became dazed when he hit the ground especially hard and was unable to protect himself from the impending danger. Seeing his master in trouble, Oswynn quickly threw his hands forward and chanted, "*Lyft bord.*" A strong wind swirled around the wizard, forming an invisible shield that deflected the majority of the rocks.

Buried, but mostly unhurt, Minaras recovered and shook the rubble off. "Many good thanks, Oswynn! Once again, you have managed to impress me with your spellwork."

"And save your life," added Oswynn with a smile, satisfied with the spell yet wondering what it would have been like to affect the falling rocks directly.

As soon as Kuril spotted an opening, he jumped from the mountainside onto the back of the giant. He clung to the creature's shirt, a patchwork of both fresh and rotting hides, and crawled toward its head. The giant reached around to grab Kuril, but his stocky arm fell short, much to the Arboreal's relief. Kuril scrambled higher, grabbed onto a lock of stringy hair, and drove his sword into the giant's neck as deeply as he could. The blade barely went in six inches, stuck in the thick layer of fat and muscle beneath his skin. The giant bellowed, "Be gone!" and violently swung his body around. Kuril flew off and fell to the rocky ground. The giant flicked the sword off his neck with his finger and turned to squash the prone Arboreal.

Minaras had to move fast to save Kuril. He picked up a stone from the fallen rubble and brought his arm back, intending to throw it while casting an enlarging spell, but on viewing the substantial pile of debris by his feet, he came up with a much better idea. The wizard waved his arms around the rubble and chanted, "*Beorg hlifian, fleogan munt.*" The entire pile rose into the air, flew toward the giant, and began circling around his head. Occasionally, one or two of the stones would smack him in his ears or protruding nose. The giant swatted at the annoying debris but couldn't rid himself of his rock-strewn halo.

"We must escape while he is thus distracted," shouted Minaras. "Make haste!"

Oswynn grabbed the horses and Kuril's sword while Minaras rushed forward and helped the Arboreal to his feet. The three sprinted past the giant, hoping he would decide not to pursue them.

Chapter XXIII

The Weapons of Power

The five adventurers shivered in the damp, chilly undersea chamber, feeling almost as wet as if they had been swimming in the cold ocean water. An unearthly sound permeated the dark room, the simultaneous muting and echoing of every noise that originated from within the hemisphere: the crunching of boots on the muddy sand, the rustling of clothing, the quiet breathing of five bodies, and the splash of water coming from a fountain in the center of the chamber. The yellow tinge of the strange symbols glowing on the walls combined with the deep blue of the water to cast an eerie green light throughout the room. Outside the magical barrier, a translucent jellyfish floated past, barely illuminated by the green glow of the chamber. The creature's beautiful but deadly tentacles flowed behind its pulsating disk and caressed the invisible shield separating the five adventurers from the depths of the ocean.

In the center of the chamber, a white jet of water sprayed up from the ground and hit the ceiling before falling back into a small circular pool. Five black pedestals of delicately carved marble surrounded the fountain, spread at even intervals around the circumference. Thulin, immediately drawn to the writing on the wall, went directly to the side of the chamber to study the magical symbols, while the other four approached the pedestals.

Halia circled the fountain cautiously, examining each of the cylindrical pedestals in detail. They were four feet tall, well polished, and inscribed with symbols, not unlike the ones adorning the chamber walls. The top of each pedestal looked like a claw with a cupped palm and five sharp talons pointing upward, just the size to hold one of the crystal spheres. Convinced there were no traps to spring, Halia took the sphere from her pocket, placed it in the palm atop of one of the pedestals, and let go. The sphere rolled out of the claw and fell. Halia threw out her hand and caught it in midair.

"Might the spheres be tied to a specific pedestal?" asked Ahriman.

"There is only one way to know," said Halia. "We must try each of the spheres."

Ahriman handed his sphere to her. She placed it on the pedestal, but it rolled out of the claw no different from the first. Xarun placed his sphere on the pedestal and met with the same result, although he wasn't quick enough to catch it when it fell onto the sandy floor with a thump. He picked it up with a grunt and brushed it off.

Ahriman looked around and saw Thulin by the side of the chamber. "Thulin, bring your sphere to Halia."

"'Tis an ancient magical language, not unlike Arboreal," said Thulin, continuing to scan the wall. "I believe I can translate it." He traced a symbol with his finger and stepped back. "There is information about powerful weapons and a great war."

"Yes, yes," said Ahriman, "you will have time to interpret the writings later. Now, bring your sphere to me."

Thulin didn't wish to have his work interrupted. Without taking his eyes from the magical symbols, he backed up and blindly handed his sphere to Halia. Then he returned to another section of the wall. Halia placed the fourth sphere in the claw and it too met with the same fate. Finally, Arwold placed his sword, hilt down, on the pedestal but had no better luck.

"You wish it should stay?" Xarun nudged Halia out of the way, slammed his sphere onto the claw, and held it there. "It stays!" he growled.

Ahriman shook his head. "Thulin, does the writing describe how to use the spheres and the pedestals? Perhaps there is a trick to unlocking the weapons."

"Nay," responded Thulin. "'Tis about a danger, an evil. I need more time to interpret this language. Some of these symbols do not relate to anything I have ever come across in my readings, but I know I can decipher them."

Unable to think of a better solution, Halia walked over to another pedestal and held her sphere within its grasp. Likewise, Arwold held his sword, hilt down, on top of a third pedestal. Ahriman shrugged his shoulders and placed his sphere in the claw of the fourth pedestal.

"Thulin," he commanded, "take your sphere from Halia and place it on the final pedestal."

"Did you not hear me?" the apprentice asked. "There is a danger here. You must allow me more time to translate these symbols before—"

"Make haste!" Ahriman yelled. "You may finish your research later! I will even help transcribe the entire wall for you to read at your leisure in Seaton."

Thulin backed away from the wall, staring at the symbols and talking to himself. "taking over the mind … I am almost—"

"Now!" the sorcerer demanded. The other three were too curious about the pedestals to notice how desperate Ahriman was to unlock the treasure before Thulin completed his work.

Thulin grabbed his sphere from Halia and placed it on the empty pedestal. As soon as the crystal touched the marble, there was a loud click as the fingers of each claw closed around the spheres, locking them in place. The five adventurers immediately let go, surprised by the sudden movement. Slowly, the pedestals retracted into the floor. The group collectively took a step back and watched in amazement. Arwold, mesmerized by the display, didn't have a single thought about his family sword as it sank into the ground, disappearing along with the other spheres. By the time the motion had stopped, only the tip of the claymore remained above the sand.

While the pedestals sank, the jet of water in the fountain subsided in proportion to their height, ultimately turning into a trickle. A golden weapons rack stood in place of the fountain. Five magnificent weapons glistened on the rack: a Great Axe, a War Hammer, a Claymore, a Long Sword, and a Staff. Each one was a perfect representation of its type, the pinnacle of human and Terun achievement, from the completely smooth hardwood handles, precisely carved to fit the shape of a hand, to the expertly forged metal, sharpened to a point unattainable by ordinary blades. The adventurers stood enthralled, gazing at the exquisite weapons for quite some time.

Thulin broke the silence, "No one must touch these weapons before I finish studying the writings. There is a reason why they have been hidden here, and I have nearly uncovered the truth."

Ignoring Thulin's request, Ahriman threw his own wooden stick aside and grabbed the Staff of Ogma. It alone looked different from the other four weapons, carved from a single piece of ebony in the shape of two vipers intertwined. At its tip, the heads of the two snakes pointed up and away from each other. With their forked tongues extended, it seemed as if the Staff sported a pair of demonic horns.

Unable to resist the temptation, Halia and Arwold took the Long Sword and Claymore respectively. The weapons fit comfortably in their hands, as if they had been wielding the blades their entire life.

Finally, Xarun reached for the Great Axe. "It be perfect," he said, tossing it between his hands and feeling it out for weight and balance.

"I have never seen its equal," Halia noted. "This is a magical weapon no doubt."

Thulin stepped in front of her. "Please, Halia, you must return the sword and wait for me to complete the translation. This blade may present a danger to you and, perhaps, the rest of the world."

So enchanted was she by her new sword that Halia didn't hear a single word coming from his mouth. She ran her hands up and down the spectacular blade without blinking once, afraid the sword would disappear. The other three stood similarly spellbound by their new weapons.

"Ahriman, you must help me with these symbols," whined Thulin, his frustration building. "Together, it shall take no time at all."

"Why not try picking up the War Hammer, child?" responded the sorcerer. "You are still young enough to learn the ways of a warrior."

"I am a wizard!" Thulin turned in a huff and bumped into Arwold. The tall warrior held the Claymore in front of him, his eyes focusing on the long blade to the exclusion of all else. Thulin, frowning, put his hand on the weapon. "Arwold, since we met, you have wished to know the history of your sword. The answer may be here in this chamber, on this very wall behind you. Give up this blade while I—"

Thulin never completed his sentence. Arwold had driven the Claymore deep into his chest. He fell to the ground, dead.

Xarun immediately snapped out of his trance and shouted, "What have you done, Arwold?"

The tall warrior stood motionless. He stared past Xarun with his eyes glazed over and his lips curled upward in a slight grin.

"The death of the lad was regrettable," Ahriman's unemotional voice rang out in the chamber, "but it is done now." He showed no concern over the murder of Thulin. "Shall we leave this chamber? With these weapons, we may fulfill our dreams."

Halia felt that something terrible had just happened, but she couldn't regain control of her mind or her body. Her eyes drifted onto the fallen apprentice, yet she was still unaware of what had transpired not ten feet from where she stood. With great effort, she managed to force a couple of words through her lips, "The weapons … are evil … drop them." Even as she spoke the last two words, the sword was drawing her attention once again. She ran her fingers over the blade, thinking how impressive a weapon it was.

"A murderer you be!" accused Xarun, squeezing the Great Axe.

Arwold replied, "And you are nothing but a thief and a bully. You do not deserve to wield the weapon of a hero!" He stepped toward Xarun and took a swing with the Claymore. Xarun raised the Great Axe and successfully blocked the attack. They proceeded to trade heavy blows with neither fighter able to gain an early advantage over the other.

Ahriman, growing impatient with these petty quarrels and wishing to return to dry land, pleaded, "Halia, this is your chance for riches. Shall we not go together and claim what we have so long deserved?"

She ignored his request, completely enamored by the Long Sword.

"Come now, Xarun. You never did care for Thulin."

"He has grown on me," Xarun shot back. "He be like a kid brother."

Those last few words evoked a distant memory in Halia. "Brother," she repeated softly, then louder, "Brother!" Her mind snapped away from the blade as she screamed, "Thulin!" She threw the sword to the ground. Dropping beside his body, she tried to stop the flow of blood from his wound but soon realized it was too late to save the young man.

"You knew these weapons were evil!" she shouted, pointing an accusing finger at Ahriman. "Did you think we would all become your slaves?"

She darted at the sorcerer, removing her old long sword from its sheath.

"Are they evil?" challenged Ahriman. He waved the Staff at the remnants of the fountain and chanted, "*Forgiefan ealdor lagu.*" A water spirit sprang to life, rising from the nearly dry pool in the shape of a gigantic amoeba. "Ho!" the sorcerer exclaimed, taken aback by the ease with which he had completed the spell. "This staff is even more powerful than the legends have told!"

The spirit extended a large tentacle and clobbered Halia with a blast of water, throwing her full across the floor of the chamber and soaking her from head to toe. Several thinner tendrils of water stretched out from the spirit and entangled Xarun. He sliced through a few of them but quickly began gasping for air as the sheer number of appendages wrapping around his neck overwhelmed him.

"Come, Arwold, we are the only ones who truly understand the nature of these weapons," stated Ahriman. "Let us leave the others to their watery grave and return to civilization."

Arwold was in no mood to comply. "You are no less a thief than Xarun, and perhaps more so. I will see you brought to justice as well."

Ahriman knew the tall warrior was completely under the influence of the Claymore and ignored his threats. He raised the Staff to summon more aid, and with a minimal amount of effort, four large air spirits immediately sprang to life, even without pure air to complete the spell. Ahriman imagined what he could accomplish if he set his mind to it. With a quick word of command from the sorcerer, the spirits whisked him and Arwold out of the water chamber and up through the passageway.

Xarun gagged on the tentacles covering his mouth and neck. Unable to breathe, he had little time to escape the slippery yet deadly grasp of the water spirit. He swung wildly with the Great Axe, slicing through its appendages, while he pressed closer and closer to the body of the creature. Once he was within reach, it took only one swing of the Great Axe to fell his opponent. The spirit collapsed to the ground with a splash. Xarun gasped, filling his lungs with a huge breath of saline air before falling to his knees in a fit of coughing.

Halia returned to Thulin's side and touched his face. "Thulin is dead," she lamented.

"Arwold ... murdered ... the boy," Xarun said with a hint of vengeance in his voice, still recovering from his ordeal with the water spirit.

"These weapons are evil, Xarun. We must destroy them all, beginning with the War Hammer."

Xarun dropped the Great Axe and unsheathed his trusty old weapon. He grabbed the War Hammer from the weapons rack and placed it on the muddy ground. It, too, was a beautiful weapon, but he trusted Halia and saw with his own eyes how the Claymore had affected Arwold. Bringing his axe high above his head, he chopped down on the hammer lying at his feet. Smash! The old axe shattered on impact, leaving the War Hammer jostled but otherwise unscathed.

"Try using the other axe," suggested Halia.

With a nod, Xarun picked up the Great Axe and tried again. Holding it in both hands this time, he swung it fiercely downward, breaking the War Hammer in two.

From within the broken shaft of the weapon, a small dark shadow emerged. It rose into the air and began circling the chamber, growing larger and gaining more substance with each circuit. Round and round it went. Larger and larger it grew. Slowly, its features took on a demonic form with fangs, claws, wings, horns, and a tail. "We may have made a mistake," said Xarun.

The shadow circled the chamber one final time before it became corporeal. It made a shrieking noise that sounded like a sinister laugh, and then, with a whoosh of its wings, flew straight up and crashed through the roof of the chamber. Water began pouring through the hole in the invisible barrier.

"Doubtless it was a mistake," yelled Halia. "Run!"

CHAPTER XXIV

A NEW ALLIANCE

Instinctively, Halia grabbed the Long Sword before she dashed for the exit. Xarun, with the Great Axe already in hand, followed her out of the chamber. They ran through the water passage as fast as they could, hoping the magical barrier would hold until they reached the safety of the shallows near the beach. Behind them, seawater poured through the hole in the ceiling, quickly filled the chamber, and barged into the passageway as if it were furious at its years of restraint. With the wave of approaching water threatening to overtake them, Halia and Xarun dashed to the beach. They heard the rumbling behind them and felt a wet spray against their legs and arms, but dared not steal a single backward glance. The barrier, which for centuries held back the might of the ocean, collapsed just when the pair could see the dry sand of the secret cove.

Halia and Xarun, drenched and panting, slogged the last few feet through the shallow water before throwing themselves onto the hot ground. Surprisingly, they were far from exhausted, their hearts racing only because of the excitement from their narrow escape. Within seconds, there was no longer any indication that either the undersea chamber or the invisible barrier had ever existed. The waves had resumed their rhythmic pounding of the shore, the gulls walked the beach in search of unsuspecting crabs, and the ocean remained rela-

193

tively calm. Halia and Xarun lay on the sand staring at the sky and wondering what to do next. Their reprieve was short-lived, however, for they soon heard the whinny of horses in the distance.

"Ahriman and Arwold?" asked Xarun.

"No," said Halia, sitting up. "They could not have found horses in these mountains. Besides," she pointed at the source of the noise, "there are three figures approaching from yonder cliff."

Xarun stood and readied his axe, watching as the three figures left their horses and climbed down the mountain into the secret cove. One was old, one was young, and the third was tall and thin.

"Lower your weapon, Xarun. I know some of these travelers."

He dropped the axe and fell back onto the sand, his heart still pounding with adrenaline.

Having seen Halia and Xarun emerge from the water in time to avoid the disruption of the ancient spell, Minaras knew something had gone wrong. He rushed to their aid, followed closely by Oswynn and somewhat further by Kuril.

"Minaras, I did not expect to see you here. How did you manage to find us?" Halia asked.

"It was not you we were expecting to find," responded Minaras. "We had hoped to find the undersea chamber and dispel the magical barrier, but you seem to have completed the task for us."

"But it would be impossible to find this cove without the spheres," said Halia.

Minaras smiled. "Not if you received instructions from the one who hid the treasure."

"Are those two of the weapons?" interrupted Oswynn when he eyed the two weapons on the ground. He reached for the Long Sword.

Halia quickly yanked the sword away before he could touch the blade. A fierce look from Xarun convinced him not to try for the Great Axe.

"Keep away from these weapons, Oswynn," Halia explained. "They are quite dangerous."

Kuril strolled up to the group and glared at Xarun. Although he didn't fight the big warrior at the fortress, Xarun fit the description the two guards had given him. His hand strayed to his sword as he took one more look and thought only of revenge.

Minaras became increasingly worried as he scanned the secret cove. "Where are the other three weapons, Halia? What has happened here?"

A surge of emotions flooded Halia's mind. She felt a combination of grief, anger, and remorse as the events of the past hour flowed through her mind. Holding back her tears, she said, "He killed Thulin. I was unable to stop him."

Kuril's jaw tightened, the mention of murder erased any lingering doubts he might have had. It was time for revenge. "You attacked our fortress and stole the crystal sphere!" He drew his sword, prompting Xarun to place a hand on the Great Axe and rise to his feet.

"Many of us were killed at the hands of your summoned magma spirit," said Kuril. "You shall pay dearly for your actions!"

The Arboreal leaped at Xarun and swung like lightning. The big warrior barely had time to jump away, receiving a gash on his side as Kuril's sword pierced his leather armor and punctured his skin. Xarun raised the Great Axe over his shoulder and was about to take a swing at the Arboreal when Minaras and Halia squeezed themselves between the two.

"Kuril, please restrain yourself until we learn what has transpired here." Minaras chuckled briefly as he continued, "We seem to have traded places. You are acting on impulse and I now sound like an Arboreal!"

Kuril saw no humor in the situation and pressed forward into the wizard. "It is because of his foul deed that I mourn for my brethren. Do you deny he is the one who stole the sphere from our fortress?"

"As Arboreals stole the fortress," Xarun replied. "It once belonged to humans." He pushed his weight against Halia as much to be near her as to intimidate the Arboreal. Halia dug her feet into the sand to hold him back.

"I do not trust him," Kuril said flatly.

"You need not trust him yet, Kuril. I ask only that you to listen to him and save your judgment for later."

The Arboreal relaxed his stance and stepped back, sheathing his sword. It took another nudge from Halia before Xarun reluctantly did the same. Minaras turned to Halia and asked, "What happened to Thulin? Where is he?"

Halia stared at the ocean, her eyes watering. Oswynn followed her gaze. He understood the implication but refused to accept the truth. In his mind, Thulin was merely somewhere else at the time, probably with his nose in a book. Minaras, on the other hand, fully comprehended what Halia didn't need to say. He dropped to the ground and held his head, releasing a flood of tears onto the sand.

Oswynn watched his master weeping on the beach. "Is he really … dead?"

Halia nodded slowly. Oswynn still couldn't believe it, although reality was beginning to sink in. Thulin was gone forever.

"This is my fault," Minaras groaned. "I should never have sent him to Zairn. He was not ready to be on his own."

"He was not on his own, Minaras. I was with him." Halia tried to comfort the old wizard, placing her hand on his shoulder, when a feeling of guilt overcame her. "He was my responsibility," she chastised herself. "I should have protected him!"

"Why did you not listen and send me to Zairn in his place?" argued Oswynn, becoming angry with his master. "We both knew Thulin could not cast the most basic of spells!"

"You may have been correct, Oswynn. I thought the journey to Zairn would do him some good, but I seem to have been a bit mistaken."

"Nay," countered Halia. "You would have been proud of your apprentice. He proved himself an intelligent, resourceful young man many times over. By the end of our quest, he had displayed a courage and self-confidence you would not have recognized in the child you sent forth so many weeks ago."

Minaras felt somewhat comforted by her kind words, but knew in his heart that the blame was his to bear.

Meanwhile, Xarun had become impatient with all the talk and grieving. "We must catch them," he huffed. "They must not escape!"

Minaras raised his head. "Catch whom? Halia, please give me all the details."

"We have no time!" Xarun continued to rant.

Kuril, still wary of the big warrior, said, "There is always time. We will hear the whole story before making any further decisions." It gave him a minimal amount of satisfaction to oppose the big warrior, and he smiled at the sight of the frustrated Xarun while he sat on the sand beside Minaras.

With an exasperated look, Xarun turned to Halia. "You saw what they did!"

"Aye, Xarun, and I shall not rest until they feel my blade," said Halia. "But we do not know where they went, nor do we know anything about the shadow we released from the War Hammer. Allow me to explain it all to Minaras."

"And if he delays further?" asked Xarun.

"We shall go together and avenge Thulin's death."

Xarun took a couple of steps toward the mountains. Then he looked back at the group, shook his head, and slumped onto the beach. He didn't even feel like throwing a pebble at a gull that had wandered within range. Instead, he listened to Halia recount what had happened since she and Thulin left Seaton. After she finished her story, the five gathered into a circle surrounding the two weapons.

"We face a difficult dilemma," noted Minaras. "The weapons offer unmatched power along with an insidious danger. Destroy them and we would be more likely to fall at the hands of Ahriman and Arwold; keep them and the weapons could take over your minds, forcing you to commit evil deeds."

Halia had already made her decision. "Destroy them we must," she demanded.

"It be a shame," moaned Xarun. "They be fine weapons."

"As much as I would like the warrior to be wrong," said Kuril, "I must agree with him. We may need their strength against the others."

"With the Staff of Ogma at his command, Ahriman will be a formidable foe," admitted Minaras, making his decision. "We cannot destroy the weapons yet."

Halia remained skeptical, remembering how strong an influence the Long Sword had on her. What would happen if it took over her mind once again? She peeked at Oswynn, wondering if he would die at her hands.

"You need only resist the sword until we recover the Staff and the Claymore," said Minaras. "Then we will do what should have been done many centuries ago … send the entrapped demons back to the netherworld. Do you have the strength to control the weapon, Halia?"

She didn't know for sure, but nodded anyway, thinking of Thulin, Arwold, and Ahriman.

Kuril, still upset with Xarun, said, "We would not have had this problem if you had not—"

Xarun cut him off. "Ahriman would have found another."

"That may be so."

"He be very persuasive," the big warrior continued.

"You should have stopped him when you realized—"

Minaras broke up their argument. "Need I remind you that we have a demon on the loose as well? We must cooperate to rid this world of the evil Ahriman has unleashed. Please put aside your differences until after we have accomplished this one small task."

"I will do as you ask," agreed Kuril.

Xarun nodded and grabbed the Great Axe from the center of the circle. "What now?" he grunted.

Halia took her old sword and jammed it blade down into the sand by the high water mark. Then she picked up the Long Sword and quickly sheathed it. In the brief moment she held the weapon, she could almost hear it calling to her, beckoning her to yield her mind. At least for the moment, she was in control.

"Are you sure you did not see them?" she asked. "They escaped the water chamber only minutes before us."

"If we saw them," replied Oswynn, "we would not be standing here jabbering."

"Then they must not have taken the same passage whence you came," responded Halia.

"Unless they were invisible," Minaras speculated. "But that would have been difficult for Ahriman. He was never skilled with illusions."

"Aye, he be a sorcerer," said Xarun.

"The spirits he summoned were invisible," recalled Halia. "They lifted him and Arwold off the ground in the weapons chamber."

"Summoning air spirits was always his favorite spell as a student," said Minaras. "They must have flown out of this cove. The Staff of Ogma would afford him the energy to command the spirits for a long time. It will be impossible to track the two of them, for they are no longer forced to walk."

Oswynn threw his hands up. "So we are lost," he said with a sigh.

"While we still live, we will never give up hope," said Kuril, placing a finger on his scar.

Xarun, irritated at the thought of losing Ahriman's trail, kicked sand at a gull, causing it to fly away. Upon seeing the bird in the air, Halia thought back to her recent conversation with the sorcerer and said, "I saw Ahriman send his familiar to the southwest one night."

"That," said Minaras, "is as good a direction as any."

The four air spirits carried Ahriman and Arwold high over the Pensorean Mountains on a direct route toward Krof. The views from the sky were spectacular: snow-capped peaks reflecting the moon's light and brightening the night sky, rocky valleys carving their way through the tall mountains, even a bird's eye view of Terun city, but neither the wizard nor the warrior noticed. Each was completely absorbed in thought, planning what to do with their newfound power.

As they passed over the Castle in the Mountain, Ahriman glanced at his fellow traveler. "Arwold," he called out, but there was no response. "Arwold!" he yelled louder.

"Release me or you shall die, sorcerer!" the warrior responded briskly.

"You speak strong words," said Ahriman. "If my air spirits were to release you now, do you think you would survive the fall? The weapon must control your mind."

Arwold shook his head. "This sword does not control me!" he growled. "'Tis nothing more than a guide."

"Does it guide your hand to murder?"

"If need be," replied Arwold. "The life of one or two means little to my greater quest."

"I see." Ahriman couldn't have hoped for a better response. Whatever Arwold desired, he would find a way to exploit it. "And what would your quest be, Arwold?" he inquired.

The warrior displayed a proud grin. "I seek to end all evil in this world, and with this sword, I shall be much closer to my goal." He stared at Ahriman with a fierce look in his eyes. "If you wish to kill me, have your foul spirits drop me now. Otherwise, you shall feel my wrath as soon as our feet touch the ground. No one shall stand between me and the fulfillment of this dream, least of all you."

"Indeed, you are on a noble quest, and I intend neither to kill you nor even oppose you. In fact, I wish to join your cause. Might I offer you some aid to accomplish such a lofty goal?" asked Ahriman.

"I knew not that you shared my vision. What have you in mind?"

"I, too, seek an end to evil. Together, we will wage a war against all who prey on the innocent, against all who have taken what they did not deserve, and against all who refuse to atone for their sins. Our united strength will bring justice to those in need, to those who have waited patiently for mil—" Ahriman caught himself before blurting out millennia, then continued, "many years, and we will begin with the center of all evil in this land, the decadent city of Zairn."

Arwold smiled, imagining a world without evil. He would cleanse the lands and be hailed a true hero.

Chapter XXV

The War Hammer Demon

As the bright afternoon gradually turned into a shadowy evening, Halia, Xarun, Minaras, Oswynn, and Kuril drew closer to the entrance of the secret tunnel. The old wizard stopped his horse not far from the spot where they had encountered the giant. He looked at the darkening sky, where the only sources of light were the fading remnants of sunset and the tiny white specks of stars appearing one at a time.

"We will camp here for the night," he said.

"Why do we stop," protested the big warrior. "I be not tired."

"Nor I," agreed Halia. "Let us continue at least to the underground passage if not farther."

"If neither of you are tired," said Minaras, "then you would not mind keeping watch while I get a bit of sleep. Besides, we should allow the horses to rest. We may need to make haste once we have cleared the mountains … no later than mid-morning I would expect."

"We should have gone southwest," grumped Xarun.

"And spent even more time battling the difficult terrain?" asked Minaras. "No, we will be out of the mountains and onto flat ground much sooner by traveling through the passage."

Oswynn and Kuril rode up to the rest of the group, the young apprentice letting out a substantial yawn.

"You and Oswynn may rest now, Minaras," offered the Arboreal as he dropped from the horse. "I will take the first watch." He didn't trust the newcomers, Xarun especially, and intended to keep a close eye on them until morning. They could easily have hidden the weapons and killed the other apprentice. "I will not let them do the same to these two while they sleep," he vowed to himself.

Halia soon found a sheltered area in the rocks beneath a pair of overhangs, one for the horses and the other for the humans. She had barely set up camp before Minaras and Oswynn fell fast asleep. Although neither she nor Xarun felt tired, their bodies were exhausted, and they too were asleep within minutes.

Kuril sat atop the ledge and thought of his home, longing to be within the comfort of a forest. There were a couple of trees scattered about, but they were too few for him to feel at ease. "Besides," he thought, "the giant must have planted them. They appear at too regular an interval to be natural." He would have preferred to continue their march and have the mountains behind them by sunrise, but he understood the need for the humans to rest.

From the perch above his sleeping companions, he sat quietly for several hours. Up the trail was the pile of rubble from the rockslide of their fight earlier in the day. Kuril knew that Xarun and the others were the cause of the giant's agony as well. Before long, the campfire began to fade, but because this night was particularly balmy, Kuril decided to forgo the hunt for wood and allow it to die out. Burning wood, even though it was already dead, bothered him. It became very dark, with only a crescent moon, mostly obscured by the mountains, adding to the weak starlight.

Kuril's gaze returned to the sleeping humans below, his mind filled with many questions. "Were they telling the truth? Should I trust Xarun and Halia? Why was Ahriman so determined to retrieve the weapons? Would this be a matter for the elders to decide?" Suddenly, the horses began to whinny and stamp their feet, interrupting his thoughts. Kuril lifted his sword and stood up. He looked around but saw nothing out of the ordinary. The horses, however, were becoming more agitated by the second, spooked by something in the area. If it had been a predator, the Arboreal would have heard or smelled the intruder with his keen senses.

Descending from the ledge, Kuril crept slowly toward the horses. They were clearly restless, stomping on the ground, gnawing on the ropes around their necks, and kicking at the air. As the Arboreal came closer, he noticed the two horses looked different from before. Their legs and bodies seemed more muscular, their tails longer and slimmer, and their teeth much sharper. Their eyes glowed bright red as they breathed heavily and stared back at him with a burning hatred.

Kuril reached out to stroke their manes as he had seen Oswynn do on several occasions. "What troubles you on this peaceful night?" he asked in a soft, lilting voice.

The horses let out a vicious growl and jumped at him, easily breaking though their partially chewed restraints.

"Awake, Minaras!" the Arboreal shouted, immediately pulling his hand away from the beasts. "The horses have gone mad!"

Xarun rose at the first sound of trouble, grabbed the Great Axe, and rushed to the center of the commotion, hoping Ahriman or Arwold was to blame. Initially disappointed when he saw Kuril trying to tame the two horses, he felt renewed excitement when he saw their glowing eyes and pointed fangs. Just when he reached Kuril's side, the two horses simultaneously reared up on their hind legs and kicked out with their front hooves. Xarun and Kuril jumped to either side, narrowly avoiding the danger.

Halia was the next to rise from her slumber, followed by Minaras and Oswynn who took longer to shake off their drowsiness. Even through the darkness and halfway between dreamland and full consciousness, it took only one glance at the horses for Oswynn to see something was amiss.

"Their eyes ... they glow red!" he cried out.

"Does this happen often to horses?" asked Kuril. "Or could it be some type of disease?"

"I have never seen the likes of this before!" shouted Oswynn, crawling closer to get a better look.

"Nor have I," added Halia. "Could they be some form of changeling?"

"I think not," said Minaras, who deduced the truth, having read about demonic possession in one of his old tomes and remembering Halia's description of the fiendish shadow released by Xarun.

"Take care," he warned, "the demon must be close by! It has lent its strength to the horses and in return controls their actions."

Looking at the ledge above the horses, Halia saw the dark outline of a large creature with a horned head, great wings, and a thick serpentine tail. The demon waved its arms in a circular motion and called out strange sounds in a deep guttural voice that sent a shiver across her skin and made her hair stand on end. "'Tis on yonder ledge," she yelled, pointing at the rocky overhang about fifteen feet above the horses.

"It attempts to open a gate," Minaras guessed.

Oswynn gazed at the dark creature. He could almost feel the awesome power required to accomplish such a spell. "A gate to where?" he asked.

"It summons a portal to the netherworld to call forth its brethren," responded the wizard.

"What would happen if it were to succeed?" asked Oswynn, inching even closer.

Minaras held him back and said, "It would not bode well for us or anyone else in this world."

A glowing circle formed in mid-air in front of the demon. Within the bright white outline, a gray mist began to appear. The spell was nearly finished. It would be only a few seconds before the link between the two worlds was complete, allowing hordes of demons to pour through. Acting quickly, Minaras lifted a small stone from the ground and threw it at the cliffside while chanting, "*Mara mara fleogan mara.*" The stone grew larger and larger as it neared the ledge. By the time it crashed into rocks just below the demon's feet, it had become an enormous boulder. The demon, forced from its perch, flew into the air with a piercing screech, furious at having to abandon the partially formed gate.

The collision between the boulder and the ledge caused a small avalanche of rocks to tumble onto the two warriors. A barrage of debris hit both Xarun and the horses. Xarun, more annoyed than hurt, brushed himself off and continued to battle the beasts, which didn't seem to be distracted in the least, their thickened hide providing them ample protection from the rubble.

Kuril noticed the rockslide as soon as it began. He deftly jumped out of the way, but, as soon as his feet touched the ground, a strong hoof clobbered him in the chest. The Arboreal staggered backward out of breath as the demon-horse moved in for the kill.

"Stay alert!" warned Xarun, but the Arboreal, stunned by the damaging blow, couldn't see the imminent danger.

With a loud roar, the big warrior rammed into the beast, pushing it just far enough away from the Arboreal to save his life. The hoof pounded the dirt beside Kuril's head. As the creature stumbled, Xarun slashed at its side with the Great Axe, causing the horse to let out an infernal yowl.

"That be no whinny," said Xarun, shifting into a defensive stance to protect Kuril while the Arboreal recovered from his injury.

The demon flew higher into the air and circled the campsite. After six centuries of imprisonment, it desperately wanted revenge.

"We must not let this fiend escape!" yelled Minaras.

"Can you bring it down to earth?" asked Halia, taking a deep breath and drawing the Long Sword from its sheath.

"I will do what I can."

Minaras began his familiar chant to summon a wind. Aware of the danger the wizard represented, the demon immediately dove at him.

"Master, the demon comes for you!" warned Oswynn.

Minaras looked up, but it was too late; the demon was nearly upon him. Halia pounced, landing on its back just before it smashed into the wizard, and caused it to hit the ground early. Minaras jumped back to avoid being crushed while Halia and the demon skidded along the rocks. Oswynn ran to his master's side, offering his help.

Before they rolled to a complete stop, Halia leaped off the demon's back and lunged at it with the Long Sword. The fiend, much faster than she had expected, recovered from the fall and managed to grab the weapon by the flat of the blade.

"You shall never steal this sword from me," Halia warned, twisting the blade to wrench it from the demon's strong grasp. It would have been impossible for her to recover an ordinary weapon in this manner, but the Long Sword easily bit into the creature's flesh, drawing a line of black blood and forcing it to release its grip.

Minaras began casting another spell, which again drew the demon's attention. Unfolding its left wing, it spun around and lashed out with a set of sharp spines. Halia ducked, but the spines on the wing connected with Oswynn behind her, opening a deep gash on his forehead.

"Oswynn!" yelled Halia.

The young apprentice, bleeding profusely, fell backward into Minaras and disrupted his concentration. The demon rose to its full height of ten feet, let out a piercing wail, and flapped both wings, blowing a cloud of dust and pebbles everywhere. Halia stood her ground between it and Minaras, determined to protect the wizard and his apprentice.

Kuril, back on his feet, focused his attention on the wound inflicted by Xarun. He sliced at the opening with swift, accurate jabs, causing a grunt of pain from the creature each time his blade connected with the soft tissue beneath its protective hide. The Arboreal was so single-minded in his pursuit that he didn't see the creature's tail lash out until it smacked him in the eyes. With Kuril temporarily blinded, the demon-horse reared up, once again ready to deliver a fatal blow.

"Not this time either!" bellowed Xarun. He jumped at the Arboreal and pushed him out of the way. The horse came down, its hooves pounding into Xarun's upper chest and throwing him onto the ground. He was able to survive only because he wielded the Great Axe, although the heavy blow severely winded him.

This time Kuril came to the rescue, positioning himself between the horses and Xarun. With his sword extended toward the enraged beasts, he helped the big warrior up with his other hand.

"Many … good … thanks," said Xarun, still trying to catch his breath.

Side by side, they faced the horses, this time as a team. Working together, they feigned several attacks, but kept a close watch on the possessed creatures. As soon as the wounded horse reared up again, Xarun went after its right leg. The Great Axe cleaved through the limb as if it didn't exist. The horse stumbled forward when the stump of its leg hit the ground. Kuril moved in closer and drove his sword down through the open wound, putting the creature out of its misery.

Turning their attention to the remaining horse, Kuril distracted the beast by moving to one side and constantly jabbing with his sword. Although he couldn't pierce the thick hide, he managed to draw the horse's gaze. The possessed creature unsuccessfully tried nipping at him and kicking once or twice, but the Arboreal easily avoided the attacks. Meanwhile, Xarun sneaked around to the other side and hacked at its neck with a strong blow of the Great Axe. The horse collapsed.

"And I thank you, Xarun," Kuril returned the gratitude. "You may not be as unscrupulous as I had initially expected."

The big warrior looked over to Halia and knew the fight hadn't yet ended. "Now for the demon!" he shouted. "To the netherworld, fiend!"

Halia was having a difficult time keeping the demon away from Minaras and Oswynn. The creature dodged each swing of her blade and countered with its own deadly attacks. It clawed at her, snapped its teeth, and swung its tail. Were it not for the power of the Long Sword, she wouldn't have survived long. Finally, the demon pressed forward, using its massive body to pin her against the mountain wall.

"Release me, foul creature!" she ordered.

The demon pushed its considerable weight against Halia, attempting to crush her to death, but Xarun charged at the creature and buried the Great Axe in its back. The demon whirled around and struck Xarun with its arm, launching the warrior into the air and throwing him several yards away. Then it yanked the axe out of its back and held it aloft, staring at the weapon with its dark eyes. It could feel another familiar presence nearby, but didn't understand why.

Kuril ran forward, stopping when Minaras called out to him, "Prepare the banishment spell!" With a nod, he retreated from the battle and removed the scroll from the bone case attached to his belt. He unfurled the ancient parchment and stood waiting to read the magic words.

While the demon continued to ponder the strange weapon, Halia had a chance to slip away from the mountainside. Once free of the bulk of the creature, she attacked it from the rear with all her strength. Halia knew no good would come of the Great Axe being in its possession, and she had to do something to recover the powerful weapon. Behind her, Minaras had the same thought. He picked up another stone, chanted his enlargement spell, and cast the rock at the demon.

"Halia … jump out of the way!" shouted Kuril when he saw Minaras preparing the spell.

She leaped aside as the boulder smashed into the demon, crushing it against the solid mountain wall. The Great Axe fell to the ground with a clang. Kuril rushed to the boulder and began reading the spell while Xarun recovered his weapon.

"Do not read the scroll, Kuril," warned Minaras, "until we know the demon has been defeated."

Halia crept closer to the boulder and leaned over, listening to a faint sound. "I hear a noise coming from behind the boulder!"

Just then, a bright green flash lit up the mountainside and startled a crow sitting on a high ledge. The black bird flew into the night air, heading to the southwest.

With his face bathed in the green light, Xarun moaned, "Not again!"

CHAPTER XXVI

TO RID THE WORLD OF EVIL

Ahriman and Arwold sat beside a small fire on a hill overlooking the Sinewan River and beyond it, the town of Krof. They hadn't spoken since their brief exchange in the air, but now, after they had finished their evening meal, Arwold broke the silence. "What evil do you know of in the city of Zairn?" he asked skeptically.

Ahriman thought for a moment before responding. "There is much wickedness in Zairn's leaders, and it spreads like a disease to those they command. They are not satisfied with the extent of their rule and wish their influence could reach throughout all of the human lands. Moreover, they intend to use force if necessary."

"What you say cannot be true," countered Arwold. "I have heard nothing of this, not a single rumor drifting through the streets of Krof, not one word describing Zairn's leaders as anything other than fair and just."

"Do you not realize that is exactly what they want you to believe?" asked Ahriman. "Perhaps you would have more faith in your own eyes. Observe what has transpired not one week ago."

"How would you know of the recent secrets within Zairn? We have been traveling together for weeks."

"We have, Arwold, but my familiar has not. Hafoc is quite unassuming and can easily spy on all but the most guarded of conversations."

Ahriman removed the vial of marsh dragon essence from his robe and pulled out the cork. Raising the Staff of Ogma with one hand, he spread the clear gooey liquid on the ground and chanted, "*Fero hlifian iewan gerecednis.*"

Two spirits rose from the spilled dragon essence, transformed into human figures not unlike the doppelgängers Arwold had fought in the swamp, and played out a scene from what was supposed to be the second circle of Zairn. Unbeknownst to Arwold, it was Ahriman who created this small play entirely from his imagination, the spirits merely puppets bearing a close resemblance to the leaders of Zairn.

"We must build up our army," said the first spirit in a confident voice. "We do not yet have the power to control the entire land and cannot risk spreading our men too thin."

The second spirit disagreed. "Nay, we could be ready within days if we planned our campaign well."

"Verily, how can this be?"

"We need only defeat Seaton to achieve our victory. Once we have taken their port, we shall control trade throughout the land. The rest of the cities and towns will have no choice but to follow our lead or risk being cut off from their supplies."

The first spirit laughed, enamored with the plan. "'Tis true, but Seaton is a powerful city, one that will not easily be subdued. We must start with a smaller town … a town like … Krof. It will fall with minimal resistance, and we shall force their young men into our army. With their added strength, Seaton will be unable to withstand our attack."

The second spirit thought briefly before agreeing. "You have made a good decision. By the time the autumn winds blow, we shall be the undisputed rulers."

"Alert the commanders to prepare the men. We march on Krof within the fortnight!"

The two spirits faded back into the ground, leaving behind a damp spot, which drew a gaze from Arwold that could melt steel. He believed what he had just seen, and it infuriated him. Even if he had held any lingering doubts, the Claymore would have removed them, fueling his anger.

While Arwold sat fuming, Hafoc flew down from the sky onto the shoulder of its master. After a brief discourse with the bird, Ahriman sent it flying to the south and said, "Hafoc has returned with news from his latest mission. Our friends have destroyed the War Hammer and released the demon from within. Unfortunately, they seem to have run into some difficulty with that very same demon."

"The fools should never have destroyed such a magnificent weapon," Arwold said, ignoring the part about the demon. "My men could have used it to battle corruption in Zairn."

"I agree it was a formidable weapon, but it was no match for this." Ahriman lifted the Staff of Ogma into the air. "If they do manage to escape the demon, they will no doubt come looking for us. They are dissatisfied with the weapons they chose in the undersea chamber and desire to take ours for their own purpose."

"Do they?" seethed Arwold. "I shall never let this sword fall into their evil hands!"

"Nor I this staff," added Ahriman with a smirk. He threw another branch onto the dwindling fire. "We must waste no time in gathering our forces for they will offer additional protection against Xarun and Halia. One can never be too safe."

"It shall take but a few days to recruit my men."

"Will you be able to complete this task in secrecy?" asked the sorcerer. "You must not rouse any suspicions in case there are spies from Zairn lurking about your fine town."

"I am a very influential man in Krof." Arwold put his hand on the Claymore, "now, even more so. I shall do my part well enough, and any spies I come across will meet the fate they deserve."

Ahriman grinned, stood up, and walked to the top of the hill. He stared at the river winding past Krof, its waters carving their way through seemingly impenetrable earth and stone toward the ocean. "We must not lose our advantage of surprise. You have two days to gather your men, after which we will follow this river to Zairn."

Arwold stepped beside Ahriman. "This is my home," he stated, pointing from one end of Krof to the other. "'Tis a town of good, hardworking people. I will not allow Zairn to spread its evil to those who live here or anywhere else in this innocent land. We shall meet on this spot in two days time." Arwold set his foot down where shadows cast by the campfire danced on the grass.

Trapped within an ethereal prison by the War Hammer demon, the five adventurers suffered a few moments of disorientation before realizing they were no longer on the same rocky mountain path as before. The world around them looked almost the same but was shadowy and translucent. The mountains, the trail, and the boulder were present but took on a dreamlike appearance. In addition to the ghostly facade, everything in the outside world moved at high speed: clouds raced through the sky in a blur, the sun rose and set within a course of minutes, and all but the slowest animals were invisible.

"Be this the netherworld?" asked Xarun.

Minaras shook his head. "It is not, but I do think the demon has sent us to another plane of existence." He looked around and added, "It is obvious that we share a connection to our own world but are physically trapped elsewhere."

Oswynn, his face and hands ashen, let out a soft groan. Minaras knelt beside his apprentice and tended to the serious wound on his head. "This would never have happened if I did not force you to join me on this quest," he whispered. "You must recover or I will never forgive myself." The old wizard pulled a small vial of ointment out of his pocket and spread the greasy paste onto the heavily bleeding gash. The treatment staunched the flow of blood and cleansed the wound, but not before Oswynn had fallen unconscious.

"This is no place for an apprentice," Minaras lamented.

"A student learns from his teacher," noted Kuril, replacing the banishment scroll in its protective case.

Minaras lowered his head. "That is so, Kuril. This is no place for a teacher."

"This be no place for anyone," Xarun said.

"How do we return to our own world?" added Halia. "We seem to be losing hours every minute we remain here."

The four looked at one another, but none of them had any idea of where they were or how to escape. Halia, near the boulder, reached out to lean on the rock and found nothing solid to support her weight. Her hand disappeared as it passed into the stone, nearly causing her to topple over.

Intrigued by Halia's discovery, Kuril attempted to pick up a stone from the trail, but his hand passed through the small rock as well. "We see the outside world as a shadow in this realm and cannot interact with it."

"Then why do we not fall through the ground?" Halia asked.

"We might," answered Minaras, "if we move too far from this spot. There could be an endless void not four paces from where you stand."

Without thinking, Kuril took a small step closer to the wizard.

"The sun peaks already!" complained Xarun.

Halia waved her hand in and out of the boulder in a playful manner, fascinated by the ability to send parts of her body through what appeared to be solid rock. "Can you not cast some spell to bring us home?" she asked.

"Such magic is far beyond my ability," admitted Minaras, wiping the blood from Oswynn's face with a clean cloth.

The apprentice shivered. Halia generously offered her clock to Minaras, who used it to cover Oswynn's body.

"He does not look well," said Halia. "Will he survive?"

"He must," Minaras prayed. "I will never outlive the guilt if he follows Thulin to the afterlife."

"Oswynn will live," said Kuril. "Death would not stop that boy from becoming a powerful wizard, and he has more to learn before realizing his dream."

Minaras grinned, knowing the Arboreal spoke the truth. "Halia, you and Xarun should search the area. Perhaps one of you can find a clue to help me solve our little problem. I doubt the demon was powerful enough to trap us here permanently."

With a grunt, Xarun began moving slowly down the trail, the shadow world holding little interest for him. Halia, however, was curious about their immediate surroundings. She stepped cautiously into the boulder and unexpectedly bumped into something solid. With a feeling of dread, she stuck her head into the rock and pulled it back with a jerk. "The demon is with us!" she exclaimed.

Suddenly the demon let out a loud shriek and leaped out of the boulder. It swiped at Halia, spinning around with the force of the attack. Halia fell away from the boulder, barely avoiding its sharp claws as Kuril jumped forward to attack the fiend. Xarun, hearing the ear-splitting wail, charged back toward the boulder, weapon ready.

"Its wound has healed already," shouted Kuril. "I cannot see the tiniest scar on its back where Xarun buried the Great Axe!"

Halia planted her back foot on the ground to break her fall. After steadying herself, she joined the two warriors, waving the Long Sword and yelling, "Release us from this prison, foul beast!"

The three heroes, wary of the demon's tricks, kept their eyes on its wings as they fought against claws, tail, and fangs. The demon similarly knew the danger of Halia's sword and Xarun's axe. While fending off their attacks, it stayed clear of the sharp edges, touching only the flat portions of the two blades. Unbelievably, the demon was able to split its attention among all three opponents at once, matching their blows stroke by stroke and occasionally throwing in a few sneak attacks with its tail and wings. No human or Arboreal could ever hope to achieve such a feat of concentration.

For several minutes, the battle was a stalemate, until an idea to gain the advantage sprang into Halia's mind.

"Keep the demon occupied," she instructed the others, as she withdrew from the battle and hurried down the trail.

At thirty paces, Halia turned and stepped into the mountainside, vanishing into the wall of stone.

Xarun, recognizing her plan, taunted the demon. "Your time here be over!"

He altered his position slightly to draw the demon's gaze away from the mountain. Kuril took his cue and stood beside the big warrior on the offensive. The two attacked the beast as fiercely as they could. Kuril, with his speed, and Xarun, with his power, slowly pressed the demon backward. When it was within a few feet of the mountain, Halia jumped out of hiding and thrust the Long Sword deep into the demon's back. The demon screamed in agony and spun around, raking her across the abdomen with its sharp claws. Simultaneously, Kuril hacked at the back of the demon's legs with a flurry of attacks. Although he was unable to cause serious damage, his blade compounded the pain, and the demon fell to its hands and knees. Finally, Xarun jumped onto its shoulders and took one last tremendous swing. The Great Axe swooshed down and cleaved the demon's skull in half.

Immediately, the surroundings reverted to normal as the demon's body began to lose its substance, turning into a black shadow no different from when Xarun had freed it from the War Hammer.

The shadow rose slowly from the ground, making small circles as it flew upward. "Kuril," Minaras called out, "it will not take long for the demon to regain its body. You must banish it now, before it has a chance to reform!"

The Arboreal grabbed the scroll from his belt and read it at once, the words fading slightly by the time he had completed the spell. At first, nothing happened.

"The spell has failed," moaned Halia, becoming concerned as the shadow circled around their heads. She put her free hand over the gash on her stomach, surprised that the nasty wound didn't hurt as much as it should have.

"You must have patience," said Kuril calmly, "and trust Falgoran's spell."

Even as he spoke, a small blue light appeared in front of him about four feet above the ground. It grew larger and elongated, until it resembled a tiny tornado with its funnel pointed at the demon. It let out a low hum and began to suck the shadow toward its center. The demon fought back, desperately trying to escape the vortex. The more the demon resisted the vacuum, the brighter the swirling light grew. Eventually, the miniature tornado completely absorbed the shadow, and both disappeared in a brilliant flash of blue light.

"Where be the demon?" asked Xarun, rubbing his eyes and looking around to see if they had been transported again.

Kuril carefully rolled up the ancient parchment, returned the scroll to its case, and said, "That demon will threaten this world no longer. It has been banished to the netherworld where it shall remain for eternity."

"The demon from the War Hammer was the weakest of the five," said Minaras. "When we destroy the remaining weapons, we must use the scroll before the others take solid form. It is the only time they are vulnerable to the banishment spell."

"I do not wish to battle any of those stronger demons," admitted Halia as she made her way to the wizard, holding her stomach. Luckily, her wound wasn't as deep as Oswynn's, and Minaras was able to treat her with the ointment before she had lost too much blood. In the back of her mind, she knew the Long Sword had sustained her through the injury. It continually offered her its strength and asked nothing in return. She began to think of the riches available for her taking with such a powerful weapon. Those thoughts felt good.

"Kuril, I am worried that Oswynn has caused irreparable damage to the scroll. Will it be effective in banishing the remaining four demons?" asked the wizard.

"It must or we will have no recourse," replied the Arboreal.

"Is there no other way to banish the fiends?" asked Halia, sheathing the sword.

"Sigmus might be able to find an answer to your question," said Minaras, "but it could take months or years for him to complete the research."

Xarun grumbled, "Time we do not have."

Kuril agreed with the big warrior. "We must recover the other weapons before they are misused or, even worse, destroyed."

"I can travel with you no longer," said Minaras. "Oswynn has been badly hurt and requires my constant attention. I will not leave him here to die."

Xarun walked over to Oswynn and lifted the boy, holding him gently between his massive spike-studded arms. "We go now."

CHAPTER XXVII

AN ARMY GATHERS

A large group of Ferfolk warriors amassed in a forest clearing under the evening sun. Their armaments ranged from hide and leather to chain and steel reinforced armor; from pitchforks and wooden clubs to great swords, war hammers, and longbows. Several wore horned helmets, battered and old, looking as if they hadn't seen battle in centuries. Those Ferfolk stood proud, with their shoulders back and an extra spring in their step. More than a few in the group had no idea why they were there and grumbled about being away from their homes and families. Others tossed around the words "revenge" and "justice" while sparring with one another.

Ahriman made his way through the gathering, each of the Ferfolk recognizing him and standing aside to let him through. Even the largest of the warriors lowered his eyes in respect as the sorcerer passed by.

"Brothers," Ahriman called out when he had reached the center of the crowd, "the time has come for us to take our revenge!"

The entire group of Ferfolk turned to him as one and quieted down. A few of them shouted, "Revenge!" and raised their weapons, but those who had been waiting to have their questions answered quickly hushed them.

"Long have we waited for this day to arrive, and now our patience has been rewarded. Behold, the Staff of Ogma!" Ahriman raised the

Staff above his head. "It is this legendary weapon that stopped our ancestors when they valiantly fought for justice against the tyranny of the humans, and it is with this very same weapon we shall complete what they had started so many years ago! We will finally bring their dreams to reality. This staff is like no other ... its power is unmatched ... with its strength, we cannot be defeated!"

Many of the Ferfolk cheered, but Ahriman heard one voice rise above the others: "What of the other weapons?"

The sorcerer didn't let his tiny speck of anxiety show through his façade of confidence. Instead, he reassured the group with a smile. "I share your concern, my friends. The other four weapons are truly dangerous, but you need not worry about them, for one is our ally, one has been destroyed, and two have been cast from this world."

Most of the crowd was satisfied with his response, but Ahriman hadn't yet finished. "We must never forget about our banishment to the wastelands!" he continued. "Our people endured millennia of hardship and suffering! Do we not know who our enemy is? The humans will finally taste our vengeance!"

Ahriman raised his staff once again and shouted, "The humans shall fall!"

The entire group of Ferfolk echoed in unison, "The humans shall fall!" as they raised their weapons and pumped their fists in the air. Ahriman had won over even the most skeptical of the crowd.

Meanwhile, Arwold had recruited a small army of men from Krof. Some were the mercenaries he frequently employed, some were town guards sworn to protect the citizens, and others were young merchants or farmers hoping to learn a new trade. Arwold convinced them all to join his cause. They believed him when he spoke about Zairn's plan to attack Krof, listening intently as he recanted the tale he had recently witnessed. After learning of this treachery, the men were riled and vowed to defend their homes against the impending invasion. Although, at first, some may have had doubts about their ability to stand against the largest army in the land, the sight of the Claymore in Arwold's possession gave them a boost of additional courage. Not one of them questioned the danger they would soon be facing.

Early on the second day, Arwold led his army to the rendezvous spot on the hill, arriving well before Ahriman. He placed four of his trusted mercenaries on guard duty and ordered the rest of the men to practice their skills. Throughout the afternoon, he walked among them, personally training many of the younger ones who had never held a weapon before. This was a chore other leaders would have delegated to a lieutenant, but Arwold believed his men would respect him more if he showed his dedication to the unit by spending the extra time with them.

It was late in the evening when Donelar, one of the sentries, returned in a hurry and reported, "An army of Ferfolk approaches! Shall I prepare the men for battle?"

"Nay," responded Arwold, "those Ferfolk come as our allies. They shall fight beside us against Zairn."

The warrior's eyes widened, disgusted by the thought of sharing a battle with the Ferfolk. "Krof is not their home," he complained. "They belong neither here nor in any other human settlement."

"'Tis true they live elsewhere, Donelar, but still they come to offer us their assistance. You must accept it, graciously or not."

"We need none of their aid to defend our town," argued the sentry. "We shall succeed on our own. Send them back to their mud hole in the forest."

"It does not matter how we accomplish our goals," Arwold explained with a tinge of frustration in his voice. "Be it alone or with Arboreals, Teruns, or even Ferfolk."

"Our goals?" the sentry whined. "'Tis not our goal to befriend the likes of them."

"'Tis a good beginning," said Arwold, his aggravation beginning to show. "The Ferfolk make powerful allies."

The mercenary wasn't convinced; his prejudiced mind was closed to any type of logical reasoning. "What have you promised them in return for their aid?" he asked cynically. "Shall we allow the Ferfolk to live among us when the battle is over? And what of the Fracodians, shall those beasts return to Krof as well?"

"If the Ferfolk or Fracodians choose to live in peace and abide by our laws, then so be it, but that has nothing to do with the deal I have struck. Ahriman, the leader of the Ferfolk, freely offered their assistance and I accepted. There was nothing more promised."

Donelar grumbled, "But the men—"

"Shall obey my command," Arwold said sternly. "You must go now and prepare them to fight alongside the Ferfolk." He placed a threatening hand on the hilt of the Claymore, partly to intimidate Donelar and partly to reassure himself of his decision.

"I will do what I can," said the warrior, returning to his post.

As Ahriman led his army toward the hilltop, it was clear the Ferfolk echoed the feelings of the humans. When they first caught sight of the men on the hill, the Ferfolk stopped. The warriors drew their weapons, and the archers aimed their bows. The humans immediately returned the gesture, forming a line along the crest of the hill and preparing for a battle with the newcomers. The two armies stared defiantly at each other.

Donelar ran back and forth in front of the human army, shouting, "Lower your weapons! They come as our allies," but the men could sense his words were insincere.

"Then why do they train their bows on us?" one yelled back. "Shall we allow them to skewer us with arrows?"

"They are here to assist us in our defense against the warriors of Zairn," explained Donelar with a touch of venom in his voice.

One of the mercenaries called back, "We need no help from them! Send those beasts away!"

"No!" thundered Arwold. "You will fight with them or you will fight against me!"

"But they are Ferfolk," spat Donelar.

Arwold swung the Claymore at him. The mercenary raised his sword to defend, but Arwold's blade easily cut through the weapon and continued deep into his shoulder. Donelar dropped to the ground, clutching his wound.

Arwold waved the bloody Claymore in front of the men. "Choose your side well."

His outburst quieted the men, but they refused to lower their weapons, unsure of who was the greater threat. Nor did the Ferfolk help the situation. They, too, were disgusted at the thought of fighting alongside the humans.

Some whispered that they had stolen their lands. Others claimed the humans had banished their ancestors to the desert. An older Ferfolk with a horned helmet yelled, "Those scrawny farmers are not fit to stand in our shadows!"

One of the human archers, a young furrier, could stand the taunts no longer. He drew back an arrow and let it fly into the midst of the Ferfolk. A single arrow was all it took to break the fragile peace. Before Arwold could use the Claymore to reprimand the archer, the two armies had charged at each other with rage in their eyes and cruel words on their lips. It was about to be a gory battle.

The armies had barely covered half the distance when the earth between them buckled. A ridge formed, running from one side of the hill to the other. The front ranks of warriors keeled over as the ground rose twelve feet into the air and sprouted two colossal arms and a pair of legs as thick as tree trunks. The headless earth spirit raised one leg and stomped heavily on the ground. The resulting trembles caused the remainder of the Ferfolk and humans to fall over backward.

While the armies were recovering their weapons and returning to their feet, two air spirits gently placed Ahriman on top of the earth spirit. "Lower your weapons!" the wizard demanded in a ferocious voice from his perch high above the battleground. The Ferfolk complied immediately as did the humans after they received a nod from Arwold, who sheathed the Claymore for good measure.

"I do not ask you to befriend or even accept the other. In fact, I do not care if you detest one another, but you will not fight among yourselves," commanded Ahriman. "We share a common goal and will achieve it sooner by combining our strengths." He raised the Staff of Ogma. "Know that I will not hesitate to use force against any of you, be it Ferfolk or human, who do not heed these words."

He looked around and found a sea of stern faces on both sides. It was an uneasy, but sufficient truce, enforced by threats of physical violence. Slowly, the earth spirit shrank back into the ground, bringing the wizard down with it. He cast one final stare at the Ferfolk, a warning for them to behave, and then took Arwold aside.

"Shall we keep these armies apart while we make our way toward the coast?" asked Ahriman.

"That does seem to be a sound idea," agreed Arwold. "We cannot have them fighting each other when it comes time for the real battle."

"Good then. We leave for Zairn forthwith," said Ahriman.

"Should we not remain here to defend Krof?" asked Arwold. "Nearly all of its warriors already follow me. There would be no one left to protect its citizens."

Ahriman shook his head. "Between our weapons and the element of surprise, we have the clear advantage despite their greater numbers. We will defeat Zairn before they have a chance to send their army to Krof."

"It shall be a quick battle," said Arwold.

"And once we control Zairn, the rest of the cities and towns will bow to our rule."

"A rule merciless against evil," added the tall warrior.

"It will be nothing less."

"And if they do not bow?"

Ahriman ran his finger along the snakes at the top of his staff and hissed, "There is not much that can stand against the Staff of Ogma."

CHAPTER XXVIII

TRACKING THE ENEMY

After sending the War Hammer demon back to the netherworld, Halia, Xarun, Minaras, Kuril, and Oswynn followed the secret passage out of the Pensorean Mountains and turned southwest through the lightly forested foothills. Within a few days, they had arrived at the Sinewan River, which wound its way from the western Dagger Mountains past Krof and eventually spilled into the ocean near Zairn. Xarun, who had been carrying the wounded Oswynn for the entire distance, placed the boy's body gently on the ground, knelt at the river's edge, and took a long drink. Although he wasn't tired, the cold water felt refreshing on this hot afternoon.

"We have lost a week!" growled Xarun.

He unsheathed his axe and swung it lightly at a sapling. Two more swings brought the tree down, but Xarun didn't feel any better. He wanted nothing more than to find the others and punish them for Thulin's death. Xarun dropped the axe and circled around the others.

While the warrior mumbled to himself, Minaras attended to his apprentice, who hadn't yet returned to consciousness. The bandages on Oswynn's head had turned a deep red, bordering on black. The wizard rummaged through his pockets for some new cloth but found none. Instead, he tore a strip of fabric from the bottom of his robe and called to Halia, "I need some fresh water to wipe Oswynn's forehead. His wound could use a bit of cleansing."

On his next trip around the wizard, Xarun stopped at the river's edge and cupped his large hands to carry some water back. He bent down carefully and allowed Minaras to soak the cloth. Then he splashed the remainder on his face and returned to the river to fetch another handful.

"Xarun, 'tis not like you to help when there is no battle involved," said Halia. "Has the heat of the summer sun addled your brain?"

"Nay, the child be hurt," responded Xarun in true sincerity. "He deserves not to die."

Kuril eyed the ground suspiciously. Scurrying back and forth among the small bushes and reeds that lined the river, he gently caressed a few leaves. Many of the tiny branches were broken and didn't have time to heal. Something had recently trampled them. "A large group has passed this way not long ago," the Arboreal announced. "They travel downstream following the course of the river."

"That could be anyone," said Halia, "a hunting party from a nearby village, a group of bandits, or even a few Fracodian raiders venturing forth from the mountains."

Kuril thought otherwise. "These signs are far too widespread for a small group of hunters or bandits, and unless the Fracodians are preparing for a war, they would not show up in such large numbers."

"It be Ahriman," snarled Xarun.

"If there is more you know about the sorcerer, then you must tell us now," said Kuril. He was neither suspicious of Xarun nor angry with him. True to Arboreal nature, he simply wanted all the facts before making any decisions.

Xarun stood directly in front of Kuril and stared at him. "It be an instinct," he replied crossly.

"Although I trust you as a warrior, you have shown your instincts to be less than reliable," scoffed Kuril.

Halia gazed at the river and became concerned. "I feel it too," she concurred. "We must head downstream after them."

Kuril stared at the river beside Halia and shook his head. "This must be a human trait for I feel nothing … or could it be those weapons manipulating your thoughts?"

"Perhaps the demons are lonely for their brothers and guide us to them," said Halia. "I say we fulfill their wishes and send them all to the netherworld!"

"If only we had a boat," Xarun hoped.

"I would much prefer to travel by foot," said Halia. "We are sure to gain ground if we continue hiking through the night. 'Tis difficult for a large group to move quickly."

"Alas, we have no choice," added Kuril sarcastically, agreeing with Halia's desire to go by land.

"Enough talk," said Xarun. "My axe yearns for battle."

Satisfied with Oswynn's condition for the moment, Minaras arose and waded into the river up to his waist. He winced as the cold water rose up his body but felt comforted by his favorite element. The wizard lowered both palms into the river and chanted, "*Awendan brim hwierfan saebat.*" Slowly, the water around his body began to solidify, much like the path he created across the lake. It formed into the shape of a small skiff with a transparent hull and five seats. The boat lifted Minaras up and carried him to the riverbank.

"A boat, as you requested, Xarun," said the wizard, taking the front seat. "Let us discover who precedes us."

Apprehensive, Halia sidled up to the boat and poked it with her finger. Then, she banged the side with her fist and exclaimed, "'Tis solid enough. Will it hold us all without sinking?"

The wizard grinned. "That it will," he said, offering his arm. Halia smiled but placed both hands on the side and leaped into the boat on her own, taking the seat in the back.

"'Tis far better than riding a horse," said Kuril as he, too, climbed aboard.

Xarun carefully lifted Oswynn from the ground and handed him to Halia and Kuril before joining the others. Once they had settled down, Minaras uttered a single command and the boat lurched downstream. It raced swiftly through the water, faster than the river current, yet provided an exceptionally smooth ride. Even Halia felt comfortable, despite her extreme dislike of both water and boats.

"Oswynn would have enjoyed this ride," said Minaras, peering at the riverbed through the bottom of the boat.

"Can you not call forth this boat when he has recovered?" asked Halia.

"If we survive ... although he will no doubt want to learn the spell," Minaras chuckled.

They hadn't gone far when Kuril noticed something in the distance. He leaned over the wizard, fixing his eyes down the river. With a wave of his hand, Minaras stopped the boat, suspending it in mid-stream. "What do you see?" he asked, his voice nearly drowned out by the loud rush of water passing by the skiff on either side.

"There appears to be a large campsite extending from the riverbank deep into the forest. I see a mass of figures but cannot determine who or what they are."

"Is it the sorcerer?" asked Halia. She looked into the sky for Hafoc but didn't see the bird.

"If it is Ahriman, we must continue on foot," replied Minaras.

"Bring me to shore for a closer look," said Kuril. "I will sneak into the campsite and return with as much information as I can gather before we take any further action."

Minaras guided the boat to the riverbank and allowed his spell to dissipate once all the passengers were safely on land. The boat vanished into the river, leaving only a drained wizard as proof that it ever existed. Having expended a decent amount of energy during the short trip downstream, Minaras dropped to the ground for a much needed rest while Kuril, with a few silent leaps, disappeared into the forest on his scouting mission.

Several hours later, the Arboreal hadn't yet returned and night was rapidly approaching. While they were waiting, Halia and Xarun had repaired their armor and polished their weapons, put together a small campsite, and hunted down a decent meal. Minaras, after his short rest, tended to Oswynn, changing the bandages and applying another coat of the healing ointment. Although he was glad the bleeding had abated, he became worried that the boy hadn't yet awoken from the trauma. During the course of the past few days, Minaras seemed to have grown twenty or thirty years older, now looking every bit his age. Despite his considerable efforts to focus on the present, his mind constantly wandered to thoughts about how he could have avoided this situation. "What if I had left Oswynn and Thulin in Seaton and taken care of these matters myself? Have I been neglecting my students all along? Should I have uncovered Ahriman's deception when he lived with me?" The return of Kuril, who had reappeared as silently and as suddenly as he had gone, interrupted the wizard's meandering thoughts.

"Two armies have set up camp downstream," explained the Arboreal. "Arwold leads a human army of about four score soldiers while Ahriman leads a much larger army composed of Ferfolk warriors and what appear to be farmers. The two armies have been traveling apart from each other and likewise maintain separate camps with the command tents surrounded by a large contingent of guards."

When Kuril paused briefly, Halia asked, "Is there nothing more you have learned? You have been gone for quite some time."

"You humans are impatient, but do not worry, Halia. I have committed to memory the full layout of both camps, which will no doubt be useful in planning our strategy. The human army, closer to the river, seems more susceptible to a surprise attack than the Ferfolk army."

"Ferfolk," Minaras thought aloud, his furrowed brow broadcasting a deep concern about the upcoming battle. "An army of Ferfolk does make sense. Ahriman intends to continue the crusade against humans, which his ancestors began six centuries ago, but this time they have the Staff of Ogma on their side. Why did I not realize this when Falgoran told us of the Great War?"

The wizard turned his gaze from the others and happened to lay his eyes on his unconscious apprentice. A younger mind might have pieced this puzzle together soon enough to save Thulin's life. "Is it too late for Oswynn as well?" he wondered. "Am I too old for the life of an adventurer?"

"Your task has become more difficult," sighed Minaras. "The Ferfolk are highly resistant to magic."

"Why did you say 'your task'?" asked Halia, concerned about his last statement. "Are you not going to help us defeat the sorcerer and banish the demons?"

"I have an obligation to my apprentice. I refuse to leave him alone and unprotected in this dangerous forest. Besides, my magic will be less effective against an army of Ferfolk. You must do without aid from this old wizard for now."

"I may be able to relieve you temporarily of your duty to the young boy," offered Kuril as he collected several green leaves and placed them on the ground beside Oswynn. He began to sing a beautiful song in Arboreal. As the enchanting words flowed from his lips, the leaves grew larger and larger, eventually overlapping. They wrapped around Oswynn's body, covering him from his feet to his head and forming an airtight shell. Finally, long vines extended from the branches above, cradled the shell, and lifted it into the air. When the song was over, Oswynn slept peacefully within his green encasement hidden deep within the thick canopy.

"He cannot breathe!" Xarun yelled, grabbing the Arboreal. "Release the boy now!"

Kuril shook off the big warrior and replied, "Oswynn will be quite safe in the cocoon I have made. It may even help to heal his wounds, although the human body is somewhat different from the Arboreal."

Minaras was still worried. "No harm must come to Oswynn."

"I assure you, Minaras, your young apprentice will be completely protected until the sun rises in the morning. He may even be awake to greet you."

"'Tis more than can be said of us," added Halia. "Shall we plan our attack now or charge right in and hope for the best?"

"The former I believe," said Kuril. "We should not rush into a battle against two armies, a sorcerer, and the demonic weapons without an appropriate strategy."

The four of them surrounded the campfire to discuss how best to defeat Ahriman, knowing a long night lay before them.

CHAPTER XXIX

THE MIDNIGHT AMBUSH

In the darkness, Kuril led Halia, Xarun, and Minaras closer to the armies, making little sound as they crept through the forest. He brought them to a small overlook with a partially obstructed but otherwise satisfactory view of the surrounding area. Hidden beyond the trees, the unsuspecting city of Zairn slept soundly, the elevated castle barely discernable as a small patch of sky curiously devoid of starlight. The four heroes huddled together at the base of a thick tree trunk to survey the scene and review their strategy one last time.

Below them, the flames of a few campfires cast their flickering light on thin wisps of smoke rising up into the air. The outlines of sleeping men and Ferfolk were visible within a few paces of each fire. A dozen guards remained awake to patrol the grounds while awaiting the pre-dawn call to signal their march against the great city. A clear dividing line of tall trees separated the two armies.

"It is just as you described, Kuril," noted Minaras quietly. "The humans and Ferfolk are more than a bit wary of each other. They keep their distance even while they sleep."

"And they travel none too close as well," added the Arboreal. "I would not be surprised if the humans forded the river in the morning to attack Zairn from the other side. It would offer the greatest dis-

233

tance between them and the Ferfolk, forcing the men of Zairn to defend two separate incursions."

"It is that very mistrust which gives us a chance to break the communication between the two armies. We must use this to our advantage and play upon their mutual hatred, enticing the humans and Ferfolk to turn on one another before morning. We will not have much time before Ahriman knows what we plan. If he organizes the Ferfolk and summons additional aid, even the axe and the sword may be insufficient for us to win this battle. Are we in agreement that our best hope lies in breaking Arwold free of the Claymore's web of deceit?"

"Aye," said Halia, Xarun, and Kuril together.

Minaras turned to face the others and spoke in a solemn tone, "Even though you carry powerful weapons, so do they. Ahriman will not easily give up an ally such as Arwold, a strong, skilled warrior under the influence of the demon in his sword. Do not underestimate either one of them."

"What if the sorcerer responds quicker than we expect?" asked Halia.

"If we fail tonight, many innocent lives will be lost tomorrow," replied Minaras.

"Victory shall be ours!" Xarun stated with confidence.

"Even so," Minaras explained, "if things go astray, head to the river as fast as you can. It is in the water where my spells will be most effective at protecting us from Ahriman's powerful sorcery."

"I do not run from battle," grumbled Xarun.

"You must not think of it as a retreat," said Kuril. "We will merely regroup and add our remaining strength to the Zairn army in defense of the city. Although it would be best to avoid the war altogether, if we fail tonight, we may yet decide the fate of this land as long as we do not unnecessarily sacrifice our lives."

"Let us hope it does not come to that," said Halia. "I do not wish to carry the burden of this sword for another night."

"Then we shall see to it," promised Xarun.

"Halia, Xarun," said Minaras, "you must break Arwold free from the grip of the Claymore. Think of nothing else. If you succeed, I expect he will turn on Ahriman and even the odds. Kuril, do not risk yourself in battle. You must be prepared with the banishment spell when the demon has been released from the weapon."

"And what of the sorcerer?" Xarun asked.

"I will attempt to draw him away from his army. Although he may deny it, I do believe Ahriman is under the influence of the Staff. If I am correct, he will come for me directly rather than dispatch his men. He had always wanted to prove himself the more skilled wizard ... I only hope he still carries that desire."

Minaras pulled a tinderbox out of his pocket and added, "May your blades strike true."

Halia, Xarun, and Kuril climbed down the hill. The Arboreal disappeared into the foliage when the others separated on their way to opposite sides of the human camp. Of the three, only Halia had any fears, worrying about what would happen when she drew the Long Sword. Could she control the weapon for this final battle, or would she turn on her friends—the only ones she had ever had? Her heart pounding, she pulled her hood tightly over her head. The stain of Oswynn's blood augmented her courage as she sneaked into the campsite.

Xarun boldly approached one of the outlying guards. Before the soldier had a chance to call out, the big warrior struck him on the head with the flat of the Great Axe, sending him to the ground unconscious. Xarun hoisted the heavy body onto his shoulder and carried it into the woods. He thought for a moment before donning the guard's helmet as a disguise and continuing toward Arwold's tent, casually striding through the center of the camp.

Halia crawled along the tree line dividing the two armies. It was the obvious choice for her as both the humans and the Ferfolk tended to keep their distance from each other. It didn't take long before she had penetrated deep into the campsite and turned toward the command tent on the human side. Along the way, she passed several drowsy guards and many sleeping soldiers, but her mind remained glued to the Long Sword. "I will not yield to your lies. I alone control my actions," she whispered, desperately trying to convince herself. Halia inched closer and closer to Arwold's tent, drawing her sword when she was a few steps from the two guards posted by the entrance.

As soon as it was free from its sheath, the Long Sword called to her. Although it didn't speak with words, she could understand its language. It tried to entice her, urging her to give in to her desires, to its desires. Halia stared at the blade and ran her finger along its sharp edge, her eyes glazing over. The devious weapon was beginning to win the battle of wills when Halia thought back to the undersea treasure chamber and how the Claymore had corrupted Arwold. Suddenly, she dropped the sword and cried out, "I cannot do it! I refuse to give in to your deceit!"

At the sound of her voice, the two guards spun around. "Who goes there?" they demanded. Upon seeing Halia, they raised their weapons, ready to strike her down without any further discourse.

"I was—" Halia started to explain when Xarun, in his minimal disguise, suddenly appeared and knocked out one of the guards, whose body fell with a loud thump.

A shuffling noise came from within the tent. "Arwold has arisen!" warned Halia. "Take care!"

The second guard fell to another blow from Xarun as Arwold emerged from the tent, Claymore in hand. "Xarun … Halia … I thought you to be trapped in another world."

"'Twas a simple matter to defeat the demon," boasted Halia. "And there is another one of those fiends in your weapon, deceiving you. Release your sword to us before anyone else is killed."

"Ahriman knew you were jealous of our weapons, but you shall not have them!" swore Arwold. "Guards, come forth and capture these intruders!"

Just as he let out his yell, an enormous wall of fire tore through the trees separating the two armies. Trunks, branches, and leaves burst into flames, with a sound deeper and fiercer than the rumble of thunder from an angry storm cloud. Chaos ensued.

On the Ferfolk side of the inferno, Ahriman rushed out of his tent, clutching the Staff of Ogma. He stared at the flames not fifty paces away and thought to himself, "An elementalist is near. Might it be you, Minaras?"

With a wave of his arm, four lieutenants appeared beside him. "Gather your men to secure the perimeter of our camp. Be mindful of any outsiders," ordered Ahriman, pointing at the first two.

"Shall we take prisoners?"

"We have no need for prisoners," Ahriman said with a smirk. "Kill anyone whom you do not recognize."

The two lieutenants rushed off while the sorcerer turned to his other two men. "Forge a path through these flames and make sure that Arwold is safe. We must protect the Claymore from falling into the enemy's possession."

"It may be faster to skirt the fire completely."

"Faster it would be, but more dangerous as well," responded Ahriman. "Our enemy might have set traps for us on either end of the flames. They will not expect us to go straight through."

The second pair of lieutenants put their fists together before heading for the burning trees.

Ahriman called silently to his familiar, which flew out of the command tent and into the night sky. "You know who to look for, my friend," he called after the bird.

"Shall I do a little investigating of my own?" he asked himself. Raising the Staff into the air, Ahriman chanted, "*Lyft gast lyft gast, beran min bodig faeste.*"

Two air spirits instantly materialized and lifted the wizard high over the campsite. From his lofty view, he could see the Ferfolk methodically following their orders while the human camp was in utter disarray. Then, his eyes caught sight of the scuffle at Arwold's tent, confirming his fears. He ordered the spirits to carry him closer, but before he reached the battle, an odd vision at the river distracted him. A wave, large enough to be battering an ocean coast during a hurricane instead of rolling down a lazy river on a tranquil night, traveled downstream at a fast pace. Upon its crest rode Minaras, as if he were an acrobat standing on a trick horse.

"Minaras, how unexpected," Ahriman said to himself as he changed course to intercept his old master. "You should not have drawn attention to yourself, for this river will be your grave. I shall best you within your favorite element."

Below him, human warriors rushed madly around their campsite, moving gear away from the flames, waking those who had managed to sleep through the conflagration, and trying to find anyone who knew what had happened. Many of them suspected the Ferfolk had caused the blaze in a failed attempt to wipe them out but were too distracted to care. As they slowly became organized, more soldiers forgot about the fire and surrounded the melee near Arwold's tent.

Xarun jumped forward on the offensive, hacking up and down with the Great Axe. His attacks were fierce, but Arwold matched him blow for blow. The weapons clanged against each other, with sparks occasionally brightening the darkness.

"You cannot beat me, Xarun. 'Tis but a matter of time before justice prevails, even with the Great Axe at your command. Renounce your evil ways, and I might be persuaded to spare your life."

Xarun grunted his refusal and pressed on, unsuccessfully jabbing at Arwold. The big warrior tried to sneak in a knee to the groin, but Arwold stepped aside and brought the pommel of the Claymore into his face, nearly breaking his nose. On Xarun's next swing, one of the guards came closer and stabbed at him. Xarun knocked the sword aside and answered with a swift punch to the gut. As the guard fell, three more moved in to take his place.

"I must help him before he is overwhelmed," thought Halia. "A few guards would pose no problem, but eventually they will swarm around him, restrict his movement, and leave him vulnerable to a finishing blow by Arwold." She took a deep breath, reached down slowly, and lifted the Long Sword. Once again, it began to exert pressure on her mind, but by concentrating on helping her friend, Halia resisted its temptations and joined the fight.

While Xarun fought Arwold, Halia held the three remaining guards at bay. The Long Sword moved as if it were as light as a dagger, which more than compensated for the disadvantages she had in physical strength and number. Despite the fourth guard rising from the ground and adding his sword to the others, Halia was just beginning to gain an advantage when three more soldiers appeared, wielding spears. The added length of their weapons allowed them to push Halia back without risk of injury to themselves, eventually separating her from Xarun. The four swordsmen then slipped past her guard and closed in on Xarun again.

High above the battle at the tent, the two air spirits carried Ahriman to the river and deposited him in advance of the wave. The sorcerer aimed his staff at the water and chanted, *"Brim fero, lagu fero, hlifian micel mara."*

As soon as he completed his spell, the river rose into the air and formed a huge torso with massive arms. The gigantic being, a liquid twin of the earth spirit, drew so much water into its body that the level of the river dropped noticeably. Minaras saw the water spirit ahead of him but couldn't stop in time. The wave crashed into the gargantuan body and came out the other side without the wizard, its rider trapped within the powerful arms of the water spirit.

Minaras struggled to free himself, but was unable to escape from the creature's vice-like hug. Tighter and tighter, it held onto him, squeezing his chest until he could no longer breathe. With the last remaining puff of air in his lungs, he weakly managed to cast one spell. A tiny ripple of water formed at the base of the spirit. It traveled up through its body, growing larger as it moved until finally, a huge wave erupted from its headless shoulders.

Both Minaras and the water spirit dropped into the river with an enormous splash. Moments later, the wizard's head popped up, gasping for air. He spat out a mouthful of water and waded to shore, collapsing on the muddy riverbank.

Surprised to see his former master still alive, Ahriman called out, "You are more powerful than I remember, old man, but there will be no escape this time." He raised the Staff and began summoning another spirit to do his bidding.

Minaras, winded and breathing heavily, merely grinned, knowing his plan would be successful whether he lived or died at the hands of his former student. He gazed toward the wall of flames, hoping the others would soon complete their mission.

Xarun, focusing exclusively on Arwold, received several cuts from the guards because of his careless lack of attention. He was so furious that he didn't even notice the bloody wounds along his arms and legs. Halia could see he was losing the battle but was unable to help him, pinned back by the spearmen. One of the guards dropped out of the melee and slipped silently behind Xarun. He smiled as he prepared to take down the big warrior. Up went his sword when Kuril leaped from behind the command tent, kicked him in the chest, and sent him flying backward onto the ground. The Arboreal knocked over a second soldier on his way to Arwold, thinking he could take advantage of the surprise and disarm the tall warrior with one accurate stroke.

Xarun had other plans. "Leave, Arwold!" he roared. "Rid me of those guards!"

At Xarun's request, Kuril stood against the swordsmen. With quick strokes and carefully planned footsteps, he lured the guards away from the tent until it was just Xarun against Arwold. Xarun, tiring of this battle, shifted his stance to give Arwold a slight opening for attack, which the tall warrior accepted with a passion. Arwold lunged forward with the Claymore, already claiming victory.

The big warrior, however, hadn't only anticipated the move, he had been counting on it. Xarun sidestepped the blade and rammed his shoulder into Arwold, knocking him off balance. "Prepare the spell!" yelled Xarun as Arwold tumbled into the tent, bringing it down in a flurry of leather and rope.

Now, with a clear advantage, Xarun would be able to destroy the Claymore. He raised the Great Axe ready to strike, when Hafoc swooped out of the sky and flew into his face.

"Begone, wretched bird!" he bellowed, swatting at the crow with both his weapon and his free arm.

Hafoc continued to pester him, flying back and forth, up and down, claws and beak everywhere. Whenever Xarun attempted to take a swing at the Claymore, the bird would fly into his face, scratching at his eyes and cheeks. With every passing second, Arwold had further time to recover, time which Xarun couldn't afford. It wouldn't be long before a mass of human and Ferfolk warriors would surround him. Xarun looked over and saw Kuril holding off the four swordsmen. The Arboreal should never have joined the fight and put his life at risk. Without him to cast the banishment spell, Xarun couldn't risk releasing the demons from the Claymore and the Staff of Ogma.

After wrestling with the canvas for longer than he would have liked, Arwold fought his way out of the remains of the tent. "This battle is at an end! Kill them all!" he ordered.

Rolling onto his knees, Arwold put his hand down to steady himself. For one brief moment, the Claymore lay flat on the ground. Xarun saw this, and knew it would be his last chance. Allowing Hafoc to shred his face with its sharp talons, he brought the Great Axe down onto Arwold's blade. The Claymore shattered, releasing the black shadow trapped within.

Arwold fell to the ground on his elbows and knees, his face sinking into the dirt. He clutched his head and screamed, "No! This cannot be!"

"Now for you," thought Xarun, faking an attack on Hafoc. The bird flew under the blade but was blindsided by the back of Xarun's gauntlet when the warrior whipped his free hand around and smacked it in the beak. Dazed, Hafoc retreated into the sky with a weak caw.

"You shall escape me never again," Xarun yelled after the crow.

Acting swiftly, before the demon could gain its full physical form, Kuril leaped behind Halia for protection. "You must hold off the soldiers until I can read the banishment scroll!" he shouted.

Halia nodded and kept her sword moving in a blur. "Arwold!" she demanded. "Call off your men! You still have time to make things right!"

Xarun moved into position to protect Kuril, but spent most of the time wiping blood from the innumerable scratches on his face. The guards surrounded the three and closed in, relying heavily on the spearmen to engage the Long Sword and Great Axe.

"Get off the ground, Arwold!" urged Halia. "Or do you still bow to the sorcerer?"

Arwold groaned, full of self-loathing and shame. He refused to move.

Out of the corner of her eye, Halia noticed two Ferfolk lieutenants approaching rapidly with weapons drawn. Xarun saw them as well, and while he was distracted, one of Arwold's soldiers broke through his guard and stabbed Kuril, slicing the Arboreal in the side just below the ribs. Kuril fell to his knees, still holding the scroll in front of his eyes. His vision blurred, but he kept reading. Xarun grabbed the back of the warrior's shirt and flung him aside. Seconds later, Kuril succeeded in completing the spell before he blacked out. The vortex of blue light appeared and sucked in the shadow, banishing the demon to the netherworld.

More soldiers appeared, ready to end the fight through sheer numbers, when Arwold rose to his feet and commanded, "Abide! We have been deceived by the sorcerer!"

His men looked at him in confusion. "But what of the Zairn army?" they asked. "Are these not assassins sent to kill you?"

"They are my friends," admitted Arwold, "though I denied it before. I know now that Zairn had never threatened our town—it was a lie told by Ahriman to coerce us into attacking the city. He tricked me into assisting him with his wicked plan, and I, in turn, brought you with me. I would not be surprised if his Ferfolk warriors had planned to turn on us after the city fell."

The entire human army had begun to gather around the group. Word spread quickly from one to another.

"This sword has clouded my mind as Ahriman knew it would," he fumed, pointing at the claymore. "It has used me to commit deeds most foul. Ahriman is the evil one! He is our real enemy!"

Halia turned to Kuril, tying her versatile cloak around his waist to stop the flow of blood from his wound. She then folded the parchment and returned it to his scroll case. Before she knew it, Kuril had awoken and tried to stand.

"No," she cautioned, "you must lie still or risk bleeding again."

"The wound is painful, but not serious. I cannot rest until we have dealt with Ahriman."

With her help, he was barely able to stand, leaning on her for support. Xarun stepped beside them and offered his shoulder, which Kuril gladly accepted. By then, the Ferfolk lieutenants were almost upon them.

"The Ferfolk approach," noted Xarun.

Arwold glanced at them with a sobering look. "Men, you know what to do."

His entire army raised their weapons and glared at the approaching Ferfolk. Sworn not to fight the humans and heavily outnumbered, the two lieutenants spun around and ran back to the wall of fire. Most of Arwold's men followed, hoping to catch them before they reached the safety of their own campsite.

Arwold lifted the broken claymore and stared at the blade, this time in disgust instead of adoration. He gripped it tightly and said, "Having walked down the path of the damned, I now see evil for what it really is. I shall deal with the sorcerer forthwith."

The tall warrior ran toward the commotion at the river, followed by three of his men and Halia. In a single motion, Xarun wrapped his arm around Kuril's legs, hoisted him up, and charged after Arwold, unwilling to miss any of the action.

Near the river, a dark figure, the size of a small hut, formed around Ahriman. The air itself came alive, its inky blackness hovering above the ground, roughly spherical but constantly changing shape. Tentacles formed and disappeared. Various appendages, both human and otherwise, grew out of the amorphous creature only to dissolve back into its body moments later. The spirit, a floating nightmare, drifted slowly toward the river.

Minaras looked up from his muddy seat on the riverbank. "What loathsome being have you summoned this time, Ahriman?" he asked himself, throwing his arms forward from the river toward the creature. "You would have done better to bring forth an earth spirit, but then again you always preferred form to function."

A large jet of water flew out of the river, directly at the black blob. Just as the water was about to collide with it, however, the spirit opened a hole in its body, allowing the stream to pass harmlessly through and strike a surprised Ahriman. The force of the water threw the sorcerer back against a tree and knocked the wind out of him. The hole in the night spirit closed as it continued its slow progress toward the river. Minaras crawled out of the water, exhausted but content to accept his fate now that Ahriman was incapacitated. "It will take more than a single wizard to stop such a powerful creature," he thought.

Upon seeing the dark shifting outline of the spirit, Arwold called to his men, "Destroy that foul beast while I put an end to the sorcerer!"

The three guards surrounded the night spirit, unsure of what to expect from the disturbing sight they now faced.

"What is that thing?" asked Halia as she ran to Minaras.

"A night spirit," cautioned the wizard. "You must ... stay away ... it is too ... dangerous!"

Halia didn't listen to his warning. Instead, she readied her weapon and closed in on the creature, compelled to assist the men who, until moments ago, were her enemy. One of the guards poked the creature with his spear, but the sharp tip failed to penetrate the rubbery membrane surrounding its body. Black tendrils formed and wrapped around the shaft of the weapon, inching their way closer and closer to the guard's hands. He tried to pull the spear away, but the creature wouldn't release it. The tendrils extended further, encasing the entire spear and grabbing his hand. As soon as it made contact with his skin, the guard screamed and fell dead.

Minaras, meanwhile, had crawled behind Halia. "Do not … let it touch you," he warned.

Halia needed no convincing. "This I can see."

It wasn't long before the second soldier suffered a similar fate to the first. The third, deciding to forgo the inevitable, dropped his weapon and ran. The spirit lashed out at Halia. Instinctively, her sword went up. The black tendrils began wrapping around the blade, trying to make their way to her hand. Halia yanked her weapon and hacked them off, each one vanishing in the night air before touching the ground.

"The Long Sword has no trouble cutting through the spirit's appendages," thought Minaras, gaining a second wind.

"Your blade has wounded the creature," he said. "We may be able to defeat this spirit with a bit of luck. Do you trust me?"

Halia looked at the creature, then back at Minaras, and gave a single nod. "We must make our way beneath the spirit," he instructed, "and do remember to keep the tendrils at bay or we will end up like those two unfortunate souls."

Minaras put his arm around Halia and, together, they moved closer to the spirit. The Long Sword practically moved on its own, slicing each appendage the spirit sent at them. Soon, they were directly beneath its bulbous mass. The night spirit formed into a large bubble with an opening at the bottom, enveloped the two, and began to contract. From inside, Minaras pulled the tinderbox out of his pocket and began chanting while Halia's sword was in constant motion, keeping them safe for the moment.

"Halia, drive your sword into the creature!" ordered Minaras as flames sprung from his fingertips.

She did as he said, reaching up with the Long Sword and making a deep incision directly above her head. Before the spirit was able to heal its wound, fire flew from the wizard's hand and ignited it from the inside out. The resulting blast disintegrated the creature instantly, but the impervious membrane spared the two humans.

Minaras fell to the ground, exhausted. "I do remember reading about the night spirit," he explained. "It is nearly invulnerable, with an outer layer that resists most weapons, acids, cold, and fire, but its insides are susceptible to flame."

Had he opted to teach his students only about elemental spells, he would never have known about the spirit's weakness. Halia was so amazed about having suffered not a single burn that she didn't hear the wizard's lecture. Without thinking, however, she did offer her hand and helped him to his feet.

Ahriman, drawing energy from the Staff, recovered in time to see the warriors approaching. He knew immediately that he had lost an ally.

Arwold raised the broken claymore and shouted, "Sorcerer, you shall pay for what you did to me!"

"Did I do anything that was not already within you?" asked Ahriman. "I placed no enchantments on your mind."

Ahriman lifted his staff into the air and called forth several forest spirits. Leaves, sticks, and dirt from the ground coalesced, quickly forming into a half dozen spirits. They darted toward the warriors, growing larger with each step.

Xarun let go of Kuril and took the first swing, cutting through the leg of one of the spirits. Immediately, a new leg formed, drawing debris from the ground. Arwold tried swinging downward, slicing the spirit in half, but only managed to create a pair of smaller ones. The spirits returned the attack, sending a barrage of twigs and dirt at the warriors. Xarun and Arwold protected their eyes, but the bombardment stung any part of their body left exposed.

Minaras came to their aid with a final "*Lyft bord*" before falling unconscious. The two warriors sliced and hacked at the spirits while a strong wind scattered the debris across the forest floor.

Arwold shouted at the sorcerer, "You can hide behind your spells no longer!"

"It is not too late to side with me," offered Ahriman. "I could grant you whatever you most desire." He raised his staff in the air and, as if he had read Minaras's mind, began chanting the spell to summon an earth spirit.

"I most desire to rid this world of evil, beginning with you," Arwold responded.

He let out a battle cry and rushed forward. Ahriman needed only a few more seconds to complete his powerful spell, and Hafoc came to his aid. The familiar dove straight for Arwold, seeking to gain a few precious moments for its master. Xarun saw the bird and launched the Great Axe. It spun through the air, straight for Hafoc. The shaft made a direct hit and knocked the crow to the ground by Ahriman's feet.

The earth began to tremble as an enormous rocky hand burst from the ground. Arwold jumped over the rising fingers and was upon the wizard when Kuril let out a cry, "Arwold, go no further! Do not destroy his staff while he casts the spell!"

Arwold, filled with rage, couldn't stop himself. He swung the broken claymore clean through the Staff, causing a powerful explosion, which consumed both him and Ahriman, incinerated Hafoc, and even singed the hairs on Xarun's head. The still-forming earth spirit crumbled into a pile of dirt.

As Kuril read the banishment scroll, a dark shadow, twice the size of the previous two, emerged from the broken staff. The gate to the netherworld opened and absorbed the demon in a great swirl of light.

CHAPTER XXX

DESTRUCTION OF THE WEAPONS

By dawn, a blanket of high clouds rolled in, reflecting the early sun in a burst of fiery red and orange that matched the color of the smoldering embers where the wall of flame once burned. The armies, both in confusion now, ignored each other and began to disperse. The Ferfolk, many of whom never wanted to participate in the fight to begin with, headed back to their remote town near the border of the wastelands. The humans, still suspicious of the Ferfolk, avoided any further contact and returned to Krof. They became local heroes even though there was never any real threat to the town.

Halia, Xarun, Minaras, Kuril, and Oswynn, who had recently regained consciousness, sat in a circle around a lone campfire near the river, each one battered and weary. Halia held the blade of the broken long sword and sighed. The powerful weapon represented a dream she could have realized. Looking at her four companions, however, brought a smile to her face. Instead of the vast treasures of gold and jewels that she would have desired only six months ago, Halia had found something even more valuable: true friends. She threw the blade to the ground. It landed near the Great Axe, still intact, leaning against a rock. "'Tis time to destroy the axe, Xarun," she said.

The big warrior shrugged, "It be a good weapon."

"Waste no more time with your talk," urged Oswynn. "I wish to see Falgoran's spell banish the demon. Have I not waited long enough?"

Kuril unfurled the old parchment for the last time, the Arboreal symbols barely legible. "There is more of a reason to destroy the axe than for Oswynn's entertainment," he said. "Xarun, you have a strong will to resist the temptations of the weapon so easily, but eventually, the axe will belong to another. It may be years and it may be centuries, but some day the demon would gain its freedom and haunt this world."

Xarun couldn't argue otherwise. He lifted the broken claymore and delivered a swift, clean blow, breaking the Great Axe in half. Kuril read the banishment scroll before it faded completely and tossed the blank parchment onto the fire. A moment later, it was nothing but ash.

"Over the past few weeks, I have gained a new respect for humans," said Kuril. "I would like to stay with you longer, but I must report back to the elders. Please know that you are welcome in my home any time you wish." Then, with a few limping strides, the Arboreal disappeared into the forest.

By midday, the four heroes had made the short trip into Zairn, heading directly for the Great Library.

"Minaras, my old friend," greeted Sigmus, "you look like you have been on quite an adventure. Would you and your friends care for a hot meal and a comfortable bed?"

"A large meal would do," accepted Xarun.

"We could have used your wizardry last night," said Minaras. "Do you not feel the desire for excitement, danger, and the thrill of victory?"

Sigmus laughed. "It is exciting to learn of ages past, thrilling to impart my knowledge on others and, even you must admit, better to forgo the danger at our age."

He reached for a pile of old tomes on his desk and continued, "Halia, I have found some books that may be of interest to your friend Thulin. Is he not with you today?"

Minaras lowered his head as Halia gave the old scribe a sad glance.

"I see," said Sigmus quietly, putting an arm around his friend. "It is one of the risks associated with such an ... active ... life."

"A life he did not choose but was forced on him," Minaras moaned. "Thulin is dead because I refused to give up adventuring and grant my students the attention they truly deserved."

"You should not blame yourself, Minaras," offered Halia. "I was the one who led him to Krof. After he had guessed the truth about the glowing spots, he was ready to return home, but I convinced him to continue on the quest."

"That may be true, but had you and he returned to Seaton, I would not have been there." Minaras looked at the scar running across Oswynn's forehead. "Our little adventure was nearly the death of you as well."

"But I did not die, Master," Oswynn chimed in, "and you were triumphant in a quest even the Arboreal elders considered dangerous. I have no doubt they will still be debating the matter when Kuril returns to the fortress."

Minaras put both hands on his shoulders and stared into his eyes. "Nevertheless, it is time that I made a difficult decision." He took a deep breath and continued, "I am sorry, Oswynn. You have great potential as a wizard, but I will not be the one to guide you."

Oswynn's face fell as he kicked one of the books on the floor. "What am I to do? I do not wish to return to the life of a farmer."

Minaras turned to Sigmus. "Oswynn, young as he is, has already mastered some basic elemental spells but is more interested in transmutation."

"Then he has found a new mentor," responded Sigmus.

A glimmer of hope entered the boy's mind. "Are you a transmuter?" he asked, raising his eyes.

"It is a difficult school of magic to learn, but quite rewarding."

"And powerful?" hoped Oswynn.

Sigmus gave him a wink, drawing a large grin from his new apprentice.

Oswynn stepped beside his new master and, with a mischievous look, asked, "What will you do, Minaras?"

The wizard replied with a smile, "My taste for adventure has grown recently."

Minaras removed the blades of the great axe, claymore, and long sword from his robes. "I do believe the Teruns may be able to re-forge a couple of weapons from this metal, without any demons entrapped this time. What do you say if we went on a bit of a journey?"

Xarun grinned, "A new axe I do need."

Halia looked at her friends and said, "To the Teruns we shall go!"

The End

978-0-595-46404-3
0-595-46404-1

Printed in the United States
200465BV00001B/1-105/A